A Nobleman's Bride
Sara Blayne

**ZEBRA BOOKS
KENSINGTON PUBLISHING CORP.**

Dedicated with love to John, Nelda, Mark, Kyla, Lori, and Jason.

ZEBRA BOOKS

are published by

Kensington Publishing Corp.
475 Park Avenue South
New York, NY 10016

Copyright © 1991 by Marcia Howl

All rights reserved. No part of this book may be reproduced in any form or by any means without the prior written consent of the Publisher, excepting brief quotes used in reviews.

First printing: May, 1991

Printed in the United States of America

The new Zebra Regency Romance logo that you see on the cover is a photograph of an actual regency "tuzzy-muzzy." The fashionable regency lady often wore a tuzzy-muzzy tied with a satin or velvet riband around her wrist to carry a fragrant nosegay. Usually made of gold or silver, tuzzy-muzzies varied in design from the elegantly simple to the exquisitely ornate. The Zebra Regency Romance tuzzy-muzzy is made of alabaster with a silver filigree edging.

AN ENJOYABLE INTERLUDE

"The sea," he drawled cynically, "is an unforgiving mistress, intolerant of fools who succumb to her allure. You are better off tending your sheep, Miss Morgan."

"And you, milord?" she came back at him, driven by curiosity and something else she did not quite fathom. "Had you it to do over again, would you have resisted her allure?"

"No, Miss Morgan, I should undoubtedly have done just as I did." For a moment he held her his unwitting prisoner with eyes that searched her face. Then, with mesmerizing deliberation, he lowered his head toward hers.

She returned his kiss with a sweet, innocent abandon. And when he released her, she suffered a sharp pang of regret. Slowly her eyelids fluttered open, and she stared dazedly into the Demon's orbs, brilliant and black in the moonlight.

His breath ragged in his throat and his eyes dark with barely controlled passion, Malvern took note of her flushed cheeks, of her eyes, dusky with the emotion he had aroused in her . . .

"I am afraid you will have to give up this dream of yours to go to sea," he remarked, his smile curiously askew. "You, my love, are very much a woman. Admit it. You enjoyed this little interlude every bit as much as did I."

ZEBRA'S HOLIDAY REGENCY ROMANCES CAPTURE THE MAGIC OF EVERY SEASON

THE VALENTINE'S DAY BALL (3280, $3.95)
by Donna Bell

Tradition held that at the age of eighteen, all the Heartland ladies met the man they would marry at the Valentine's Day Ball. When she was that age, the crucial ball had been canceled when Miss Jane Lindsey's mother had died. Now Jane was on the shelf at twenty-four. Still, she was happy in her life and accepted the fact that romance had passed her by. So she was annoyed with herself when the scandalous—and dangerously handsome—Lord Devlin put a schoolgirl blush into her cheeks and made her believe that perhaps romance may *indeed* be a part of her life . . .

AN EASTER BOUQUET (3330, $3.95)
by Therese Alderton

It was a preposterous and scandalous wager: In return for a prime piece of horse-flesh, the decadent Lord Vyse would pose as a virtuous Rector in a country village. His cohorts insisted he wouldn't last a week, yet he was actually looking forward to a quiet Easter in the country.

Miss Lily Sterling was puzzled by the new rector; he had a reluctance to discuss his past and looked at her the way no Rector should *ever* look at a female of his flock. She was determined to unmask this handsome "clergyman", and she would set herself up as his bait!

A CHRISTMAS AFFAIR (3244, $3.95)
by Joan Overfield

Justin Stockman thought he was doing the Laurence family a favor by marrying the docile sister and helping the family reverse their financial straits. The first thing he would do after the marriage was to marry off his independent and infuriating sister-in-law Amanda.

Amanda was intent on setting the arrogant Justin straight on a few matters, and the cozy holiday backdrop—from the intimate dinners to the spectacular Frost Fair—would be the perfect opportunities to let him know what life would be like with her as a sister-in-law. She would give a Merry Christmas indeed!

A CHRISTMAS HOLIDAY (3245, $3.95)

A charming collection of Christmas short stories by Zebra's best Regency Romance writers. *The Holly Brooch, The Christmas Bride, The Glastonbury Thorn, The Yule Log, A Mistletoe Christmas,* and *Sheer Sorcery* will give you the warmth of the Holiday Season all year long.

Available wherever paperbacks are sold, or order direct from the Publisher. Send cover price plus 50¢ per copy for mailing and handling to Zebra Books, Dept. 3401, 475 Park Avenue South, New York, N.Y. 10016. Residents of New York, New Jersey and Pennsylvania must include sales tax. DO NOT SEND CASH.

Chapter One

Brigida Morgan waited impatiently as her grandfather, Commodore Tavis Llewellyn, Esq., retired, polished off his fourth helping of Morgay soup and settled back in his chair to savor the last of the Madeira her brother Collin had procured for him by rather questionable means. The sun had set an hour or more earlier, and the full moon must be well on the rise by now, the tide at its ebb-flow, she thought, hardly able to contain her frustration at this unexpected delay. Heavenly days! The best of the crabs, lobster, and crawfish marooned in the rocks below Tal Carn would be picked over before she ever got there! She would be left to "twitch" eels from the sand with the children, and her grandfather would be deprived of the crab pie steeped in white wine to which he looked forward after every spring tide. How then would she explain to him that the money for such luxuries was long gone, his pittance from the crown and the little left over from what she had received for her mother's diamond necklace and earrings were all that kept them from debtors' prison?

"You're uncommonly quiet this eve, Mistress," rasped the commodore, eyeing his granddaughter appraisingly. "An' 'twould seem 'ee has lost the taste for good Cornish dog fish. Did I not know better, I'd say thee was ailing."

"Our Brie's never been sick a day in her life, Commodore," spoke up Collin Morgan, the grin breaking across his handsome face full of the devil. "Belike she's only moonstruck at the notion that 'Demon' Drake's come to claim his bride at long last."

"Oh!" gasped Brie, her sea-green eyes flashing. "I've far better things to occupy me than the infamous Captain Drake, I assure you. Not the least of which is the wish that you will both remove yourselves that Fionna and I might clear away the leavings. I promised Mrs. Guthrie she might go home early this eve."

"Methinks you protest too much, Brie of Gullan Carn. Are thee sure 'tis not yourself who would be off while the moon is yet full and round?" laughed the youth, his blue eyes dancing as he unfolded his lean length from the chair. Strolling easily round the corner of the oakwood table, he chucked his sister playfully beneath her delightfully pointed chin. Brigida was the image of her dainty, coppery-haired mother, but Collin, at two and twenty, had more the look of the Morgans, for he was tall, with the slim-hipped build of their seafaring father and the same rebellious lock of fair hair falling carelessly over his forehead. "You've the guilty aspect of the schemer, me love," he warned, tilting the back of his head significantly toward the old commodore. "Can it be some foolish young blood has usurped the sea captain's place in your heart? Take care you don't find yourself all aback. From what I've heard of the new Earl of Malvern, he'll not stand idly by while another seeks to take what he considers his by right."

"Eh? What's this?" the commodore grunted, heaving his not inconsiderable bulk upright as he bent a keen glance upon his granddaughter's suddenly flushed face. "Are thee up to some devilry, girl? I warn 'ee, I'll not stand for it. You're a Llewellyn and a Morgan. You'll not go back on your father's given word."

"Shall I not?" Brigida cried, springing impetuously to her feet. "My father was wrong to give it, as he himself admitted before he passed on. Shall I be made to pay for his error? Would you have me like Cordelia Drake? Broken and old at nine and twenty? I should rather be dead and buried."

"Aw, 'tis not so bad as that, Brie," Collin groaned, a look of chagrin darkening his youthful features.

"And what would 'ee know of it, Collin Morgan?" Brigida demanded, slipping unconsciously into the dialect her old governess had worked so hard to eradicate from the young girl's speech. "Thee, a man, free to do as 'ee plaise?"

"Nothing, Bridgida love, nothing. Except that whatever you decide about Malvern, you know I'll always stand by 'ee, come what may."

Brigida tossed her coppery curls and turned her back on the guilty look of entreaty in her brother's eyes. With her whole heart she wished Collin Morgan to the devil for his meddling. He well knew she fairly itched to be away and that, furthermore, her grandfather, having declared that now her bridegroom was returned to Cornwall she should cease to behave like an ill-mannered hoyden, had forbidden her to partake of the springtide harvest along the beach and beneath the crags. Oh, *why* did not the commodore retire to the study to enjoy his Brosely pipe and his customary libation of smuggled French brandy? she fretted.

Tavis Llewellyn might be a trifle eccentric, commanding the inhabitants of Gullan Carn, the old stone house perched on the cliffs overlooking Whitsand Bay to the east and the Looe to the west, as if they were the crew of the old *Sybil*, his former flagship — and, indeed, he was more than a little notional, losing himself more often than not in the past in which he had commanded a king's squadron during the American Revolution—but he was neither blind nor a fool. He had an uncanny ability to know whenever she was plotting one of her "acts of insubordination," as he was in the habit of calling them, and she had no wish to arouse his suspicions, for he was quite capable of ordering her to her room and locking her in. In the normal course of events, it would have little signified. After all, it would not be the first time she had slipped out her window and down the weathered oak that hugged the house and stolen along the smugglers' trail to the *Mere-Magden*, her skiff, beached in one of the many narrow inlets below the cliffs of Gullan Carn. But word was out that "Demon Drake" had taken up residence at Malvern, and that placed a whole new complexion on things. Indeed, it had recalled to the commodore's erratic memory the hitherto nearly forgotten agreement that pledged Brigida Morgan in marriage to Captain Drake, the new Earl of Malvern, a circumstance which she found anything but felicitous.

Brie, having been left from the tender age of thirteen to the guardianship of her eccentric grandparent and the timorous Miss Moresby, her governess, had soon found herself taking charge not only of the previously poorly run household but of the commodore as well. With the result that what had once been a very precocious child had soon developed into a highly independent female with a mind very much her own. In truth, Brigida Morgan, long accustomed to a degree of independence denied most of her feminine contemporaries, had long since determined that what was erroneously described as "wedded bliss" was in actuality naught but a trap from which there could be no escape. Small wonder, then, that she found herself out of all countenance with Collin, whose persistent teasing only wedged the notion of matrimony more firmly in the old gentleman's mind. Matrimony, moreover, with a man who had in the four weeks since his return to Cornwall shown a decided lack of interest in the woman he was sworn to wed, not to mention the eighteen years before that spent at sea! She thought with what could very well have been a trace of pique.

No, my girl, she told herself, it were better to bridle your temper and use woman's wiles than to fly into the boughs only to find yourself treed good and proper. Besides, she could never stay mad at Collin long, no matter how she might like to, once he turned on the old Cornish charm. Oh, he was a sad scapegrace, he was, but he was her old playmate as well, *and* her closest friend. She could never deny him anything.

"Enough!" she laughed, albeit a trifle grudgingly, and, turning, boxed in mock vexation at Collin's ear. "You may both cease to plague yourselves or me about any fancied beaus, for I have none. Doubtless Demon Drake himself has long since forgotten my father's pledge to his that we should wed. And 'twere better so, for he can have little wish to take to wife the dowerless Brigida Morgan," she declared a trifle bitterly, but her head nevertheless held high. "Now begone. I've work to do before retiring. And as for you, dearest gramfer," she added, going to kneel beside the commodore, " 'tis time you were abed."

"And who made 'ee captain of this ship, mistress?" demanded the old gentleman, his glance yet fond as he beheld the girl's lovely face turned with tender concern up to his. "I may be old and forced into retirement before me time, but I'll not be ordered about by any managing female. Your mother, God rest her soul, was reared a lady. Soft-spoken, she was, and gentle mannered, as befitted the squire's granddaughter, who won the heart of a lord's second son. Trevor Morgan may have died penniless, but he was a gentleman born. In birth thee are no less than Damion Drake, Earl of Malvern, and for dowry, thee has the Ferris diamonds that were your grandmother's and your mother's before 'ee. So say not again that the sea captain will not have 'ee, for he shall, or Tavis Llewellyn, Esquire, will know the reason why."

"Oh, Grandfather!" Brigida murmured, hastily averting her face. Heaven help her, for the fat was in the fire for certain now. And yet she could not bring herself to tell him that the diamonds were gone and her dowry with them, sold to put the new roof on Gullan Carn and to purchase the high-bred Suffolk ram needed to improve the slowly growing flock of sheep upon which all their hopes depended. All their hopes, that is, save for the commodore's, she thought bitterly. *He* would persist in the newly resurrected notion that the means to their salvation lay with her marriage to the wealthy house of Drake. After all, was that not why she had been provided a governess till the age of sixteen, that she might be molded into a lady worthy to be chatelaine of Malvern Castle? And, indeed, not since Cordelia Drake had given birth to a stillborn son had there been any doubt that one day Damion would inherit the earldom from his elder brother Duncan, for the countess had been unable to bear further offspring.

Oh, what a damnable coil it was! And yet not even to save them all from the poorhouse would she let herself be sold to the demon of Malvern, she vowed, a dangerous glitter igniting in the marvelously green eyes. Suddenly she rose to her feet, and drawing a deep breath, flung both woman's wiles and caution unflinchingly to the wind.

"Even so, dearest Gramfer," she said, "I doubt not that you will be disappointed in this absurd plan of yours. Not even you can say what happened to the marriage contract drawn up long ago by my father and the earl's. 'Tis gone, and with it any proof that Brigida Morgan was ever pledged to Damion Drake. Yet if we *had* it in our possession and *if* his lordship could be brought to honor it, you would still have *me* to contend with. I'll never wed the Earl of Malvern, Grandfather. You cannot make me."

"*Now* ee's gone and done it," groaned Collin Morgan, rolling his eyes ceilingward, but he might have been talking to an empty room for all the attention his two companions paid him.

"What's this? Not wed, say you?" the commodore blustered, growing red of face. "Heed well your words, me girl, for they've the ring of mutiny about 'em."

"Nevertheless, you force me to them," declared Brigida, her lovely chin jutting just a fraction higher.

The old commodore bit off a low-muttered curse. Egads, one had only to look to see that the gel had run out her guns and was cleared for action, and, as he well knew, not the devil himself could make Brigida Morgan back down once she had shown her colors. The devil fly away with mulish females, he fumed, for he little doubted they had been placed on earth solely to plague the existence of straight-thinking men. Any fool could see his granddaughter's only hope of security lay in marriage, and what better match could she ask than to be wed to a titled gentleman of wealth, one, moreover, who had made a name for himself in the King's Navy? Stifling a sigh, Tavis Llewellyn came heavily to his feet to pronounce sentence on the unrepentant mutineer.

"Then 'tis to the brig with 'ee, Brigida Morgan, till 'ee shall learn a civil tongue."

"Or till the commodore requires his breakfast," mused Collin Morgan philosophically as he watched his grandfather march the culprit up the stairs to her cell beneath the eaves.

* * *

Hardly had the bolt slid home and the echo of the commodore's footsteps retreated down the hall, than Brigida had shed her gown and was busy shrugging on a coarse shirt and patched duck trousers. With a grimace, she forced bare feet into low-quartered shoes and covered her copper-colored curls with a black wig salvaged long ago from a trunk in the attic. At last, cramming a floppy brimmed hat down low on her forehead, Brie paused briefly before the cheval glass to make certain of her disguise.

Suddenly she uttered a low gurgle of laughter. If only Demon Drake could see her now, she mused wryly as she stared at the slender figure indecently attired in male garb. Save for the green eyes, luxuriously lashed, she looked every inch a young boy of the lower orders. Nor was this the first time she had ventured forth in male disguise, yet for some odd reason, she was suddenly tempted to give up the scheme. After all, if her identity were ever discovered, she would be utterly ruined, and while such an occurrence would most certainly put to a period any possibility of her ever marrying Damion Drake, or anyone else for that matter, she could not like to bring disgrace down on her grandfather's house.

Botheration! Such considerations had never troubled her before, she fumed, wheeling in exasperation from the looking glass. Why they should now, simply because the new Earl of Malvern had taken up residence once more in the ancient pile sprawled atop Tal Carn, the crag overlooking the bay a scant four miles east of Gullan Carn, she could not have explained even to herself. In truth she could not quite suppress a slight shiver as she tried to formulate a mental image of the man to whom she had been promised in marriage upon the event of her first birthday. She was nineteen now, well of an age to have made her come-out in Town had there been the funds for such an extravagance and had both her parents not been drowned in a sudden gale off Dodman Point some five years past, but never once had she laid eyes on the naval captain who was legendary throughout the realm for his daring exploits against the French.

"Demon Drake," she murmured softly, the lovely purity of her brow marred by a frown, as it came to her to wonder just how apt was so unfelicitous a sobriquet. The younger of the late earl's two sons, he had proven wild and unruly as a lad, falling into one scrape after another, until his dismissal from Eton at the age of thirteen had prompted his father to obtain an appointment for him as midshipman in a king's ship of the line. Apparently the sea had appealed to the young hellion, for he had chosen not to return to his home in Cornwall even following the untimely demise of his father seven years later or the tragedy of his elder brother's death some eighteen months ago. He would be about one and thirty now, she judged, and did he resemble his brother, the late earl, at all in appearance, would be as stout as a bull and with a face and temperament to match.

Duncan Drake had been overly fond of the homebrewed Cornish mead called "metheglin," and fond of sloe gin and good French brandy, too—when the "gentlemen" had managed a successful run against the "picaroons," which was the Cornish name for the preventive men. In all probability it was the smugglers who had done for the earl, though no one was foolish enough to voice such a thought out loud, for the likes of Kermit Lachlan and Lincoln Kane, the two biggest flaskers in southeast Cornwall, would not take kindly to such an aspersion. Even so, the rumor had gotten around that Duncan Drake had invested in a sizable run which in turn had fallen foul of the coast guard, and being Duncan Drake, he had gone off half-cocked, threatening to turn his nefarious associates over to the preventive men lest they come up either with the money or the goods. His body had been found washed ashore on Whitsand Bay, and no one had mourned his passing overmuch, least of all Cordelia Drake, his childless widow, who had not lingered after the funeral, but had made straightaway to Torpoint and her three spinster sisters.

Poor Cordelia, mused the commodore's granddaughter compassionately. The countess was no beauty, but she had ever been a gentle soul possessed of a kind heart. She had deserved far better than Duncan Drake and Malvern Castle, both of which had sapped her youth and broken her spirit. And now it looked as if fate intended for Brigida Morgan to take her place as chatelaine of the dreary stone fortress atop Tal Carn.

That less than heartening reflection might have sent another girl into a sudden fit of the doldrums, but Brie Morgan was made of sterner stuff. Drawing herself up to her full five feet in height, the commodore's granddaughter thrust her arms defiantly into the sleeves of a disreputable duck smock, which was of the sort worn by the Cornish laborer.

"Neither the devil nor Demon Drake shall keep Brigida Morgan from going her own way," she vowed, and crossing the small chamber made cozy with poster bed, chest, wardrobe, and vanity, let herself out the window.

Chapter Two

The moon was climbing steadily over the channel as Brigida crossed the bourne, which emptied into the sea at the west end of the crags, and gazed out over the sweeping shore of Whitsand Bay. Already a sizable number of cottagers from East Looe and roundabout had gathered to wrest the harvest from the leavings of the ebb tide. Brie, lantern in hand and an empty wicker swinging from the end of the iron crook slung boyishly over one shoulder, was careful to keep the wide brim of her hat pulled low as she made her way past the score of more shrieking urchins hunting sand eels along the beach. There would be time enough to fill her own basket with the agile creatures later. For now, her goal lay among the rocks along the base of the crags.

She had removed her shoes and concealed them in a rocky niche as soon as she came to the bottom of the cliff below Gullan Carn, and the sand, yet damp from the receding tide, gushed deliciously between her toes as she walked. The night was warm for May, the moonlight shimmering silvery on the water, and Brie, her troubles forgotten, succumbed to the lovely spell cast by the sea and the Cornish coast at night. Nevertheless, she felt a keen bite of disappointment when she came at last to the foot of the crag, for she knew as soon as she saw the swarm of men and boys combing the nooks and crannies for shellfish that the rocks would already be nearly picked clean. For a moment she hesitated, reluctant to return home with nothing more rewarding than the basketful of lance eels that might still be gotten along the beach. She had counted on at least five lobsters, three of which would have brought a fair sum from the proprietor of the Riverside Inn in East Looe, enough, in fact, to provide the *Mere-Magden* with a few much-needed refurbishments. The other two had been destined to soften the old commodore's heart toward his errant granddaughter, an object Brigida deemed of only slightly less importance than the fitting of her beloved sailboat.

Suddenly she straightened to her full height, a determined gleam in her eyes. The tide had been out a bare two and a half hours or so, which meant there was still time to search the narrow inlets, or "zawns," which some Cornishman long ago had whimsically named "the Grottoes." The tale was yet told among the simple folk that the place was haunted by the spirit of Inness Glen, an owler who, half a century past, having been caught with his smuggled wool, had escaped to the zawns, only to be drowned by the incoming tide. And now the ghost of Duncan Drake might well keep Inness Glen company, Brie reflected with a slight shiver, for the excisemen suspected the earl had likewise met his fate in the grottoes. Indeed, they had even searched the recesses for the missing contraband. That they had found nothing surprised no one very much, for the grottoes had been similarly combed countless times before and always with the same negative results. Dismissing with a shrug her grandfather's strict orders never to set foot in the treacherous recesses known to be used by smugglers, Brie skirted the reaches and made for the southeastern face of Tal Carn along the bottom of which the grottoes were to be found. The "gentlemen," after all, preferred moonless nights to do their work, and, besides, the grottoes were the one place the harvesters never went, for the Cornish were both a superstitious and a practicable people, and few would care to risk the wrath either of Inness Glen's ghost or of the considerably more dangerous flesh-and-blood smugglers.

Perhaps another quarter of an hour had passed before Brigida came at last to the grottoes, which, actually little more than deep gouges carved from the limestone cliffs by the sea, were hardly deserving of their name. Of course there *was* the hollow known as Smugglers' Cave. Possessed of a wide vaulted ceiling ten or more feet at its greatest height, the cave extended as far as twenty feet or so beneath the crag and thus afforded a convenient chamber for the concealment of a "gentleman's crop of goods" if he happened to be hard-pressed by a coast guard cutter. It was there that Inness Glen had met his end, or so the story went, and high above it, perched on the knoll, was Malvern Castle.

With the adeptness of long practice, Brie soon spotted a fine lobster marooned in a narrow cleft between the rocks. Her iron crook shot out and down, catching the luckless creature and flipping it deftly out of the fissure to the boulder on which she stood. Instantly Brigida closed strong slender fingers about the carapace and dropped her catch into the wicker half submerged in a shallow pocket of water. 'Twas a fair beginning, she thought with a deal of satisfaction and fell to with a light heart.

Without pausing for a rest, Brie worked feverishly, till her back ached from stooping to peer into the cracks and crevices among the rocks and her fingers were numb from gripping the iron crook. She had accumulated a fair catch of cockels and mussels as well as four prime lobster and numerous crabs, when she straightened at last with a sigh and brushed the damp hair from her forehead with the back of a soiled hand.

It must be close to midnight, she judged, and time to make for the safety of the beach above the tidal mark. Yet she was reluctant to leave, for she had still to find the fifth lobster, which was to have helped purchase new canvas for the *Mere-Magden*. This Brie had deemed a dire necessity, since several weeks earlier she had been caught out in a storm that had worked havoc on the small vessel. Indeed, it was only by the sheerest luck and her own levelheaded sailing that she had made it back to shore at all with the mainsail ripped nearly from head to foot. She had been left high and dry for longer than anytime she could remember since first her father had set her hand to the helm when she was nine, and to Brie, who felt happiest when sailing before a stiff breeze, that was tantamount to being confined to prison. With a stubbornness well known to her intimates, the commodore's granddaughter quickly decided that before giving up the means of returning the *Mere-Magden* to a state of seaworthiness, she would hazard a look in Smugglers' Cave.

The time was growing dangerously short, but Brie yet lingered a moment longer, reluctant somehow to follow through with her impulse, not because she was afraid of the ghost of Inness Glen, but because of a rather silly incident that had occurred only a few days past.

Rory Gale, the squire's ne'er-do-well younger son and her brother's friend since childhood, had called for Collin in the evening, as was his wont when he found himself pockets to let and of a mind to carouse in the seamier establishments of East Looe, both of which circumstances occurred far too frequently to Brie's way of thinking. Yet no matter how often she might remonstrate with her brother for allowing Rory Gale to use him so, Collin would only laugh and, chucking her fondly under the chin, declare he'd choose his own way to perdition without a nagging woman's tongue to drive him there, thank you. This particular evening had been no different from the rest, save only that Rory, having made his appearance, as usual in time to be included in the evening meal, had brought with him the latest tidbit of gossip going the rounds of the neighborhood. It seemed, he had reported with a sly wink at a stone-faced Brigida Morgan, that the spirits of Inness Glen and Duncan Drake had been joined by yet another tormented soul—the newest Earl of Malvern, to be precise. Oh, aye, 'twas the God's own truth, he vowed, for he himself had seen the caped figure atop the sheer jut of rock that everyone knew marked the exact location of Smugglers' Cave. Like a monument carved from stone, he was, and staring out to sea, as if he thought at any moment to behold the French fleet come to invade Cornish shores. It was then that Collin, entering into the spirit of the thing, had declared that no doubt the Demon of Malvern thought to lure the poor souls to their deaths on the rocks and laughingly had named the crag "Demon's Perch."

That was all there had been to it, but the account had left Brie strangely moved, for she little doubted that it was neither French ships nor doomed souls that drew the sea captain night after night to his lonely perch, but only the sea itself. Unaccountably she felt an odd sort of pang as she conjured up an image of the brooding figure silhouetted against the darkening sky at dusk. Did Demon Drake so yearn for the sea, why did he not return to it? she wondered, thinking with envy of the graceful schooner moored below Malvern Castle. For not once had *The Aimless* been taken out since it had appeared like a lovely phantom skimming across the bay and dropped anchor at Men-aber, the earl's private dock set at the mouth of the bourne where it met the sea. Indeed, so far as anyone knew, the new Earl of Malvern had not set foot from the home grounds since he had disembarked from the schooner four weeks earlier, a circumstance which was bound to cause a deal of speculation among the close-knit gentry. *They* naturally looked with eagerness to the exchanging of social calls with so illustrious a peer, one who was, moreover, considered the catch of the marriage mart both in London and his native Cornwall.

Well, it was none of her concern, she shrugged, dragging the wicker out of the water and kneeling to slip the hemp strap over her shoulder. She cared not a whit whether Demon Drake should ever see fit to show himself. Indeed, she would vastly prefer it if she never had to lay eyes on the man whose mere presence at Malvern Castle had been enough to disrupt the even tenor of her life. The bite of the rope into the tender flesh of her shoulder as she stood brought a grimace to her lips. Almost she gave up the notion of the last, cherished lobster as she considered the necessity of lugging the already burdensome catch up the cliffside of Gullan Carn. Still, sacrificing all hope of a new canvas would be a deal harder to bear than making the tedious climb up the smugglers' trail with the precious lobster snug on her back, she thought with a wry smile and resolutely began to pick her way across the treacherous rocks to Demon's Perch.

The moon had passed its zenith, leaving the grottoes in darkness so that the feeble glow from Brie's oil lamp cast weird shadows over the jagged outcroppings of rock. Brie shivered, a chill coursing down her spine as she came at last to the wide, gaping mouth of Smugglers' Cave. Almost one could believe the cave really was haunted, she thought, her grip tightening instinctively on the handle of the lantern at the sudden rustle of an eel writhing among the rocks. Imperceptibly her breathing quickened as she kept doggedly to the search, which led her ever deeper into the murky recess.

It was the shimmer of silver in the lantern light that first attracted Brie's attention and brought her to the edge of a fissure concealed by a jutting ledge of rock. Her curiosity aroused, she bent to retrieve a silver medallion from the sand, its severed chain caught beneath a chunk of limestone that had evidently broken off the ledge. Suddenly a low cry was startled from her as she recognized the fine craftsmanship, which she knew to be the work of a certain Spanish silversmith in the far West Indies. Indeed, its twin hung even then around her own slender neck.

"Now how can this have gotten here?" she murmured, her brow puckered in a frown. Then the soft scutter of something moving among the rocks caught her ear, and leaning far over the ledge with the lantern held high, she spotted what she had come for.

Pocketing the medallion for later speculation, Brie quickly divested herself of the wicker and knelt to peer down into the crevice partially filled with water. The lobster, measuring a good foot or more in length, was wedged between two overlapping shelves of rock just above the waterline. Careful not to damage the creature, she lowered the iron crook and tried to ease the lobster from its niche.

"Botheration!" she muttered as the crook slipped from numbed fingers and clattered into the fissure. Now what was she to do? By heavens she had not come this far only to give up in defeat! Gritting her teeth, she lay full length on the rock and reached blindly beneath the murky surface for the lost implement. Her pulse abruptly quickened as her fingers found not only the crook, but a rough surface, which further exploration revealed to be the top of a submerged wooden cask.

"So that's where they hide it!" she exclaimed and, retrieving the crook, backed hastily from the smugglers' cache, her mouth suddenly dry as she realized the dire implications of the medallion's presence in the close proximity of a smuggler's concealed crop of goods.

"Quite so, my lad," drawled a soft voice behind her. Brigida, her heart leaping to her throat, wheeled to search the shadowed depths of the cave with frightened eyes.

"Who is it?" she called out, raising high the lantern. "Show thyself, if 'ee's man enough."

She gasped as a ghastly figure garbed in black detached itself from the shadows.

"I might be the ghost of Inness Glen. Or the spirit of Duncan Drake," remarked the intruder, observing her out of eyes that glittered in the lantern light. Like black diamonds, they were, set in an abnormally pale, but strikingly handsome face, which was marred only by the thin line of a scar across a high-boned cheek.

"But thee's not," Brigida retorted belligerently, not one to be easily taken in. Indeed, it was not ghosts she had to fear, but something far more sinister, for she knew well the peril inherent in her unlooked-for discovery. No matter what they might be pleased to call themselves, the flaskers were no gentlemen, but dangerous cutthroats who had been known to commit murder on more than one occasion to protect themselves and their secret dealings. Deliberately she set the lantern down, her fingers tightening on the iron crook as slowly she rose to her feet. The blackguard might have caught her red-handed, but he would not take her without a fight.

The blackguard, however, appeared in no hurry to take her on. Indeed, if anything, he seemed in a peculiarly whimsical mood.

"But can you be so certain?" he queried with an oddly cynical quirk of the lips. "Behold the scarred visage, the pallid complexion and reflect: Is it in truth a creature of flesh and blood who stands before you or rather the poor remnants of a man?"

"Thee'll not bam the likes o' me with naught but a wee scar an' words meant to frighten children," Brie instantly rejoined, but a frown knit her brow. Who the devil was he? He had neither the look nor the manner of a flasker. Indeed, from what little she could make out in the dim light, his bearing was more that of a gentleman born, for though he was slender and not above average height, there was about him the compelling air of one used to command, and, what's more, he spoke with the cultured accent of the gentility. Suddenly Brie stiffened, as with a start she realized that while she had been puzzling over the stranger's identity, he had drawn imperceptibly into the circle of the lantern light.

"That's far enough, gov'nor," she warned, holding the crook significantly before her. "Spirit or not, thee'll feel the hard side of me rod does 'ee come any closer."

The hint of a smile played briefly about the thin lips.

"You're a plucky little bantling, are you not. And yet one with more bottom than brains, 'twould seem. Even an infant, is he a true Cornish lad, must be aware that the moon has passed overhead. Listen," he said, a slender white hand cautioning her to silence. "The tide is already to the reaches."

Even as she turned her head to hear the sea crashing against the rocks below the caves, Brie sensed him coming at her and swung with all her might. A hand shot out to catch the rod in a strong clasp, and suddenly she found herself staring mesmerized into black, steely eyes scant inches from her face.

"Drop it, you little fool," he rasped, his breath whistling in his throat. "The sea is your enemy, not I."

A defiant retort rose to Brie's lips. Then to her amazement, she saw him waver, beheld a grimace of pain twist across his face.

"You're ill!" she cried and without thought, let go her hold on the makeshift weapon and pressed against his side, one arm going about the lean waist as she felt him sag against her. The iron crook dropped harmlessly to the cavern floor, and for a breathless moment Brie wondered if the stranger would as well, but almost immediately he had himself in hand again.

Forcing himself upright, he gazed down into the young face turned anxiously up to his, and suddenly a rueful laugh seemed dragged from him.

"Who are you, boy?" he said, an odd expression flickering in the coal black eyes. "What are you doing here?"

Instantly Brie drew back, her heart pounding beneath her breast, as his words recalled to her the dangerous charade she played.

"Br-*Brian*," she stammered in a gruff little voice and ducked her head to hide the sudden flush of her cheeks as she searched her mind frantically for a pseudonym that might suit. "Brian Murdoch. I be come for the springtide harvest, nothin' more, gov'nor. I swear it. 'Twas the lobster I were after, but I dropped me crook, an' when I went to fetch it out'n the crack, I found what weren't never meant for none to know. Plaise, gov'nor. I'll not tell a soul. On me maither's grave, I swear. Thy secret's safe with me."

"*My* secret!" he echoed, one dark eyebrow shooting toward his hairline as he bent a piercing gaze upon her.

The girl struggled not to squirm beneath the man's pointed scrutiny as all her instincts warned her to flee. Indeed, she doubted if in his weakened condition he could stop her. Yet something kept her from making her escape. She told herself it was the medallion and the need to discover what the stranger might know of it, but if she were to be completely honest with herself, she would have to acknowledge it was the man himself who held her where she was.

There was that about him that both fascinated and perplexed her—the hint of suffering in the fine lines about his mouth, for example, and the gleam of recklessness behind the hard glitter of his eyes. From the manner of his speech, she doubted not that he had been gifted with a quick wit and keen intellect, and despite the cynical curl of finely molded lips, she suspected he possessed as well a strong capacity for passion kept rigidly in check. Then, too, she could not but detect in the stubborn jut of the firm jaw, the intimation of a will to match her own. What it was, however, that seemed to draw her to him she hardly understood herself. She knew only that he was ill and that somehow, villain or not, she could not leave him to face the peril of the incoming tide alone.

All at once Brigida jumped at the man's ironic bark of laughter, followed by an ungentle hand grasping her familiarly by the scruff of the neck.

"Impertinent little whelp, you think that *I*—," he began, his voice vibrant with a wry sort of amusement. But then abruptly he broke off what he had been about to say as he was treated to a glance from magnificent green eyes ablaze with purely feminine indignation.

And, indeed, for the briefest moment Brie had forgotten her assumed role before the bewildering sensations aroused by the contact of masculine fingers against bare skin. No man other than her father, her brother, and her dearest gramfer had ever before dared to lay a hand upon her, and for a single, appalling instant flames had seemed to leap beneath this stranger's touch. Frightened by what she felt and did not understand, it was perhaps not surprising that Brigida should have erupted suddenly into a fit of anger.

"Take your hands off me!" she cried and, twisting sharply from beneath his grasp, turned to face him defiantly. Who was *he,* after all, to insult Brigida Morgan? she fumed, little guessing at the sudden shock that coursed through her assailant's frame as unintentionally he was granted a glimpse of the vital creature lurking behind the unprepossessing guise of an urchin.

Only the sudden narrowing of his gaze upon her face brought her to an awareness of how perilously close she had come to utterly betraying herself. Blushing furiously, she glanced nervously away.

"No one lays a hand on Brian Murdoch," she muttered in a feeble attempt to retrieve her error.

"I see, and thus, no doubt, you think to be applauded," commented the gentleman acerbically. "Yet it occurs to me that an ill-mannered pup is better served by a hand properly applied. And so I shall inform your unfortunate sire when I meet him."

"I haven't a father. Or a mother," declared the ill-mannered pup, her heart suddenly fluttering at the appalling notion that he should ever encounter anyone even remotely related to her, let alone Collin Morgan or her grandfather, the commodore. "I takes care of meself."

"No doubt that explains why you are to be found in such unwholesome surrounds when you would be better off at home tucked in your bed," he observed, apparently unmoved at her unfortunate lack of familial ties. "However, that is neither here nor there. 'Twould seem it devolves upon me to extricate you from an untimely demise by drowning." And, indeed, the tide had risen sufficiently to send swells washing past the lower reaches of the cavern mouth and into the cave itself. "You, my lad, will be best pleased to come with me," he ended and, grasping her by the arm, began to pull her ungently toward the back of the cave.

"No!" Wrenching free, Brie backed warily from the man, her mind reeling with fear and an odd sense of disappointment. What a fool she had been to fall victim to a handsome face and her own soft heart! In truth his soul was demon black, and he'd meant from the first to do away with her.

"Now what foolishness is this?" he demanded, his well-modulated tones edged with impatience.

"Did 'ee think I should go gently to me death?" she retorted incredulously. "I be not so great a fool as that."

"No, only fool enough not to realize I could have knocked you over the head and left you for dead when first I came up behind you — had that been my intention. And in truth the notion grows more tempting by the minute. Doubtless it would have saved me a deal of trouble."

"Aye, and would still," declared the girl, unconvinced. "For 'tis plain 'ee meant to throttle Brian Murdoch and leave his body wedged among the rocks at the back of the cave."

"I am sorry to disappoint you," he answered with a cold gleam of a smile, "but unless you plan to succumb to my murderous intent without a struggle, I fear I simply cannot oblige you. I find this rather unprepossessing souvenir of my inglorious past quite useless, you see." And lifting his left arm to his chest, he revealed the once supple hand now hideously scarred, the fingers curled in upon themselves like tortured claws.

Brie felt the bile rise to her throat and, swallowing hard, had to force her eyes from the poor, disfigured member. How cruelly he must have suffered and from the looks of him, suffered still! she thought compassionately and was suddenly grateful that the floppy brim of her hat hid her face in shadows. Carefully schooling her features to reveal nothing either of her horror or her pity, she glanced up to find him watching her, the thin lips curled in bitter self-mockery.

"Law, gov'nor!" she exclaimed ingenuously. "There's a scar to put to shame ole Fergus Doyle, who lost four fingers and an ear in a tavern brawl. Belike thee could tell a tale or two that'd make a body sit up and listen!"

For a breathless moment she feared she had overplayed her hand as she saw the muscle leap spasmodically along the lean jaw. Then all at once his head went back and the cavern reverberated with his laughter.

"No doubt you are in the right of it," he managed when he had got his breath back again. "And now, if you are satisfied that I am harmless, perhaps we can proceed to more congenial surrounds."

"Not so fast, gov'nor," Brie demurred, standing her ground. "No one ever said 'ee was 'harmless', nor ever could, to my way of thinking, without he was to tell an awful fib. Perhaps a spirit like 'eeself can pass through walls of solid stone, but Brian Murdoch'd rather take his chances with the sea, if thee's no objection."

"You are, of course, free to do exactly as you wish. It does occur to me, however, that you might conceivably find the Earl of Malvern's private exit a trifle less tedious than a midnight swim. But suit yourself. I'm a reasonable man, you see." And with that, he retreated to the rear of the cave and applied his shoulder to a section of the wall. There was a low rumble, and what had previously appeared as solid rock was soon revealed to be a cleverly wrought stone slab set on a pivot, and behind it, a turret stair carved from the limestone cliff itself.

Anything but a slow-top, Brigida was not long in putting two and two together, or in this case, the stranger and the Earl of Malvern's secret stair.

"Oh, Lord," she groaned, " 'tis Demon Drake himself!"

"Even so, bantling," drawled the Earl of Malvern,

ironically inclining his head toward his startled young guest. "And now that you are aware that I am neither a murderer nor a smuggler, I really must insist that we depart."

Still Brigida hesitated, stunned at the realization that she faced not only Demon Drake, but her own certain ruination. Indeed, for an instant she was half tempted to dare the incoming tide rather than submit to the inevitable unveiling of her true identity. Then, ever of a practical inclination, Brie quickly discarded the desperate notion. Her death by drowning, after all, would avail her nothing, she reflected wryly, and there was still the chance, small though it was, that she might yet carry the thing off.

Drawing a deep breath, Brie took a reluctant step forward, only to come once more to a halt, her head sweeping up in an unconscious gesture of defiance. Indeed, it had suddenly occurred to her that if she were truly to be sunk into ill-repute for this night's work, she should at least have the fruits of her labor, and the devil fly away with the odious Demon Drake.

"Be with 'ee in the shake of a lamb's tail, gov'nor," she called a trifle wildly, and ignoring the earl's blistering oath, wheeled to retrieve the iron crook from the cavern floor.

This time luck seemed to be with her, as she lowered the crook and deftly twitched from its niche the lobster that had been the cause of her own plunge into deep waters. No sooner, however, had she consigned the troublesome creature safely to the wicker, than a wave, crashing through the cavern mouth, knocked her off her feet. Her head struck something hard, and darkness threatened. Then an iron hand snatched her from the receding swell, so that she came up, sputtering, to meet the Earl of Malvern's icy stare.

"You, my lad, are fast trying my patience," observed

Demon Drake in a voice all the more chilling for its velvet softness, and Brie, still clinging with a death grip to her precious wicker, was dragged ignominiously toward the safety of the stair.

Chapter Three

"Just *what* did you think you were doing?" demanded the Earl of Malvern as he ushered a bedraggled Brigida Morgan past the astonished butler and into the great hall. "Did it once occur to you that a mere lobster, no matter how delectable when served up on a platter, is hardly worth the risk of drowning?"

Brie, who had been battered and dazed from her unlooked-for adventure and who thus far had suffered herself in silence to be herded up the turret stair to the promontory of Demon's Perch and from there along a steep trail to Malvern Castle, found her tongue at last.

"Thee's a fine one t' praich, when 'ee's a lord's castle and a rich man's purse," she uttered scathingly. "Me *Mere-Magden*'s all I got what's mine. 'Tweren't never meant for the likes of Brian Murdoch to dine on a rich man's fare. But three prime lobster'll buy food to feed a poor Cornish family a se'ennight or more. Or, better, bring blunt enough to fit out me sloop with canvas. And to my way of thinking such is worth a wee risk or two."

"I shouldn't doubt it for an instant," the earl acidly agreed. "You, my blockish young friend, are foolish beyond permission." Then, apparently becoming aware of the presence of his scandalized superior servant, who was eyeing with obvious distaste the urchin bedecked in sodden rags, its hair hanging in clumps about its dirty face, and its shivering form streaming rivulets of sand and seawater to create a slowly spreading puddle over the immaculate parquetry tiled floor, he added blightingly, "If it is not too much to ask, Griffith, I would suggest that you cease to stand with your mouth agape and instead try if you can make yourself useful. If indeed you can bestir yourself, you may summon my man Hartwell to me at once. After which you will no doubt be pleased to fetch black coffee, a cold collation, and a strip of court plaster to the 'Aviary.' "

"Very well, m'lord," sniffed Griffith with the wounded air of one unjustly impugned of gross impropriety, and, bowing stiffly, exited the hall in the grand manner.

"And as for you, you impertinent young whelp," the earl continued with hardly a pause, "*you* will come with me."

"Ifn it's all the same, I'd rather not, gov'nor," Brie demurred, her pulse suddenly erratic as she glanced up into black, Celtic eyes. Indeed, from the first moment she had beheld the Demon of Malvern emerge like a wraith from the shadows, she had been subjected to a veritable panoply of unfamiliar sensations, none of which was calculated to add in any way to her comfort. In short, she thought she must go mad if she did not soon escape the man's bewildering presence, not to mention the fact that every minute spent with him only increased the likelihood of her eventual unveiling. The earl, however, seemed odiously determined to prolong her visit.

"I was not issuing an invitation, Brian Murdoch," he drawled significantly. "You will do exactly as I say, or I shall be forced to report your findings to the excisemen. Do I make myself clear?"

"Thee wouldn't dare!" Brigida yelped, her face

blanching beneath the smudges of dirt. "Not even a fine lord like 'eeself'd risk the wrath of the flaskers."

"Indeed not?" his lordship queried, fixing her with a piercing glance. "And my brother Duncan, no doubt, is the proof of the pudding, is he not?"

Brie stifled a gasp. So that was what the Demon was after, prowling about the perch at night. He was looking for his brother's murderers, and who must he find instead, but Brigida Morgan! Oh, Lord, it did not bear considering.

"I—I never said any such thing. I haven't the barest notion who might've d-done the deed," she stammered, feeling the medallion heavy in her pocket. "And ifn 'ee was to claim I did, 'twould be a lie."

The Demon's lips curled in a soulless smile.

"Quite so, and yet who but you and I would know it?"

For a moment Brie stared dumbfounded into the saturnine countenance, her stomach feeling peculiarly hollow, for it was only the truth he had spoken. There was no one to swear Brigida Morgan had not accused the smugglers of Duncan Drake's death. Nor would it matter overmuch if there were. The likes of Lincoln Kane and Kermit Lachlan would not care one whit that she was innocent. The merest whisper that she had in any way betrayed "the gentlemen" was enough for them to murder her in her bed and afterward burn Gullan Carn to the ground with all the inhabitants in it. And yet, who was to say Brigida Morgan had anything to do with this smuggling business? she reflected with a sudden start. Unless the Earl of Malvern discovered her true identity, it would be the fictitious Brian Murdoch they would be looking for.

The realization was enough to send her bolting for the door. Coming up hard against the solid barrier, she fumbled for the latch and at last felt it give. Her breath sobbed in her throat as she yanked the door open and lunged for freedom. Too late. From out of nowhere a strong, burly arm closed about her waist and snatched her, kicking and screaming, into the air.

"Put—me—*down!*" she panted, perilously close to tears, as she suddenly found herself slung, rather like a sack of potatoes, beneath the brutish arm of a veritable giant of a man and borne ignominiously back into the Demon's presence.

"I congratulate you, Hartwell, on your timely arrival," commented the earl, sublimely oblivious to the vociferous protestations issuing from the helpless captive.

"It wasn't nothing, sir. The little rogue never seen me comin'. An' what was ye wishful of doin' with th' banty, Cap'n? He's a lively little cock. Shall I knock 'im aside th' head an' feed 'im to th' sharks?"

Brie went suddenly rigid. Good God, this *could* not be truly happening to her. But the Demon's hatefully cool tones soon put to the rout any such vain hopes.

"I think not, Hartwell," he drawled negligently. "Inexplicable as it may seem, there might be someone who would miss the young thatchgallows, and I should find an investigation at this time exceedingly tedious. You may convey him to the aviary for the present, and see that he has what he needs to render himself more presentable, if you will."

"Aye, Cap'n," cheerfully replied Brie's burly captor as he started up a magnificent circular stair that climbed gracefully to a stone apse met on either end by more ascending stairs. Upon which, Brigida Morgan was at last jarred from her stunned paralysis.

"No! Thee can't keep me against my will," she shouted, twisting in the giant's grasp to peer furiously back at the trim figure poised languidly at the bottom of the staircase. "There be laws against abduction!"

Nevertheless, laws or no laws, several minutes later

Brie found herself firmly ensconced in an elegant, if subdued, paneled chamber, remarkable for the carved oak wainscot along the ceiling, which depicted with intricate detail various and sundry birds in marvelous attitudes of motion.

"Here ye be, lad," rumbled the giant, setting Brie on her feet, and with arms crossed over the massive barrel of a chest, proceeded to sweep her from head to toe with a measuring glance. "A mite on the puny side, ain't ye," was his astute observation, "but never ye mind. Might be that ye've time yet t' fill out an' sprout an inch or two, ifn ye behaves yerself. Now, off wi' yer togs loike a good lad, afore ye catches yer death of cold."

For the barest instant Brie froze, her glance flying in horrified astonishment to the man towering above her. Dressed in white trousers and a checked shirt, he stood well over six feet, every inch of which seemed to bulge with muscle. He had the unmistakable look of the British sailor, with deeply tanned skin, light blue eyes, and sun-streaked brown hair tied in a queue at the nape of his neck. The clean-shaven face was rugged and, oddly enough, not unpleasing in appearance, for there was about it a sort of humorous tolerance evidenced in the easy quirk of rather full lips and a knowing twinkle in the steady gaze bent patiently upon her.

"Come now, lad," he urged. "No need fer modesty 'twixt mates. Jack Hartwell may have th' look of a bugbear, but he'll not eat ye."

"Even so, Brian Murdoch strips for no man," declared Brie, having decided that in the circumstances a bold front was the only avenue open to her. "I be not afeared of 'ee or your Demon Captain Drake."

"So ye've heard the tales told o' the cap'n, have ye. Well, I'm not sayin' they ain't th' truth. I've seen 'im when there wasn't a man jack who'd not shiver in his timbers before 'im'. An' I've seen 'im wi' those black eyes aglitter wi' th' fire o' battle. Eyes what'd make a youngster like yerself come awake screamin' in the dead o' night. But there's not a jack tar what's served under 'im who wouldn't go up agin Boney or the devil himself if Demon Drake was to ask it of 'im. Meself included. So ye'd better do as the cap'n ordered, or ye'll have Jack Hartwell to answer to."

Brie's heart sank like a leaden weight. Clearly the loyal Hartwell was prepared to go to any lengths for his precious cap'n, but no less determined was Brigida Morgan to thwart him. Slowly she backed before the big man's purposeful advance, her every sense alert to discover even the most desperate avenue of escape. Like an answer to a prayer she glimpsed the billow of satin drapes off to her right. Then Hartwell made his lunge. Quick as thought Brie ducked beneath the grasping arms and darted for a casement window, the sashes left ajar by some negligent servant. Bounding from the window seat on to the ledge, she clutched suddenly at the mullion, her head spinning as she teetered on the precipice. For a seemingly endless moment she stared in terrified fascination at the sea crashing into the cliffs two hundred feet or more below her. Then a movement from behind brought her head around.

"Stand back!" she cried. "Try to lay a hand on me, and I swear I'll jump."

Her voice, sounding fey and wild even in her own ears, brought Hartwell up short, a shadow of uncertainty flickering in his eyes. Brie swallowed hard. Lord, what now? she thought, trying to resist the morbid impulse to look down. She had got herself in a real toil, and it behooved her to keep her wits about her. Then Hartwell grinned, revealing a gaping hole in the midst of even white teeth.

"Now we both know ye doesn't mean it, lad," he crooned, edging closer to the window.

Brie, her ears ringing from weariness and the blow she had suffered earlier in the cave, swayed drunkenly, little knowing what she meant to do. Then a soft voice cut across the taut stillness.

" 'Twould seem our guest has unaccountably taken you in aversion, Hartwell. Has he proven to be too much for you, it were perhaps better to call in reinforcements than to drive the infernal brat to the rocks below. Doubtless Griffith would be happy to oblige, or Cook. In any case, I suggest you ease off for the present."

The big man stiffened to attention, a dusky red deepening the swarthiness of his sunburnt cheeks.

"But, Cap'n," he said, spreading wide huge hands as he turned half pleading toward the slim figure observing them with acerbic interest from a doorway that led to an adjoining room. " 'E took me by surprise, 'e did, but ifn ye was to give me just a minute longer, I swear I'll have the little bugger tamed fer ye."

To Brie's amazement, she saw the frosty glint of the Demon's eyes relent before the giant's pained discomfort. A shadow passed fleetingly across the austere features, and the chiseled lips curved in a rueful smile.

"Never mind, Hartwell. You need concern yourself no further," he said wearily. "Doubtless I should have warned you of our maggoty young guest's proclivity for falling into distempered freaks. For that I assume full responsibility. Meantime, you are free to retire. I shan't need you further tonight."

Reluctantly Hartwell muttered a disgruntled "Aye, sir," then, casting a darkling glance over his shoulder at Brigida, he retreated grudgingly from the chamber.

"And now, Brian Murdoch," murmured the Earl of Malvern, crossing to stand with his back to the fire crackling invitingly in a carved Gothic fireplace set in one wall, "you will kindly explain what you are doing on that window ledge."

Brie, gritting her teeth to stop their sudden chattering, eyed the nobleman warily. He had taken time to change out of his wet clothing and now wore over ankle-length trousers a magnificent example of the deshabille, belted at the lean waist. Hair, the bluish-black of ravens' wings, clustered close to a well-molded head in the style known as the Brutus crop, and on his feet were soft leather slippers known as "mules." His maimed hand thrust casually into a corded pocket below the waist, he presented the perfect picture of a wealthy gentleman fitted out for a quiet evening at home, she thought a trifle wildly and suppressed an insane urge to giggle.

"Well?" prodded the earl, when it seemed no answer was forthcoming.

"The ape wanted me to take me clothes off," she declared with a fine show of defiance, though her voice shook ever so slightly with the cold and she was sure her lips must be an unbecoming tint of blue.

"A hideous prospect, I've no doubt," Malvern magnanimously agreed. "Far more disagreeable, in fact, than contracting a fatal inflammation of the lungs, which is what you risk do you continue to play the gaby."

"Fudge! I'm not like to cut me stick from a little wetting," the girl retorted, then, despite her heroic efforts, immediately succumbed to the persistent tickle in her nose with a stentorian sneeze.

"Quite so," cynically pronounced the earl, upon which, a slight scratching at the hall door announced the arrival of Griffith, bearing a tray laden with savories the likes of which made Brie's stomach protest its hollow state.

Brie heard her host calmly instruct the stone-faced butler that they would serve themselves and then with a murmured thank-you, coolly dismiss him. Whereupon Griffith, obviously a personage of great condescension, departed with staid deliberation from their presence. As if it were an everyday occurrence for the inmates of Malvern to have persons flinging themselves in desperation from the battlements, she reflected with a sense of having entered Bedlam. And then the earl's sardonic drawl obtruded on her private musings.

"If you are not irrevocably set on putting to the period your brief existence," he commented negligently as he turned away to fill a plate with hot Cornish pasties, pickled pigs' trotters, and a generous portion of savory meat custard swimming in almond milk sauce, "perhaps you would care instead to withdraw to the adjoining closet to relieve yourself of all your dirt. Purely a suggestion, mind you, but it would be a shame, would it not, to allow such an admirable collation as this to go to waste?"

"Well, so long as 'ee puts it that way, gov'nor," Brie assented, exceedingly relieved to be spared not only the ignominy of having herself stripped bare by the Demon of Malvern, but the necessity of remaining further on the dizzying brink of self-immolation as well, "I suppose I *could* do to hang about a mite longer. But no tricks, mind 'ee. Brian Murdoch plays straight with them what plays straight with him."

A smile twitched at the earl's handsome lips, but his answer, when it came, was properly grave.

"Then it is agreed," he murmured, and, leaving the plate on the tray, crossed leisurely to the window. Brie watched with the fascination of a bird confronted unexpectedly by a cobra as Demon Drake extended a slender white hand up to her. "No tricks, I give my word," he said, a disquieting glint in his eyes, "for just as long as Brian Murdoch shall choose to deal in plain pounds with me."

Not surprisingly, Brigida *cum* Brian Murdoch suffered a slight twinge of unease at the pact that was offered. Indeed, she had the oddest sense of having bartered her soul as hesitantly she placed her hand in Damion Drake's and allowed herself to be helped from the precipice to the floor.

Chapter Four

It was with a distinct feeling of unreality that Brie stood some time later upon the threshold of the oak-paneled chamber, her soiled clothes rolled in a bundle in her arms. Her slight form was rather more elegantly, if outlandishly, arrayed in a collarless skirted coat, knee-length waistcoat, blue satin small clothes, white silk stockings, and leather slippers with brass buckles, all of which had been neatly laid out for her in the dressing room adjoining what she had soon discovered to be the earl's bedchamber. From this she had quickly deduced that the "aviary" must be his lordship's private sitting room, and, indeed, the caffoy-covered settee with matching wing chairs, the Oriental carpet, and the Louis Quinze secretaire bookcase replete with leather-bound volumes would seem to bear her out. In fact, the one thing she had yet to determine, and that which troubled her the most, was her own enforced presence in the Demon of Malvern's inner sanctum with her person decked out in the fashion of a noble's pampered son. It passed the bounds of all reason, unless, of course, the hero of countless tales of daring happened to be Roman in his private pursuits of pleasure.

Good heavens! she thought, her glance flying in horror to the gentleman seated before the fire, his unfathomable gaze fixed and brooding on the flames. She had read of such things in her father's books on antiquity, but to believe that Damion Drake, no matter how black his reputation, could be so decadent and depraved was simply too dreadful for contemplation. For a moment she hesitated, uncertain whether to make known her presence or to try a desperate dash for the hall door in the slim chance of achieving an escape. In an agony of indecision, she found herself probing the unnaturally pallid features for some clue as to the man's inner musings.

That his thoughts were unrewarding was evidenced by the slight furrow between the finely drawn eyebrows. Furthermore, the shapely fingers of his good hand drummed a monotonous pattern against the armrest. *Something* plagued the Demon, she decided, but he hardly had the look of a man contemplating an imminent debauchery. Rather, with his guard down, he appeared worn to the nub, the disturbing eyes wreathed in shadows and the stern-lipped mouth a thin, white line of fatigue and pain. Doubtless he was as hardheaded as most of his gender, who, without a woman to look after them, were like to drive themselves into a sharp decline rather than to take to their beds when they should. Indeed, she had yet to meet a man who had a lick of common sense when it came to having a proper care for himself, she mused, then drew herself up sharply as she realized that she was laboring under an unfamiliar urge to soothe the bleak lines from about her heartless abductor's eyes and mouth.

This will never do, Brigida Morgan, she told herself and wondered with a wry quirk of her lips if the Demon of Malvern had cast some sort of spell over her. For, unlike her mother, who at an early age had been fortunate enough to marry the first and only love of her life, Brigida had ever demonstrated a marked indifference to the various unattached males of her acquaintance. Thus far, her heart had remained untouched, and, having ever considered herself a wholly sensible female, she was more than content to leave it that way. She had better things to do with her life, after all, than to let herself become enamored of some man who would expect to rule both her heart and her head, and she certainly had no intention of becoming an unwitting victim of the infamous Demon of Malvern. Indeed, she had to contrive somehow to remain Brian Murdoch until such time as she could make her escape. And that time had better come soon, she realized with a sinking feeling, as she heard the ormolu clock on the mantelpiece strike the hour of two.

"So, you've decided to join me after all," observed the earl, glancing up to find Brie watching him uncertainly.

Startled from her reverie, Brie visibly winced.

"Aye, but then 'ee didn't leave me much choice in the matter, did 'ee," she retorted bitterly and hastily ducked her head to hide the angry glitter of her eyes. But almost immediately she looked up again, as if compelled. Indeed, she had to know. "Would 'ee truly have turned me over to the picaroons?" she asked gruffly, hardly knowing why she should doubt it for a moment.

"As surely as your name is Brian Murdoch," he answered without the flicker of an eyelid.

"But *why?* I've done nothing agin 'ee or any of thy house, and I doesn't know anything about the store of goods sunk in Smugglers' Cave. Yet thee'd feed me to th' sharks without so much as a never 'ee mind. And 'ee shan't claim ignorance that me life'd not be worth a pickled herring was I to earn the name of 'informer,' for there's not a soul what'd believe it, meself least of all."

"Indeed, you would be exceedingly foolish to assume anything so patently unlikely," agreed the earl chillingly. "I am well aware of the Cornish motto, 'All and One,' which enjoins entire communities to silence out of misguided loyalty and fear. Undoubtedly without such connivance the 'Free Trade' would long since have been laid to rest. That is why you will do exactly as I command you, Brian Murdoch, do you wish to continue in good repute with your neighbors."

"But what can 'ee want from me?" she queried harshly, a clamp seeming to close on her vitals as she stared into the Demon's cold, black eyes and shivered in spite of herself. "I be naught but a poor orphan without polish or learning. But I've tried t' be an honest lad. What use could the likes of Demon Drake have for one such as meself?"

"Possibly none," admitted his lordship. "It has, however, occurred to me that I am in need of a pair of eyes and ears to see and hear what is denied the Earl of Malvern and his kind. A homeless waif like yourself, for instance, who is in the confidence of the local element. You, my little rag-mannered and scurrilous young whelp, are about to become my page."

Brie, torn between fear and outrage at the nobleman's unscrupulous maneuverings, instantly bridled.

"I'll be no man's slave," she declared with flashing eyes, "nor a sniveling blab for the likes of 'ee. I'd as lief sell me soul to the devil."

"Oh, but you have already, if only you can be made to see it," murmured the earl, his smile enigmatic. "For you belong to me, Brian Murdoch, as surely as if your name had been entered in a legal contract pledging you till death to Demon Drake. You have no choice but to obey me."

Brie stifled a startled gasp. Good God, if he only knew how near he was to the truth! Indeed, if she were not so properly in the briars, she would have been tempted to laugh at the absurdity fate had dealt her. As it was, she could not but admit he was odiously in the right of it: for the present she must play the dupe till she could see her way out of the coil she had wrought for herself. After all, it was not only her life at stake, but whatever dreadful secret surrounded the silver medallion now hanging with its twin about her neck. And, besides, she comforted herself, she need only pretend to demean herself till such time as she could make her escape from the Demon's castle, upon which, not only would Brian Murdoch cease to exist, but Brigida Morgan would be home scot free. And the devil fly away with Damion Drake.

The commodore's granddaughter schooled her features to what she hoped was a sullen acceptance of defeat as she glanced up to meet raven eyes observing her intently from beneath heavily drooping lids.

"Well, Brian Murdoch," the earl drawled, hatefully cool. "What is it to be? The picaroons or servitude to Malvern?"

"Why, since 'ee puts it that way, gov'nor," she managed with only the smallest quiver of suppressed fury, "I reckon I could do worse than enter into the service of a fine *upstandin'* gennelman like yourself. Might be I kin learn a trick or two from the devious Lord of Malvern."

"I don't doubt for a moment that ere we're through you shall have learned a great deal more than you had bargained for," commented the earl quite affably. "Indeed, I shouldn't wonder if you discover we deal extremely, so long as you keep to your word to play strictly on the up-and-up."

Unaccountably, Brie felt the blood rise to her cheeks as it came to her that the odious creature was laughing at her. And, indeed, for the barest instant she was sure she had detected a flicker of unholy amusement in the soulless orbs, but then a shutter seemed to descend over the handsome features, and the moment was lost as her thoroughly detestable master commanded her to approach him that he might have a closer look at his latest acquisition.

Instantly her ever uncertain temper flared. Acquisition indeed, she thought, biting her tongue to keep from delivering his lordship a stinging retort. Lord, how she would like to be quit of her abominable disguise that she might tell him exactly what she thought of a man who apparently would hesitate at nothing, not even abducting and coercing children to do his will. Nevertheless, she was well aware that she had no choice but to play her part out to the bitter end. Studiously fixing her gaze upon the elegant pattern of the Oriental rug, Brigida Morgan did as she was bid.

Thus she did not see the curious twitch of Damion Drake's lips as she came to stand before him or the devil lurking in his eyes as he ordered her to kneel. For a moment she thought she must surely erupt with the fury building up inside her, but again she managed to curb her tongue and bridle her temper, though the effort that it cost her left her trembling within. Determined that he should not get the better of her, she dropped stiffly to her knees. But then she recoiled as if stung at the unexpected touch of his fingers gently pushing a lock of the unsightly wig back from her forehead.

"*Softly,* repellent boy," he said quellingly. "I've a particular aversion to having crackbrained young lobcocks bleed all over my floor. And since it was due to your own iniquitous behavior that you have received what can only be considered your just recompense, it behooves you now to stand buff. This may hurt a bit."

It was only with the greatest effort that Brie came at last to understand not only that the earl was referring to a gash on her forehead, sustained, apparently, during her mishap with the wave in Smugglers' Cave, but that, incredibly, he fully intended to minister to her hurt as well. What a strange creature he was to be sure, she thought as obediently she settled back on her knees before him and steeled herself to remain still as the Demon of Malvern cleansed the wound with soap and warm water, which waited in readiness on a tray beside the chair.

The cut, while not serious, was attended by a sizable goose egg and the added complication of sand granules ground deep in the wound. Thus the earl's warning that there might be some slight discomfort attendant with the operation soon proved to be an understatement. But the pain was as nothing compared to the bewildering sensations aroused by his touch and, worse, by his lordship's disturbing proximity. Not only was she forced to endure the appalling notion that she had somehow contracted a slow-mounting fever, which had the disquieting side effects of disordering her thoughts and rendering her mouth peculiarly dry, but she must also find her senses unfairly assailed by the heady scents of shaving soap, tobacco, and clean linen at exceedingly close range. It was all she could do to keep from crying out in frustration, but at last her torment came to an end with the Earl of Malvern's sudden, low-muttered, "Hellsfire!"

Brie glanced up in startled wonder to behold the nobleman eyeing with unwonted malevolence an innocuous strip of sticking plaster, which somehow had become affixed to the fingers of his uninjured hand. Instantly grasping his dilemma, she acted without thought.

"Here, let me," she said and leaned forward to clasp his hand in hers.

"If I require your aid, I shall ask for it, you misbegotten puppy," he growled, wrenching to one side with such abruptness that his maimed hand came into jarring contact with Brie, nearly sending her sprawling.

"*Damn* your meddling!" gasped the earl, his face gone parchment white as he clutched the crippled member to his chest.

"My meddling!" exploded the commodore's granddaughter, pushed beyond the limit. "Why 'ee crossgrained, puffed-up swell! Who *asked* 'ee to play the nursemaid? Not me! And for that matter, who gave 'ee leave to drag me into your bloody old castle or to make me your blooming prisoner? I've me own life, and I'm me own master, and if thee's in need of a poor soul to bullock, then thee had ought to take a wife. Though 'tis plain thee'd have the devil's own time finding a female henwitted enough to have 'ee."

"No doubt you are in the right of it," Malvern chillingly rejoined. "Only a fortune hunter or an idiot would willingly shackle herself to one so hideously disfigured."

"Fudge!" Brie retorted in disgust. "A wee scar or two'd not phase a female worth her salt. Rather would she see them for what they are—the record of a brave man's deeds and nobly won. Nay', gov'nor, 'tis not thy scars what'd throw a prospective bride into the gloom, but your own tendency to the crotchets. In truth, I never seen the like for falling into the sullens as thee's shown this past hour or more. 'Tis enough to weary a saint, I tell 'ee, and that's not to mention your top-lofty manner and high-handed methods. Why, 'tis hardly any wonder if females take 'ee in aversion."

"Is it indeed," drawled the earl dangerously, though with a decidedly odd glint in the gimlet eyes. "And to what profundity of experience, I must ask myself, do you attribute such vast knowledge of women? You seem hardly of an age, after all, to so advise your elders."

Brie, thus pointedly brought to a sense of just how far her unruly tongue had led her, blanched but kept her head up, determined to stand buff.

"Why, I've me eyes and ears, gov'nor," she said, cocking her chin belligerently. "And it doesn't take much to see that if 'ee *was* to seek a wife, thee'd be like to make a mull of it, without 'ee was t' change thy ways."

"Impudent brat," said the Demon with obvious feeling. "No doubt I should be appalled at such an unavoidable humiliation as you predict. Fortunately, however, I have no need to go in search of a bride, since the marriage contract has long since been signed. Perhaps you are acquainted with the miserable little wretch who is to be my loving wife. An undisciplined hoyden, I am reliably informed, with neither polish nor countenance, and whose sole recommendations are a ne'er-do-well elder brother and an eccentric grandparent, fondly referred to as 'the Commodore.' Miss Brigida Morgan is her name, and she resides presently at Gullan Carn."

Brie stifled an indignant gasp. The knave to malign her so! And Collin and her dearest gramfer, too! Still, with an effort she curbed her rising ire and fixed the earl with a calculating glance. Now's your chance, Brigida Morgan, she told herself, to lay to rest once and for all this business of the marriage contract.

"Oh, I've heard of Mistress Morgan, right enough, gov'nor," she managed with a semblance of indifference. "An' what I've heard bain't all that bad. Still, ifn thee's little liking for th' wench, why not simply call the whole thing off? It'd hardly make sense to wed where there's a lack of kindly affection on either side, and belike there's another lady what'd suit your lordship a whole lot better."

"I collect, Brian Murdoch, that I was mistaken in you," Malvern cynically observed. "You are hardly the man of worldly wisdom I took you for do you think for one moment that *I* should be held in breach of contract.

Strange as it may seem, a gentleman does not cry off. Nor, apparently, does the lady hold me in ill-esteem, if one is to believe the protestations of profound affection communicated through her legal guardian. Indeed, Commodore Llewellyn has seen fit to assure me that Mistress Morgan is all eagerness to comply at the earliest possible convenience to the agreement drawn up by our fathers."

"*What* did you say?" Brie gasped before she thought, upon which the earl regarded her with the inquisitive arch of an aristocratic eyebrow.

"Was there something in what I have just related which is beyond your comprehension?" he queried insufferably.

"Er—no, your lordship," mumbled the commodore's granddaughter, her hands at her sides clenched into knotted fists.

"Excellent. Then perhaps I should be allowed to continue without unseemly interruption. In regards to a lady better suited to my purposes, I am, no doubt, sorry to disappoint you, but contrary to your expectations, I have found the marriageable females of my acquaintance to be excessively tedious, with hardly a measurable wit to share among them. In which case, Mistress Morgan should do as well as any other to provide the requisite heir and to run my houses. I *have* been led to understand that she at least is young and robust of health. And once she has undertaken to fulfill her wifely duty, I shall no doubt be content to leave her to her domestic tranquillity. My needs, after all, can be met more satisfactorily—and without the accompaniment of a nagging tongue—elsewhere. We should rub on well enough, does she but prove to have a modicum of sense about her."

"*Oh!*"

"I beg your pardon?" Malvern murmured.

Unable to trust her voice, Brie contrived to deny her lapse with a brief shake of the head.

"Curious. I was sure I heard something. Doubtless it was the wind then."

"No doubt, my lord," Brie uttered in a strangled voice.

"Yes, well then. Have you nothing to offer in rebuttal, I shall wish you good-eve, Brian Murdoch," announced the earl. "Doubtless a few hours sleep will serve to revive your impudent tongue."

Brie watched in a seething fury as the insufferable earl strolled languorously from the room, pausing only long enough to close the door connecting his bedchamber to the dressing room and turn the key.

Brave and noble hero of countless tales of daring — Bah! she fumed, delivering the unoffending chair that Malvern had only recently vacated a resounding kick. Doubtless they were all lies. He was despicable and vile, and without a single redeeming virtue. How she *hoped* he would come to pay her suit. Indeed, she would gladly gratify the commodore by making an all out effort to discover the whereabouts of the detested marriage contract simply for the sole enjoyment of having it to fling in the Demon's face when she refused his odious offer. But first she must make her escape, she thought, deliberately subduing her temper that she might assess her surroundings with all her wits about her. No stone must be left unturned in discovering a way out of her loathsome prison!

Dawn was scarcely an hour from breaking when Brigida Morgan found herself poised once more on the brink of destruction. Eyes squeezed shut and her back to the wall, she sent a prayer heavenward as she inched along the narrow ledge that ran along the outer wall of the great house from the sitting room window to that of the earl's bedchamber, a distance of ten feet or more. Had anyone informed her even twenty-four hours earlier that she would have attempted anything quite so lackwitted, she doubtless would have questioned their sanity. Twenty-four hours earlier, however, she had not been locked in Demon Drake's private sitting room after having been roundly insulted in the most despicable manner possible. Desperation coupled with the conviction that she could not endure another confrontation with the wholly detestable earl without succumbing to mayhem and murder had soon led her to seek the only avenue of escape left to her.

Undisciplined hoyden, indeed, she thought fleetingly as her hand groping along the wall came in contact at last with the window embrasure. *He* was a fine one to talk—an abductor of helpless young orphans and the perpetrator of the Lord only knew what other iniquitous deeds. But at least she could be grateful that, unlike most of his contemporaries who believed fresh air was the harbinger of disease, Demon Drake apparently made it a practice to sleep with the windows open wide to the breeze, she thought wryly as she slipped noiselessly inside.

For a moment Brie sank down on the window seat, feeling suddenly weak and all aquiver with the enormity of what she had just dared. Nor was she out of the briars yet, she was ruefully reminded, as the creak of a bedstead and the susurrous of someone moving between silk sheets came significantly to her ears. For the first time it occurred to her that she might very well have leaped from the frying pan into the fire, for it would hardly do to have anyone discover her in the Earl of Malvern's bedroom, least of all the earl himself. Briefly it came to her to wonder how a relatively simple excursion to gather shellfish should have developed into such an impossible coil. Then she had gathered herself to steal on tiptoe toward the hall door on the far side of the room.

Her heart in her throat, she had just congratulated herself on having passed the foot of the high four-poster bed, when all at once the silence was shattered by a blood-chilling curse.

"Where's Bramwell, *damn* his bloody soul!"

Brie froze, her heart leaping to her throat. Then the voice sounded again, this time low and bitter. "God rot him, he's sold us to the devil!" lashed accusingly out at her, and suddenly she felt herself drawn despite her instincts of self-preservation to the bedside. There, in mingled wonder and dismay, she beheld Damion Drake in the throes of a nightmare, his head turning restlessly on the sweat-dampened pillow.

"Never mind," he uttered mockingly. "The lads'll fight. You'll make them, as you've always done. For king and country and Demon Drake, God help 'em, for there's not a chance in hell we'll make it out of this one. Mr. Briggs, hold steady to the wind. Easy lads. We'll rake her across the stern. Steady now and fire as you bear. *Again,* Mr. Ingram! Full broadside. *Now,* Mr. Briggs, bring her about. Bloody hell! Anson's down. And Culver. And now the whole cursed pack's closing in. No choice now—we'll *have* to strike, but not before we've raised the bloody bill. Hard about, Mr. Briggs! We'll ram her down the Frenchman's gullet. Mr. Lowell, let the bastards think Nelson and the whole damned fleet's come on 'em. Signal, 'To *Victory.* Have engaged the Enemy. Close-action.' Now, Mr. Ingram. Fire!"

At that very moment, the door to the bedchamber was thrust open. Caught off guard, Brie barely had the presence of mind to slip unseen behind a paneled screen before the unexpected caller came to the side of the bed.

She caught a glimpse of Hartwell's burly form and heard Drake cry out, "Hellsfire! The ship's aflame!" Then she was stumbling blindly for the door.

"*Easy*, Cap'n. It's all over now. Villeneuve fell for the ruse and hightailed it for Cadiz," drifted to her as she paused for a bare instant to glance back at the big coxswain bent over the bed. "Bramwell paid the bill for his cowardice. He's dead, sir, and the bloody frogs struck to you and th' *Peregrine*."

Brigida Morgan waited to hear no more. Stifling a sob, she bolted down the hall as if pursued by her own private demon.

Chapter Five

Drake stared blankly into Hartwell's rugged face, the cold clamp of fear slowly easing as he realized he had been dreaming again. God, would it never end? he thought despairingly, his body cold with sweat as he lay back against the pillows, one arm thrust over his eyes to shut out the sight of the other man's pity. It was ten months since the *Peregrine* had come upon the rearguard of Villeneuve's squadron making for Cadiz, and still he must relive it over and over again. Two British seventy-four's pitted against two French ships of the line and a Spanish frigate. The odds had not been overwhelming—till the mists, having cleared, revealed Villeneuve's combined fleet in the distance and Bramwell, curse his soul, had chosen not to engage.

Bloody damn! Hartwell was right. It was over. Finished. Nearly three months after *Peregrine* had sunk the Spanish frigate and disabled one of the eighties, Villeneuve had been taken prisoner at Trafalgar, and Nelson, at the cost of his own life, had reduced the Franco-Spanish fleet from thirty-three to eleven ships of the line. Damion Drake was well out of the whole bloody mess, he told himself, then became aware of his former coxswain still hovering about.

"Well, what is it, Hartwell?" he demanded, fixing the

big man with bleary eyes. Lord, what now? he thought, as he saw the redoubtable Hartwell shift nervously.

"I didn't like to wake ye, sir, but I figured ye'd want to know."

Hartwell hesitated. Then the muscles about his jaw bunched with sudden grim determination.

"It's the prisoner, sir," he said baldly. "The little devil's gone."

For an instant there was total silence in the room as Drake digested this startling information and Hartwell maintained an attitude of rigid attention before the earl's sharply narrowed gaze. Then one dark eyebrow arched imperiously.

"Surely you are mistaken," Drake said. "Unless the rogue's a lock-pick, I fail to see how he might have escaped my sitting room."

"It's got me some puzzled, too, Cap'n, an' that's no lie," replied the coxswain with a furrowed brow, "fer the doors were locked tight. An' th' little bugger's fancy clothes was laid out on the couch as neat as ye please. It's loike he just vanished into thin air."

"You astonish me, Hartwell," murmured the earl, flinging aside the bedclothes and rising. "I never suspected you to be of a superstitious bent."

"I'm no more'n some an' less'n most, sir," Hartwell said as he helped the earl into the dressing gown and belted it about the lean waist. "But it struck me from the first that there was somethin' fishy about th' lad. Game as a pebble, he was, but a mite soft fer a stripling what's been on 'is own. An' no lad should have eyes like his — big and all sparkly loike a girl's. No, sir. If ye was to ask me, I'd say there's somethin' not quite right about Master Brian Murdoch."

"Indeed," murmured the earl with something less than good humor. "An intriguing notion, one which I shall no doubt give my due consideration. At the present time, however, I should be more interested in learning how the young thatchgallows has managed to give us the slip."

It was soon apparent that the solution was not to be of a fantastical nature after all, as the earl unlocked the door that connected his bedchamber to the dressing room and walked through to enter the aviary awash with the light of dawn. Sparing the interior only a single, cursory glance, he strode unhesitatingly to the window, the double sashes of which stood agape, and peered first over the edge to the crashing sea below and then, consideringly, to the left and right.

"The bloody young fool!" he muttered beneath his breath.

"Ah. Ye doesn't mean th' lad jumped to is death," groaned Hartwell, horrified.

"I doubt that was his intent, though it's early days yet as to whether it was indeed the end result of his audacity. No, I prefer to believe the little madcap made his way along this ledge to my window, then, ascertaining that I was asleep, slipped into my chamber and escaped unseen down the hall. At any rate, we should know soon enough, if you will summon Griffith forthwith."

Deliberately he pulled the sashes to and turned to stare broodingly at the satin finery laid out on the couch. "I should have thought to have the brat's own rags removed," he mused out loud, his aspect grim as unconsciously he clutched the disfigured hand to his chest to relieve the never-ending throb of pain. "Obviously I underestimated the puppy. I should have guessed he would go to any lengths to gain his precious freedom. We must find him, Hartwell. I'll not have his death on my head."

"There was no way ye could've known, Cap'n," said Hartwell, eyeing Drake with a worried frown. Lord, hadn't the cap'n enough to trouble him without this? he fretted to himself, recalling with a sense of despair the months of pain and fever in which Damion Drake had battled infection and his own tormented memories. And afterward, the weeks of waiting for new orders that never came, succeeded at last by the bitter certainty that his career was at an end. Hartwell cursed the entire bloody admiralty for their shortsightedness. Even with naught but one good arm, Cap'n Damion Drake was worth a damn sight more than the whole lot of 'em put together.

Griffith's arrival put to the period Hartwell's somber reflections, or rather channeled them in a new direction, since the burly coxswain and the exceedingly superior butler had from their first encounter entertained a mutual antipathy for one another. Indeed, it was Hartwell's considered opinion that Malvern Castle in general, and the cap'n most in particular, would improve in both comfort and cheer with Griffith's immediate removal. A regular old Brimstone, he was, forever sniffing about and kicking up a dust with the underlings, till he had them fair in a quake whether or not he was about, reflected Hartwell.

"My lord?" intoned the butler, stiffly inclining his head toward the earl, who had turned to stand with his back to the room and his gaze distant on the blue bulge of the channel at sunrise.

For a moment it seemed his lordship had not heard, as he continued to stare out the window in apparent abstracted silence. Then suddenly without turning, he spoke.

"Tell me, Griffith. Last eve I asked you to have one of the servants tend to a wicker of shellfish left in the bailley. In what manner was my request carried out?"

"I believe I did inform your lordship at the time that the staff had, with your permission, earlier retired. Naturally, having been made previously aware of your liberal views concerning the treatment of the lower orders, I assumed the matter could wait till morning. Unfortunately, I have since been informed that no sign of a wicker is to be found anywhere on the grounds. I am sorry, my lord, but I have tried to conduct the household in accordance with your own expressed wishes. If I am in someway remiss in my duties, I most humbly beg your indulgence."

Oh, he was a cheeky one, all right, thought Hartwell, waiting with relish for Demon Drake to bring the butler down a peg or two. He was, however, to be disappointed.

"That is not necessary. I was not questioning your undoubted efficiency in running this household," said Malvern curtly and turned once more to gaze out the open window. "That will be all, Griffith."

Consequently he did not see the flicker of contemptuous superiority in the butler's eyes as he bowed at the waist before withdrawing. But Hartwell saw it, and he did not like it.

"Beggin' your pardon, Cap'n," he uttered gruffly as soon as the door had closed behind the butler. "But it seems to me that a man had ought to keep a watch on his back when that un's about. There's a slickness about 'im. Like a ship's purser that's bought foul meat for fair and pocketed the difference, if you knows what I mean."

"Indeed?" queried the earl quellingly as he came about. "Really, Hartwell, you amaze me. First the boy and now Griffith. It would seem that to you nothing here is as it should be."

"And so it bain't," declared the irrepressible coxswain roundly. "Not so long as Demon Drake be grounded instead of on the decks of a king's ship where he had out t' be."

At last a flash of temper flared in the black, compelling orbs.

"You are impertinent, Hartwell," observed the Earl of Malvern.

"Aye, Cap'n," agreed the coxswain unrepentantly.

A single black eyebrow lifted toward Malvern's hairline as he eyed his loyal coxswain with scant humor.

"Not 'Captain,' surely," he murmured, the chiseled features hard as granite. "As you have so aptly pointed out, I no longer command a king's ship, but only this ancient, ghost-ridden pile." A peculiarly cynical smile curved the thin lips. "Ghosts which are made no easier by my presence."

Instantly the smile vanished, to be replaced by a singularly daunting expression.

"At any rate, I am a lord of the realm now, not a naval captain, no matter how little I might wish it to be so. And 'tis time you learned that."

"Aw, Cap'n," groaned Hartwell, sorry for what his unruly tongue had bought.

"Henceforth, you will address me according to my proper title, is that understood?"

"Aye, Cap'n — er — milord," muttered Hartwell, shifting his weight uncomfortably beneath the Demon's icy stare. "Though belike there be another what'd suit ye better," he added dourly beneath his breath, "if ever the Lords of the Admiralty could be brought to see the light!"

The earl, however, had already turned his attention elsewhere.

Dismissing Hartwell, he seated himself at the Louis Quinze secretary and, taking a shallow metal box from one of the drawers, opened the lid. For a moment he stared at the small packet of papers, a strange glitter in the coal black eyes. Then leaning forward, he removed a yellowed document and a letter from the contents of the box. The former he tucked into the pocket of his dressing gown, while the latter he unfolded.

An enigmatic smile curled the handsome lips as a miniature of a young girl with copper-colored curls and beguiling green eyes peered back at him.

"So. Miss Brigida Morgan anxiously awaits an audience with her intended, does she?" he mused sardonically out loud to himself. "Well now, 'twould be a shame to disappoint her, would it not?"

Abruptly he rose and, summoning his valet with an impatient jerk of the bellpull, vanished into the adjoining bedchamber.

Brie, feeling less than her usual self after her night's harrowing adventures, wandered fitfully about her room, a frown upon her brow. What the deuce was keeping Collin? she wondered for the umpteenth time. She had slipped him a note at breakfast requiring his presence here just as soon as the commodore retired to his study, ostensibly to work on his memoirs, but more often than not to snooze for an hour or two before the bell for midmorning tea was rung. That was better than half an hour past, and still her errant brother had not chosen to show himself. By God, if he had snuck out to meet Rory Gale, she would . . .

A soft scratching on the door perhaps fortunately interrupted that thought. With a soft swirl of her woolen skirts, she hurried to admit her brother.

"Well, don't just stand there," she whispered testily, as she met frankly amused blue eyes beneath the ever-rebellious lock of fair hair. "Come in! What the devil took you so long? Surely I made it plain enough that I had something of dire importance to discuss."

"Aye, 'twas plain, which is why I took my time. Thee's a devilish sharp tongue when thy temper's roused, Brigida love," accused her sibling, stretching himself, boots and all, out on her unslept-in bed. "Ruins a man's digestion, don't 'ee know. Now, tell me, what have I done this time to bring the sparks to your eyes?"

Brie gave the grinning rogue a withering look.

"You might as well know, 'Collin love,' " she said imitating her brother's lilting drawl to perfection, "that I went to the springtide harvest last night."

"Did 'ee now. And why, I wonder, am I not surprised. But then, what's a little thing like a bolted door to Brie Morgan, when she's a stout Cornish oak placed conveniently just outside her window."

"What indeed," murmured Brigida dangerously. "And thanks to you I was forced to use it. Collin, how *could* you be so thoughtless? You know how I feel about Demon Drake and the cursed marriage contract! If it were a pact with the devil himself, I'd not be deader set against it. But that is not all or even the worst of it. Because of your meddling tongue, I arrived too late for aught but the leavings, and 'ee knew I was counting on lobster for the commodore."

All at once a patently relieved smile, tinged liberally with amusement, spread across the boyishly handsome face.

"Is *that* what this is all about?" he laughed. "For a while 'ee had me a mite worried, Brigida Morgan. Come now, there'll be other springtides. And 'tis the money 'ee's worried about, I've a little something that'll put your mind to rest."

He took a plump purse from his inside coat pocket and tossing it negligently to the foot of the bed, settled back on folded hands against the pillow.

"And what do you have to say to that? There's enough there to pay the grocer and buy yourself some lengths of silk for a new gown or two, I'll wager. An' 'tis no more than 'ee deserve, Brigida girl. Did 'ee think I didn't know how hard it's been for 'ee? 'Tis time you had something besides our mother's outmoded gowns to wear."

If he had expected her to be rendered momentarily speechless by his largesse, he was not to be disappointed. What he could not have anticipated was that his normally robust sister should go suddenly deathly pale and weave slightly on her dainty, booted feet. Alarmed at what appeared the onset of a swoon, he scrambled hastily from the bed.

"Brie, what is it, love?" he cried, supporting her about the shoulders as he led her to a seat beside the low-burning fire. There he knelt before her and anxiously chafed her wrists. "If I'd known how deeply affected 'ee'd be, I'd not have sprung it on 'ee so suddenly."

At last huge, haunted eyes lifted to Collin's face.

"Where did you come by it? Tell me, Collin, and none of your Cornish charm. I'll know if you're fibbing, I warn you."

The boyish features took on a wounded look.

"Sure, and why should I lie about it?" he demanded. "As it turns out, Dame Fortune smiled on Collin Morgan last night at the tables."

"Stop it!" cried Brie, shooting to her feet. "Did I not tell you I went to the springtide harvest and that because of you I was too late for aught but the eels when 'twas lobsters I needed? Oh, Collin, when have you ever known me to give up when I'd my mind set on a thing?"

"Never, Brie," conceded her sorely perplexed brother, wondering if she were a trifle touched in the head after her moonlight outing. "But what has the one to do with the other?"

"What indeed," she retorted. Wringing her hands, she paced agitatedly before him, then stopped to impale him with a look that made him squirm inside. "When I found the beach picked clean, it came to me — the one place where no one would dare to go."

At last a glimmer of understanding flickered.

"Good God, Brie!" exclaimed Collin, his face going nearly as white as hers. "You didn't go *there?*" He shot a glance around the room as if he expected to find the ghost of Inness Glen lurking in the shadows. "None but a fool would dare Smugglers' Cave. And for what? A brace of lobster for the commodore's supper? Did you not once consider what the 'gentlemen' would do if they caught you?"

"Oh, aye," Brie replied bitterly. "The thought crossed my mind. But 'twas a full moon and bright. Not the sort of night for a smugglers' run, thought I."

"Ah, yes, so it was," breathed Collin, relief beginning to ease the sickly hue from his features. "I'd forgot. Still, it was a foolhardy venture, one that'd not bear repeating. I suppose we must simply be grateful 'ee made it without happening on anyone. But 'ee must swear never to go back. Does 'ee hear me? Thee's only a kid of a girl and can't have a notion what these men would do to 'ee—to all of us—if they found 'ee'd been poking thy nose in where ee'd no business to."

He saw immediately he had put it wrong, as the sparks leaped once more to the lovely eyes.

"A 'kid of a girl,' is it?" she demanded furiously. "And what does that make you, Collin Morgan? A fool and a ne'er-do-well! Or so I was informed by a certain gentleman last night in Smugglers' Cave. And now 'twould seem he was in the right of it."

Her voice broke at the end, and impatiently she turned from him to hide the glimmer of angry tears in her eyes.

Really alarmed now, Collin grasped her by the arm. "Gentleman? What gentleman?" he demanded.

"Brie, 'ee said there was no one in the cave."

"No, that's what you said, Collin Morgan. But there was someone. Oh, you needn't fear he was one of your flaskers, for that he was not. But in truth, perhaps it were better had he been. The last man I'd a wish to meet was Damion Drake, the Earl of Malvern."

Collin stared at her, a low whistle sounding through pursed lips. Then at last the story came out of Brigida's memorable first encounter with the man to whom she was pledged to marry.

"At first he claimed to be the spirit of Inness Glen — and, indeed, he had the look of the ghost about him — but Brigida Morgan's not one to be fooled by stories meant to frighten children."

Nevertheless, she shivered slightly, remembering the peculiar sensations that had coursed through her at the touch of his hand upon her. And, later, the unfamiliar yearning she had experienced to chase the gloom from those black, compelling orbs, eyes that had a strange power to make her weak and all atremble inside. The memory gave her no comfort. Indeed, she was swept anew with a fiery burst of temper.

"It was not enough that he should have snuck up on me and frightened me out of half a year's growth," she declared. "But then what must he do, but insist I accompany him to his castle."

"Lord," uttered Morgan, sinking heavily into a chair. "Now thee's gone and done it. I shudder to think what the commodore will do when he learns the Demon's caught 'ee at your old tricks masquerading as a boy. At least 'ee got what 'ee wanted. The wedding, I must suppose, is off?"

"Then you suppose wrongly," she answered tartly. "As a matter of fact, having determined that the marriageable females of his acquaintance have hardly a wit to share among them, he has decided that Brigida Morgan will do as well as any to supply him with the heir he requires. That is, after all, all that shall be asked of her, since his more intimate needs may be satisfied by any number of barques of frailty."

"Good God, you cannot mean he had the nerve to tell 'ee that?" exclaimed her brother, incensed at such a notion. "The cad. I'll—I'll have him horsewhipped. Nay! I'll demand immediate satisfaction of the blackguard for the insult he has done me sister."

Acutely conscious of the blush that stained her cheeks, she gestured impatiently.

"I pray you will not do anything so foolish," she said. "A duel is not only out of the question, it would be highly irregular since Malvern had not the least idea it was to your sister that he was speaking. The earl, far from guessing my identity, propositioned Brian Murdoch to enter his employ. To serve as his page and a spy among the common folk."

Collin's expression was incredulous.

"Thee cannot be serious. Why the devil would he be wanting to spy on his neighbors?"

Now that they had come at last to her real purpose in calling him there, Brie experienced a sudden queasiness in the pit of her stomach.

"You might well ask, Collin Morgan," she said, coming about to face him again. "And while you're at it, it might come to you to wonder what Demon Drake was doing in Smugglers' Cave."

"Well, how the deuce should I know?" Collin retorted, then stopped, an arrested expression on his boyish countenance. "Unless—" He swallowed and hastily turned his glance away.

"Unless he was looking for clues to the identities of the men who murdered his brother," she finished for him. "He means to discover who has been using Smugglers' Cave to stow good French brandy. 'Twas the devil's own luck I was before him."

Reaching up to remove the silver chain from around her neck, she dangled the incriminating medallions in front of him.

"And now tell me, Collin Morgan," she said in awful tones, "that you won your fat purse at the gaming tables."

She had the dubious satisfaction of seeing her brother's face turn an alarming shade of gray, followed almost immediately by a sickly grin.

"Now I wondered what came of that, Brie love," he said. "How clever of 'ee to find it for me."

At that moment Brie would gladly have throttled her brother, for she had little doubt now that he was mixed up with the smugglers. His face, as well as the medallion, betrayed him.

"Oh, Collin," she groaned, sinking down on the bed. "How *could* you!"

"It was easy enough, I assure 'ee. And why should I not reap a little of the harvest? Everyone does it, one way or the other."

"Because," she retorted bitterly, " 'tis a dark and dangerous business, with men who would murder their own mothers if they thought they had betrayed them. And would murder me if they knew I had discovered where they keep their cursed contraband. Just tell me thee'd nothing to do with the slaying of Duncan Drake, Collin. And pray God it is the truth you're saying."

At last an angry flush darkened her brother's cheeks.

"Thee's a fine notion of my character, does 'ee think I'd have anything to do with back-shooting a man."

"Oh, Collin, I don't think it. But if you know who it was—if you were there when it happened, you must tell me."

"Well, I was not, nor do I know who the murdering devils were," Collin sullenly declared. "I went on but a single run not more than a se'ennight past. And only then because of a wager I'd made with Rory. 'Twas a lark, nothing more."

"Then you'll not mind giving me your word that you'll not go on any more. Promise me, Collin, for you've not yet met Damion Drake. He's a dangerous man, subtle and fearless. He'll stop at nothing to uncover his brother's killers."

A spark of resentment kindled in his eye at her implication that he himself might end up in the Demon's net. But then he looked into her face, and suddenly at sight of her fear for him, he was plagued with an unfamiliar twinge of conscience.

"Well, sure, I give 'ee my word," he answered, the old reckless grin flashing in the handsome face. "And did 'ee think that I wouldn't? Now don't 'ee worry that pretty head of yours. The Demon's got nothing against me, for I'd nothing to do with Duncan's death. Upon my maither's grave I swear it."

It was an oath he would not make lightly, for they had both worshiped their mother. And yet, she had the terrible feeling that he had not told her all the truth.

"And now, if thee's nothing else of dire import to discuss," drawled Collin, placing a buss upon his sister's cheek, "I've business elsewhere."

Oh, what a coil they had got themselves in, she fretted as she watched her roguish elder brother blithely make his departure. And all because the Demon of Malvern had decided to take up residence in his castle!

"The devil fly away with him!" she uttered out loud, then immediately experienced an odd sort of pang as the memory of a man, ill and tormented by nightmares of some hideous past, rose up to haunt her. It was a thing that she had not been able to get out of her mind since her precipitous flight from Tal Carn. Anymore than she could banish the memory of the paralyzing sensations that had swept over her as he had cared for the cut on her forehead, she mused, one hand lifting unconsciously to the strip of sticking plaster concealed beneath a coppery lock of hair. In truth, he was a strange, unpredictable creature, one with the inexplicable power to fascinate and bewilder her as no one else had ever been able to do. It was a sobering realization, one that left her feeling more than a little irritable, that far from wishing him ill, she prayed that soon he would be made well and whole again.

But then, 'twas only what she would want for anyone so gravely afflicted, she tried to tell herself, and fell immediately into a daydream in which she managed somehow not only to chase the shadows from the black, compelling orbs, but to straighten the poor mangled limb as well.

At last, realizing where her thoughts had led her, she jerked to attention with a furious blush. Careful, Brigida Morgan, she thought, chiding herself for a fool. 'Twould never do to fall prey to such fanciful notions. After all, she reminded herself, it was not a nursemaid the loathsome earl wished of her, but only a brood mare to provide him with an heir.

A defiant sparkle in her eye, she picked up Collin's purse from the bed and hastily hid it in a hatbox in her wardrobe.

"There!" she declared to the empty room and, snatching up a straw cottage hat, which had seen better days, clapped it over her thick rebellious curls. "And as for Captain Demon Drake, he can just look elsewhere for a wife. For Brigida Morgan will not marry him. And there is nothing he, or anyone, can do to make her."

Satisfied that she had relegated the matter of her would-be bridegroom to its proper place, she briskly tied the frayed ribbon beneath her chin and marched militantly down the stairs. There were more important things to attend to than the Earl of Malvern. The flock, for example, on which all their hopes depended.

Tiptoeing past the commodore's study, she made her way through the Rose Room and let herself out the French doors into the garden. Moments later, she was striding across the down toward the paddock, her step eager. Fortunately, Neal, Mrs. Guthrie's eldest son, had agreed to deliver the three prime lobsters to the inn in East Looe, which freed her to check on the ewes. It was the lambing season, her favorite time of all, and though the commodore had forbidden her to actually help with the work, she always looked forward to visiting Malcolm, the old man who cared for the flock.

She found him, kneeling beside a young ewe that had already given birth to one of a set of twins.

"Oh, Malcolm," she exclaimed softly, as she came up to him and saw the tiny thing struggling to rise on ungainly legs. "No, don't get up. It appears you've your hands full. I've only just managed to get away for a little to see how you are going on."

"I fear 'ee picked a bad time fer it, Miss Brie," replied the old man gravely. "It looks t'be comin' breach. Her bein' small like she be and tuckered from the first, I don't give out much hope for either one of 'em."

"But surely there is something we can do? Malcolm, we cannot just stand by and let her die."

A doubtful frown creased the weathered brow as the old man gazed speculatively at his young mistress.

"About the only thing we can do is try to turn 'im head to fore. 'Tain't easy, but I've had a few what come out of it all right."

Immediately Brie began to roll her sleeves up.

"Then I suggest that we get started," she said, her delightfully pointed chin firm with determination. "Just tell me what you want me to do."

Malcolm, however, appeared anything but eager at the prospect. Glancing slowly at the ground then up again, he coughed to clear his throat.

"Beggin' your pardon, Miss Brie," he drawled carefully. "But might be 'ee should send one o' the lads to help. It bain't no sight fer the eyes of a young lass, gently born like thyself."

"Nonsense," retorted Brie. "I'm hardly a bit of fluff to swoon at the sight of a little blood, I promise you. Now, what do we do first?"

A single glance into uncompromising green eyes, decided Malcolm against further argument. With a noncommittal shrug, he instructed her to hold the ewe's head as best she could, while he tried to turn the unborn lamb inside its mother.

It soon turned out that indeed it was a little more than Brie had bargained for, and in spite of her boast to the contrary, she felt a surge of queasiness at first as she watched the old man go to work. It was not long, however, before she forgot everything, but the young, living thing struggling for life and the creature straining beneath her hands to give birth to it. In an agony of suspense she watched the old man and marveled at his patience. And then, wonder of wonders, the thing was done, and, feeling as if she had been witness to a miracle, Brie beheld the newborn lamb lying at the side of its weary mother.

"Oh, Malcolm, he's beautiful!" she exclaimed, kneeling to help him wipe the young thing dry. The lamb's sudden bleat as it struggled to gain its feet startled a delighted gurgle from her lips. "And hungry, too, from the sound of him."

Just as the newborn managed to get his legs under him, his twin stumbled into him and knocked him down again. Brie laughed and gathered the young creature into her arms.

"Oh, thee poor thing," she said, pressing her cheek against the velvet-soft neck. "Life, thee'll find is full of falls, but 'ee must learn always to get up again."

"That is fair advice, coming from a lass with so few years in her cup," drawled a dry, masculine voice at her back.

Like a shadow of doom looming suddenly over her, Brigida felt the sun blocked behind her. Whirling around, she stifled a gasp as she beheld a gentleman mounted on a magnificent stallion, black as the ace of spades.

"I have, have I not, the honor of addressing, Miss Brigida Morgan?" queried the newcomer, a devil of laughter dancing in eyes like black, glittering diamonds. "I was informed at the house that I might find her here."

Brie felt the blood drain suddenly from her cheeks.

"Demon Drake!" she pronounced in tones of awful certainty before she had the wit to curb her tongue.

"Indeed," murmured the Earl of Malvern, removing his hat to her and bowing. "Your servant, ma'am."

Chapter Six

As she stared askance at the slender figure perched easily atop the stallion, Brie wondered how long Malvern had been there and how much he had seen and overheard. How odd that she should feel a curious pang in the region of her heart as she noted the crippled hand concealed beneath a black leather glove. Indeed, except for the white of his silk shirt and the yard-long neckcloth, tied in the Oriental, he was garbed all in funereal black, a color which seemed peculiarly well-suited to the raven locks and unnaturally pale visage. He exhibited an attitude of unsettling calm, and yet she could feel that same aura of leashed recklessness that she had sensed in him in Smugglers' Cave the night before. He presented, in fact, the appearance of a villain from the pages of a singularly lurid romance, thought Brigida with a slight shiver, then became aware that her protracted study of the earl had brought a faint, mocking smile to his lips.

Brie ducked her head to hide the sudden flush that invaded her cheeks. Dressed in one of her oldest gowns, the skirt and bodice soiled from her recent labors on behalf of the lamb still clutched in her arms, she was acutely aware of how perfectly dreadful she must look. But even worse, she had committed an unforgivable slip of the tongue. She had called the Earl of Malvern "Demon Drake" to his face! While that was something which might have been forgiven Brian Murdoch, such a gross dereliction of manners put Brigida Morgan beneath reproach.

Oh, it was all *his* fault, the loathsome earl with those eyes that rendered her absurdly lackwitted. How dared he come sneaking up on a body like that! she fumed. And then the thought came to her that, on the contrary, she could not have presented a more felicitous picture, for was it not her whole intent to fill him with a disgust of her? A hoyden, he had said of her, and wanting in either polish or countenance. Well, she certainly had no intention of proving him wrong about her.

"Milord," she murmured coolly, dropping into a curtsy, lamb and all. "In spite of the fact that we have never been properly introduced, I should have known you anywhere."

"Not introduced? But you are mistaken, surely." At the startled parting of her lips, something suspiciously like a devil of amusement flickered briefly in the disconcerting eyes. "I distinctly recall your father presenting you to me. As a matter of fact, I held you in my arms, an intimacy which at the time I confess I did not wholly appreciate."

With an effort Brigida concealed the swift surge of relief that swept over her. For the briefest moment she had been sure he was referring to a more recent encounter.

"I hardly think that qualifies, milord," she retorted drily. "I was only a year old at the time. But now that I am a woman of more mature years, I no doubt am gratified that you have at last taken it upon yourself to call." Deliberately she lifted sea-green eyes to his face. "Even unannounced, it must naturally be a pleasure to receive you."

An expression of sublime surprise crossed the handsome features.

"Ah, but I was led to believe from your grandfather's recent communication that I should be welcome anytime. As I recall, I was to consider myself as one of the family and, as such, might even run tame about the place. Did I misread his words, I most humbly beg your pardon, Miss Morgan."

In spite of herself, Brigida felt a bubble of laughter rise to her throat at his masterfully delivered counterstroke. Never had she seen anyone less humble. Ah, but he was a devil, was the Demon of Malvern, she thought. Yet she was no pansy to be wilted by a clever wit.

"On the contrary, I am sure you did not, milord," she retorted as she set the newborn lamb on its feet and watched it totter stiff-legged to its mother. "Unfortunately, it would seem you have found me at something of a disadvantage. I am afraid I haven't time at present to entertain gentlemen over tea and biscuits. But if you wish, I feel certain the commodore might oblige you."

An appreciative gleam ignited in the coal black eyes.

"That has given me back some of my own, has it not," he remarked. "However, it was not the commodore whom I came to see."

Unwittingly Brigida experienced a disturbing flutter beneath her breast as she watched him swing lightly to the ground.

"Perhaps," he murmured, coming a step nearer, "you will have no objection if I wait until you are free to grant me the pleasure of your company."

She would have objected, vociferously, had she dared. But well aware that not even she could go so far as to order the Earl of Malvern from the grounds, she curbed her hasty tongue.

"You may do as you please, I am sure, milord," she

answered instead, assuming an indifference she was far from feeling. "Though I fear you will find it quite tedious and not at all to your liking."

"I am no doubt touched at your solicitude for my comfort," he drawled, insufferably smiling as he bent his raven head over her small, shapely hand.

A disconcerting tingle shot up her arm at the light touch of his lips to her knuckles. Angry at herself and bewildered by the unsettling effect he had on her senses, Brigida firmly withdrew her hand as soon as she decently could.

"If you will excuse me, milord," she murmured and with a flounce of her skirts, turned her back on him.

Determined not to allow his lordship's presence to spoil her morning, Brigida tried resolutely to ignore him as she accompanied Malcolm on the rounds. This, she soon found, was no easy matter. In spite of the fact that Malvern maintained a cool, easy silence, she could not keep from being aware of his disturbing presence. She could feel his eyes on her—eyes that seemed to bore holes through her back. With a queasy sensation in the pit of her stomach, she waited for the moment when finally he would recognize and denounce her as Brian Murdoch.

That moment, however, did not arrive, and presently Brigida was able to attend with at least a modicum of success to Malcolm's report on the state of the flock.

Ten lambs had been born in the night, which, taken together with the dozen that had arrived some two days before and the twins she herself had helped bring into the world, made a round sum of twenty-four to add to the steadily increasing flock. That left only a half-dozen ewes to be delivered, Malcolm informed her with distinct satisfaction.

Brigida felt a small glow of pride at what she had managed to achieve in so short a time. Three years before, she had started with a dozen ewes and an aging ram, and now their numbers had more than tripled. Soon they would require the services of a lad to help Malcolm and Lively, the sheep dog she had purchased at no little cost to her dwindling reserves. This year should see the flock bring in a profit.

If Brigida had thought to wear the earl's patience thin with her prolonged inspection of the sheep, she was to be disappointed. It was almost noon when at last she could find no further excuse for putting off her return to the house, but Malvern still waited. His elbow propped negligently on top of the stone wall, he lounged at his ease as she thanked Malcolm and turned to regard his lordship with huge, guileless eyes.

"Still here, milord?" she queried in dulcet tones. "No doubt I should apologize for having kept you so long. However, I did warn you."

Leisurely Malvern straightened.

"So you did," agreed his lordship, the look he bent upon her curiously enigmatic. "And, since I did not find the time in the least heavy on my hands, I deem an apology is in no way in order. On the contrary, I found the experience singularly informative."

"Informative?" Brie echoed, eyeing him with suspicion. "Would you have me to believe you have formulated an unexpected interest in sheep, milord?"

"Not in the least," he replied without batting an eyelid. "In fact, I can think of few things which I should find less stimulating. Obviously, however, the same cannot be said of you."

He had taken her arm as he talked and now, his mount's reins looped over his elbow, he led Brie away from the grinning shepherd and toward Gullan Carn, embraced in the distance by ancient oaks, beech, and ash trees.

"It is not the sheep which fascinate me," she demurred stiffly, acutely aware of the light touch of strong fingers beneath her arm. "But the satisfaction that comes from a successful enterprise."

"And is it your usual practice to pursue this 'enterprise' in the fields and pastures, Miss Morgan?" he queried smoothly. "It would seem, after all, labor better suited to a field hand, would it not?"

He said it so casually and with such arrogant certainty, Brie had to bite her tongue to keep from delivering him a stinging retort. Nor did it help in the least that he was odiously in the right of it. The commodore would confine her to the brig for a week on nothing but bread and water if he found out about it. Still, with a perversity well known to her intimates, she was determined to take the risk if it meant she would be free once and for all of the meddlesome earl.

"It is honest labor, milord," she answered, giving a defiant toss of the head. "Something of which I am not ashamed because it is work that is necessary. Thanks to the flock, Gullan Carn will one day grow prosperous as it was used to be in my Grandfather Morgan's time. Since the loss of my parents at sea, circumstances have not always been of the most felicitous," she added on a sober note, her thoughts straying to a time when things had looked bleak indeed.

Her face hidden beneath the broad brim of her hat, she did not see the grim tightening of the handsome lips.

"I believe I heard something of the difficulties that plagued your father in his last years," drawled the Demon of Malvern. "Some unfortunate investments as I recall."

Brie shrugged a slim shoulder.

"Father was the dearest, most wonderful man," she replied, her eyes misty with memories. "But he had not the least head for business. For a while it seemed we might even lose Gullan Carn."

"And why was the late earl never made aware of the state of your affairs?" demanded his lordship with deceptive casualness. "Surely your guardian must have known he had only to apply to my brother for assistance."

Taken off guard, Brie nearly stumbled. But quickly she recovered herself.

"And pray tell why should he have done any such thing, milord?" she exclaimed in accents of astonishment. "Whatever our circumstances at Gullan Carn, they were certainly no concern of your brother's."

"No, but they were of concern to me. I may not have been an earl at the time, but I was not without means of my own. I hardly think you would have been refused a reasonable competence until my return. At the very least I might have been assured that my promised bride would be spared the necessity of working as a common field hand."

"Might you indeed?" demanded Brigida, incensed at his high-handed manner. "Oh, you are just as I might have expected from the tales I have heard of you! Whatever our 'circumstances,' I assure you that we are not in the habit of applying for, let alone accepting, charity from anyone, and least of all from you. Furthermore, I, milord, do not, nor ever have considered myself promised to you or any man. And why should I? Never once in the past eighteen years till now have you seen fit to acknowledge that I even exist, let alone that anything of a more intimate nature might one day lie between us."

A single arrogant eyebrow shot toward the earl's raven hairline.

"Do you not?" he drawled in a manner most certain to arouse her temper. "And yet you have admitted to being Miss Brigida Morgan. Unless you have a sister I have yet to hear of, I very much fear you are indeed my future wife. Or so says the marriage contract, which was signed by my father and yours."

At last Brie turned on him, her eyes flashing dangerously.

"Marriage contract?" she flung back at him. "If there ever was such a document, I have never seen it."

"Come now, Miss Morgan. You need not put on missish airs with me. While you may be excused some slight pique at my failure to court you with billets-doux, you must know as well as I that your father left the marriage contract with mine for safekeeping."

Brie favored his lordship with a fulminating eye.

"On the contrary, milord. I know no such thing," she roundly informed him. "And I assure you that not only do I never put on airs, missish or otherwise, but the last thing I would have wished was to receive 'billets-doux' from a man I do not know and cannot like!"

There! It was out, and she could not regret it. But if she had thought to pierce his armor with such a declaration, she was soon to discover she had misjudged her man. Brigida's heart sank as she saw his hand move toward the pocket of his coat.

"No need to play coy with me, Miss Morgan," the earl assured her as he drew forth an official-looking paper, which ominously bore the seal of the Earl of Malvern. "It is hardly to the point whether you can like me or not. In spite of what you might have heard of me, I am a man of honor. You may be certain I have every intention of adhering to the terms agreed to by our late parents. I am, in fact, prepared to have the banns read immediately. June weddings are supposed, after all, to be blessed with good fortune." His smile as he handed her the detestable marriage contract was odiously mocking.

They had come to the rose garden as they talked, and Brigida, feeling suddenly as if her legs could no longer support her, sank weakly down on the stone bench beneath a trelissed arbor. The earl's eyes as he watched her turn the fateful document over and over in her lap without opening it held a curiously baffled expression in their depths. But Brie did not see it. Her mind was working furiously to find some way out of the trap which seemed to be closing in on her.

She was no prime bit of blood to be sold to the highest bidder, she thought resentfully. And no matter that *his* was the only offer she was ever likely to receive, every fiber of her being rebelled at thought of finding herself forced into a marriage she had neither asked for nor wanted.

At last her shoulders straightened, and she came to her feet to face him.

"No doubt I should be grateful for the honor you would do me, milord," she said steadily. "However, I very much fear I must cry off. I assure you it is nothing personal. It is simply that I have no wish to be married—to you or any man. And, indeed, you must see we should not suit. I am, regrettably perhaps, a woman who has grown used to a degree of independence not usually granted to others of my sex. After all, I have, since the age of thirteen, been the lady of this house. But more than that, it has been incumbent on me to make all the decisions concerning the running of my late father's estate. You will find that I am strong-willed and stubborn and quite capable of determining my own life—not at all the sort of woman to make you a conformable wife."

"And not the sort of woman either, I trust, who would be satisfied to take second place to your brother's wife, should he marry," observed Malvern, regarding her from beneath heavily drooping eyelids.

It was a telling point, one which she had not previously considered. And nor would she consider it, she told herself firmly. Not now, when the earl's nearness was making it so extremely difficult to think in a rational manner.

"Whether or not my brother marries is hardly to the point," she insisted, a slight edge to her voice. Oh, why did he not accept her answer and leave her be! "This concerns only me."

"Quite so," he drawled. "In which case you must see that as my countess you will be chatelaine of your own house. And if it is independence you require, you will find that I am prepared to allow you considerable freedom to do as you please. So long as you are discreet in your pursuits, I see no reason why we shall not rub along well enough."

At the implication in these final words, Brigida was hard put to stifle a gasp.

"I beg your pardon," she uttered incredulously. "But I believe I have made it quite clear that I do not intend to be chatelaine of your house. I prefer to determine my own independence, rather than rely on the whims of a husband, no matter how benevolent. I shall not marry you, milord. There is nothing you can say or do which will change my mind."

"But I am afraid you have no say in the matter," he had the effrontery to reply. Taking the yellowed document from her hand, he held it significantly before her. "You will find the agreement between our fathers legally binding. To cry off now would be a breach of contract."

"That is flummery and you know it," Brigida declared, her eyes flashing glorious green sparks of defiance. "The day of arranged marriages is long past. No one, not even the Earl of Malvern, can force a woman to wed against her will."

"Quite so," drawled the earl. "Nevertheless, you will marry me. Indeed, had you troubled yourself to read the contract, you would realize any attempt to break the agreement entails a sizable forfeiture. But then, perhaps your guardian is prepared to pay a hundred pounds to prevent a marriage which most would consider highly advantageous."

Brigida stared at the earl, her mouth suddenly dry.

"You must know very well that he will not," she managed hoarsely after a moment.

Malvern answered cynically. "Indeed, the commodore has already made his views on the subject abundantly clear. And why should he not? After all, he is intent on insuring his granddaughter both a title and a fortune."

Brie uttered a gasp of outrage.

"How dare you impugn my grandfather's motives!" she furiously exclaimed. "Anything he has done was done out of a wish to see me settled, nothing more. I can assure you that for himself he expects nothing in return."

"Well, not exactly 'nothing,' Brigida lass," observed a new voice from the French doors behind her. "There is the small matter of a cask of French brandy."

Well aware the fat was in the fire for certain now, Brie whirled around to face the commodore.

"Grandfather," she said, clasping her hands firmly before her. "You are just in time to greet our visitor."

"Damion Drake," pronounced the commodore, his keen old eyes going with interest to the slim figure of the earl. "No need for introductions. Duncan, now, he was the spittin' image of his father. But 'ee, lad. Thee's the look of thy mother."

Malvern's smile was sardonic.

"My father used to say I was very like her," he drawled, a hard sheen in the expressionless eyes. "Perhaps that is why he could so little bear the sight of me."

"And that rankles, does it? Well, I don't mind tellin'

'ee, the countess was one of the finest ladies I ever knew, and your father worshiped the ground she walked on. 'Tis little wonder if he demanded more of the son who took after her than of the one cut of the same cloth as himself. The earl was proud of the name 'ee earned for thyself. Never doubt it for a moment."

To Brie's astonishment, a glimmer of warmth eased the coldness from the satyrlike countenance.

"It has been my one regret, sir," replied the nobleman, "that I myself never knew her. And now, it would seem, I never really knew my father."

"Ah, well, what man does? However, it was not the late earl, thy father, 'ee came to discuss, but the terms of the marriage contract, was it not? Indeed, I'm afraid I must apologize for my granddaughter," he said rather pointedly as he came forward at last to greet his guest. "She's a hot-tempered lass, with a tendency to leap to conclusions at times. Naturally, I do not look unfavorably on such a match as 'ee have described, milord, so long as the man behind the title is one to measure up to Brigida Morgan. She's a rare handful, and for all she's my granddaughter, I do not hesitate to say that for the man with the mettle to tame her, she'll prove a treasure beyond price. I hope 'ee ken my meanin', lad, and don't take unkindly to an old man speakin' his mind. I'm obliged to make sure of any man who would claim her for his wife."

"On the contrary, I understand perfectly. It is only what I should do, were our situations reversed, I assure you."

Satisfied, the commodore nodded.

"Obviously, 'ee's a man after me own heart. I see no reason why the wedding should not proceed apace. Perhaps 'ee would care to finalize matters over a small libation?"

Brigida, who had witnessed this exchange with

mounting resentment, could not believe her eyes as she watched the commodore clap a familiar hand to the earl's back and urge him toward the house without a never-you-mind to herself. "Oh!" she exclaimed, beside herself with rage. "So, you think that settles everything."

"Now, Brigida," began the commodore on a note of warning.

"No, Grandfather. You shall not 'now, Brigida' me. How *dare* you discuss me as if I were not even present! And *you*," she said, turning contemptuous eyes on the earl. "Do you think because I am a woman, I can be bullied and coerced? That all you need do is win over my grandfather and I am yours for the taking? And all because of a stupid marriage contract drawn up by our fathers! But it changes nothing. I have already given you my answer. The commodore can confine me to my room on bread and water from now until eternity, and I still will not marry you. Indeed, milord, I should rather be dead than be forced into a marriage not of my own choosing."

Satisfied that she had unequivocally stated her position, Brie crossed her arms and waited, chin up and eyes fixed on a point above and to one side of the two men. Thus she did not see the devil of amusement leap in a pair of black, glittering orbs. To her utter amazement the earl turned and began to draw his host on toward the French doors.

"I believe, Commodore Llewellyn," an infuriatingly cool drawl drifted back to her, "you said something about a libation to seal the arrangement?"

"Er, indeed, milord," coughed the commodore, clearing his throat. "In fact, 'twould seem a drink is definitely in order."

Brigida, left staring foolishly after them, could do naught but stamp her foot in outrage. Oh, but he was loathsome and vile, was the Earl of Malvern. But she would show him she was not so easily defeated. If it needed a hundred pounds to purchase her freedom, she would come up with the sum, one way or another!

Immediately upon that thought, however, her mood suffered a sudden blight. Who in heaven's name was she trying to fool? she thought, sinking once more to the bench beneath the grape arbor. It might as well be a million as a hundred. She could not come close to raising either sum.

As if she could not bear to sit quietly when her whole world was threatening to come tumbling down around her, she shot abruptly to her feet and began nervously to pace the confines of the rose garden. There must be something she could do, she told herself, searching her mind for some avenue of escape. Indeed, the very notion of submitting without a fight was utterly repugnant to her.

And then it came to her. The purse containing Collin's ill-gotten gains! She had not even bothered to look inside let alone count up the coins. While there might not be a hundred pounds in it, from the weight of it, she had judged it was a goodly sum. For one brief moment she wrestled with her conscience. Money gotten by illegal means was tainted and sure to bring bad luck. Though she had not the least notion what she had intended doing with it, spending it had never once entered her mind. Perhaps she had vaguely thought to give it to charity, from an anonymous donor, as it were. Now she could think of no better end for it than that it should go to the Earl of Malvern to break the hated marriage contract.

The next instant found her slipping round the corner of the house to the kitchen entrance.

The commodore and his guest were closeted in the study, the door left slightly ajar. As Brigida tiptoed past the oaken barrier on her way to the stairs, the low rumble of her grandfather's voice fell on her ear.

"Aye, she's proud. And used to sailing her own course. Belike 'tis my fault for givin' in to her whims and fancies. Still, she's a lady, never doubt it for a moment. She'd a governess till she was sixteen. I made sure of that. And now, lad. 'Tis all up to 'ee whether or no she'll have 'ee."

"She will have me," drawled the Demon of Malvern. "One way or the other. On that, sir, you may depend."

Brie felt a cold shiver course down her spine at the velvet softness of that voice. And then her head came up, her eyes glittering with defiance.

"Will I, indeed, milord," she muttered softly beneath her breath. "Well, we shall just see about that!"

Lifting up her skirts, Brigida fled silently up the stairs.

Chapter Seven

"You should have heard him, Collin!" exclaimed Brigida, pacing angrily before her brother. "He is insufferably top-lofty and arrogant. He had the gall to claim I had no say in the matter. No *say* in the matter — can you believe it?"

"Well, considering he *is* a lord, *and* a naval captain of some repute, I shouldn't think it all that surprising," Collin pointed out as he settled his lean frame in the single chair in Brigida's favorite retreat, a small room, little more than a closet, located below the attic and overlooking the sea. "He's a man used to giving orders and seeing them obeyed without question. It sounds to me like thee's met thy match, me girl."

"Oh, does it indeed?" demanded his sister, coming about to face him with a look of incredulity. "And you, I suppose, think I should give in to his demands. Collin, how could you? I had thought you, of all people, would stand by me."

"Now, Brie love, 'ee knows I would do anything in me power to deliver 'ee from Malvern. But a hundred pounds? I know of only one way to raise a sum like that in such short order."

Brigida did not have to have him spell it out for her.

On his single run with the flaskers, Collin had already brought home nearly a third of the needed amount, and now Rory Gale had promised him fully twice that sum if he agreed to go on another. Of course, there was one tiny condition: the loan of the cellars at Gullan Carn in which to store the goods. Good God, it did not bear thinking on! And yet she did stop to consider it for a full minute.

"Thee's only to say the word, Brie," Collin said, studying the fingernails on one hand, "and 'tis done. 'Twouldn't be so bad. The goods'd not be at Gullan Carn more than a mere night or two."

"No!" Angry at herself for listening and at Collin for suggesting what must clearly be out of the question, Brigida whirled away to gaze blindly out the window toward the sea. "I'll not have you place yourself and Gullan Carn at risk for me. There has to be some other way. And I swear that I shall find it."

Collin, little liking the note of determination in her voice, somberly shook his head.

"Maybe," he said consideringly. "And maybe 'ee should think a little more about accepting Malvern. Most girls'd jump at the chance to be a countess. Who knows, 'ee might even come to like him, if 'ee was to give it half a chance."

"That's easy enough for you to say," Brigida bitterly retorted. "You are not the one who has been ordered to wed him. And even if I could like him, which I cannot, I should still refuse. Oh, can you not see it is the principle of it all? Why should I be forced to submit to the wedded state, simply because it is what is expected of a woman? And for what? To be ruled by a man. And not even a man of my own choosing. And in return to be obedient and—and docile, a—a creature without a will or thought of her own. Do you think I should be satisfied to give up all that I hold most sacred simply to gain a title? Would *you*, Collin Morgan?"

Collin, who was not given to contemplation of anything more momentous than the action at the gaming tables or the pursuit of the next diversion, appeared momentarily struck at the notion.

"Actually, I never thought of it in that way before," he admitted. "I suppose not, though if an heiress were to take a shine to me, I expect I'd not cavil over a thing like principle." A roguish grin broke across his face. "I'd grab at the chance to feather me nest with a fortune. Perhaps, Brigida love, 'ee should try looking at it from my point of view. They say Malvern is rich as Croesus."

Brigida threw up her hands in exasperation at his teasing.

"The devil fly away with you, Collin Morgan," she cried, flinging an eiderdown pillow at his head. "I should have known better than to think you could be serious about anything."

"Aw, now 'ee's wounded me to the quick." He laughed and, throwing the pillow back at her, headed for the door. There he stopped, one hand on the handle, and turned back to look at her. The laughter slowly faded from his eyes. "Thee knows whatever 'ee decides, I'll stand by thee. I may be a brigand and a rogue, but I'd never wittingly let 'ee down. We're Morgans, me and thee—first, last, and always."

Brie swallowed, caught off guard.

"Aye," she murmured around the sudden lump in her throat. "And now take thee off, Collin Morgan. I've my future to contemplate, and I'll not be bothered by the likes of thee."

Grinning, he opened the door and sauntered out, leaving Brie to the turmoil of her own thoughts.

It was the middle of the morning the day following the earl's fateful visit, and Brigida's night had been anything but restful. Small wonder, then, that she should find herself gazing with longing at the blue expanse of sea, tossed with waves. The breeze was freshening before the slow gathering of clouds on the horizon, and she doubted not it would be a marvelous day for sailing.

"And why not?" she asked of the empty room. Neal Guthrie had had time enough upon his return from East Looe to make the *Mere-Magden* seaworthy. The sloop waited below, and there was nothing to keep Brigida from taking her out, nothing, that is, but the distinct possibility of another visit from the earl. That thought was enough to send her bounding down the stairs to her bedroom to change for the proposed outing.

Flinging open the door of her wardrobe in the bottom of which she kept the bundle of boy's clothing, Brie suddenly hesitated. She would be taking a chance going out again as Brian Murdoch with the Demon of Malvern on the lookout for his runaway page. And yet with a storm brewing, the last thing she wanted was to be encumbered by woolen skirts.

All at once her chin jutted at a stubborn angle. The devil fly away with the Earl of Malvern. She needed to feel the wind against her cheek and salt spray in her hair. Once free of the land she would be able to clear the cobwebs from her brain.

Defiantly, she reached in the back of the wardrobe, only to discover that, save for the wig, her disguise was mysteriously vanished. In vain she got down on her hands and knees and searched every nook and cranny, and still she failed to discover any trace of the missing clothes. At last, baffled and made irritable by her failure, she stood. No doubt, she told herself, Fionna had discovered them and, thinking they were naught but mere rags, had discarded them, or some such thing. Well, she would just have to make do with some of Collin's old things. There was a trunk in the attic full of boy's clothing, things he had long outgrown and which she had never bothered to get rid of.

Snatching up the disreputable black wig, she hurried upstairs.

Brie, laying the *Mere-Magden* on the larboard tack, set a course to weather the headland. Under the press of canvas, the little sailboat fairly skimmed through the water, her stem biting into the first gentle roller and leaping out again. As her deck tilted, Brie brought her round, steady with the offshore breeze. In moments, she was running with the wind, her prow pointed toward the open water.

Brigida's spirit soared, and she felt a burden lifted from her shoulders as she put the trim sloop through her paces. Jibing and running free across the wind, the *Mere-Magden* shot through the water, following the long sweep of Whitsand Bay. A wild cry burst from Brie's throat, and in her jubilation she yanked off the hated wig and shook out her hair. Then easing sheets and coming about, she ran once again with the wind, leaving the land behind her.

As the coast melted into the haze hugging the shoreline, she felt a heady temptation to hold to her present course and never turn back. Whimsically she wondered how the French would greet her. No doubt with the dreaded blade of the guillotine, she mused wryly and tacked, bringing the little boat back to windward.

With no destination in mind and with only the wish

to flee the problems that waited her at home, Brie welcomed the first stiffening of the wind, which hours earlier had shifted to inland. Soon she forgot everything, but the thrill of tacking before the building storm. Still, she was no fool, and she had a Cornishman's respect for the vagaries of the sea. Greater vessels than hers had been dashed against the rocks. At last she paid off and sailing to leeward, headed for the safe haven of Looe Bay.

Ruefully she realized she had come in not a moment too soon. The clouds, bloated and black, unleashed a pelting rain before she had clawed past the headland. Riding the crests of the storm-ridden sea, she fought her way into the harbor and made for the narrow inlet below Gullan Carn.

She was both weary and elated as she moored her small craft, then, with numb fingers and the wind howling in her ears, fought to secure the sail. Breathless from her exertions, she stowed the sailbag below and checked once more to make sure everything was shipshape.

Only then did she think of the wig, lying where she had discarded it. With a wry grimace, she retrieved the sodden thing from the bottom of the boat and held it up between thumb and forefinger. At thought of putting it over her already wet curls, she was greatly tempted to chance making the trek up the cliffs bareheaded. But in the end caution won out over disgust. Brie pulled the thing down over her hair. Then satisfied at last that she had forgotten nothing, she slipped over the side.

Her head down and shoulders hunched against the rain, Brie waded through the shallows toward the shore. In the fury of the storm, the narrow path to Gullan Carn would be treacherous in the extreme, she realized with a wry grimace. Perhaps she should wait in the lee of the cliffs till the squall blew itself out. Then, at the low rumble in her stomach, it suddenly occurred to her that she had not eaten since breakfast and that she was quite ravenously hungry. Thoughts of hot chocolate and cold chicken before a crackling fire filled her with an impatience to be home. That, and the certainty that the commodore would be pacing the deck for her if she did not make her appearance soon. Recklessly, she made up her mind to dare the cliffs, rather than the commodore's uncertain temper.

Reaching shore, she stepped free of the shallows.

"Ah, I might have known it would be you," pronounced a steely voice. "Who, but Brian Murdoch after all, would deem a tempest fit sailing weather?"

Brigida's breath caught in her throat as a cloaked figure loomed out of nowhere to stand over her.

Her first instinct to break and run was put to the rout by a strong hand grasping the collar of her coat.

"Not so fast, my elusive little thatchgallows," warned the Earl of Malvern. "We've some unfinished business to attend."

Brie slipped in the mud and went to her knees as her captor began to drag her, resisting, along the base of the cliff. Relentlessly he yanked her up again.

"No!" Brie choked, taking a wild swing at him with a punishing left. " 'Ee can't do this to me."

Malvern laughed and stepped easily aside. Then catching her wrist, he twisted it deftly behind her back and held her, helpless in his grip.

"I can do as I please," he murmured in her ear. "You belong to me, Brian Murdoch. Or had you forgotten?"

Brie bit her lip to keep from crying out.

"I ain't . . . forgot nothin'," she panted. "An' the last I heard, there's a law against kidnapping."

Malvern's grin was nothing if not unnerving.

"I suggest," he crooned, tightening his grip enough to make his point without hurting her, "that you do not try my patience. We had an agreement, you and I. Now, do you come quietly, or must I knock some sense into that maggoty head of yours?"

Forgetting the charade she played, Brie felt her temper snap. How dared he threaten her with violence!

"Brute!" she choked. "Vile beast. I'll not be bullied by the likes of thee."

In a fit of fury she twisted foolishly in his grasp. Instantly a stab of pain shot up her arm. In anguish she cried out.

Malvern uttered a blistering oath and precipitously released her.

In an instant Brie came about and, without stopping to contemplate the consequences, connected a hard kick to his unprotected shin. To her surprise, Malvern reeled and staggered back.

"Wretch!" he growled through clenched teeth. Limping heavily, he made his way to a nearby rock and propped his weight against it. "I carry the lead of a French sharpshooter in that leg."

At his obviously extreme discomfort, Brie felt her anger dissipate.

"Well, how was I to know?" she demanded irritably. "Thee shouldn't have handled me the way 'ee done. Thee threatened me, 'ee did. And—and wrenched me arm. Is it any wonder that I took snuff?"

"Impudent little devil!" retorted his lordship, obviously in no mood to be conciliatory. "Had you had the sense not to struggle, none of this need have happened. You might at least have warned me that you were about to erupt in one of your distempered freaks."

"Warned 'ee?" exclaimed Brigida. "And 'ee, I suppose, would have politely let me go?"

"That is, as I recall, precisely what I did do," he wryly pointed out.

Brie frowned, unable to deny it.

"Humph," she snorted, hedging a bit. "And I suppose next 'ee'll be claimin' thee'd never no intent to knock me alongside the head, the way 'ee said 'ee would."

"The notion grows more enticing by the moment," confessed his lordship with such convincing grimness that Brie's confidence was momentarily shaken.

" 'Ee wouldn't dare!" she choked, fighting the urge to back a step.

Climbing stiffly to his feet, Malvern favored her with a quelling look.

"Repellent rogue," he murmured ominously. "I should not be so cocksure if I were you." Favoring his injured leg, he took a step toward her. "I may be constrained by a misplaced sense of humanity from putting a crease in your skull," he conceded, taking another step, "but I can and shall most certainly beat you if you do not comply with my demands."

Brie stood indecisively, held where she was by a sudden uneasiness at the unnatural pallor of his face. Reminded that he was not yet recovered from his wounds received in battle, she was overcome with the unreasoning fear that he was on the point of succumbing to his weakness—until at last he stood over her. "And right now," he said between clenched teeth, "it is my heartfelt desire to remove myself from this downpour. Unless you wish to feel the palm of my hand against your rump, I suggest you start down that trail at once."

At the end he wavered ever so slightly on his feet. With an effort Brie quelled a low cry of alarm.

"Easy, gov'nor," she blurted. Without stopping to think, she clasped an arm about the lean waist. "Don't be afraid to put your weight on me shoulder. I reckon I'm a mite stronger than I looks t'be."

"Yes, no doubt," he murmured, a strange glint in the look he bent upon her. Brigida, blushing, glanced away. Thus she did not see the faint twitch at the corners of the handsome lips. Wondering what the devil had possessed him to come out on such a day, she headed inland along a track that skirted the inlet. It was not long before she recognized the path they trod. A low cry burst from her as they topped an outcropping of rock and gazed down into a small protected harbor.

"Men-aber," she murmured under her breath, but her eyes saw only the graceful beauty of the schooner riding at anchor below her.

"Ah, but she's a wonder, gov'nor," she breathed. "Why, she must be all of sixty feet. A right trim lady for sailin' the seas. What manner of crew does she carry?"

The earl's look was slightly bemused as he took in her rapt young face, all aglow with admiration for the vessel.

"Two officers and forty hands," he answered drily. "None of whom are on board at present. Now, unless you enjoy being wet to the bone and battered by the wind, I suggest you save your questions till we are safely aboard."

At the prospect of being alone with the Demon on his private yacht, however, Brigida balked.

"Hold on, gov'nor!" she cried, digging in her heels. "I'd just as lief not. I'd other plans for this eve, what don't include playin' the cull for an English lord. Thee'd best get someone else to do your spyin' for 'ee. I told 'ee before. Brian Murdoch bain't for sale."

"Is he not indeed?" murmured the earl, his soft drawl edged with steel. "Then perhaps he would prefer to linger in the dungeons of Malvern Castle till the excisemen can be summoned. No doubt they would enjoy a lengthy chat with the lad who uncovered the secret of Smugglers' Cave. What think you?"

Brie swallowed hard.

"I think Brian Murdoch's betwixt the devil and the deep blue sea," she answered, wishing heartily that the ground might open up and swallow her.

Moments later she was rowing a small dinghy toward the earl's yacht, while Malvern sat in the stern and watched her.

There was an eeriness about the schooner, which was no doubt due in part to the marked absence of the crew, and yet was more than that, thought Brie as she climbed on board, followed by the earl. Perhaps it was the feeling she got as the deck rose and fell beneath her that the vessel was like some rare and lovely creature straining to be set free of its moorings. Or maybe it was something she sensed in the man, who stood, legs braced easily against the rolling of the deck, his eyes lifted out of instinct or long habit to the fluttering pennant atop the foremast. It was the act of a seaman, long accustomed to gauging the wind, and it somehow made him seem less the forbidding Lord of Malvern and more a man at last in his own element. Whatever it was, Brigida felt herself inexplicably drawn to the earl at that moment. But the beautiful *Aimless* she had loved from the first instant she had laid eyes on her.

"La, gov'nor," she exclaimed, forgetting for the moment that she was the Demon's captive. "Were she mine, I'd not leave her to pine for the open water. I'd sail her to the farthest reaches of the earth. She's a spirited lady what doesn't deserve to be left cooling her heels at anchor."

"I collect that that is meant in the way of a criticism," drawled his lordship with a repressive lift of an eyebrow.

"Thee can take it anyway 'ee wants," Brie retorted. "But 'tis only the plain truth."

"I take it as an impertinence, coming as it does from a crackbrained young idiot with more bottom than brains. Only a fool would take a skiff out with a storm obviously building."

Instantly Brie bridled with resentment.

"At least I bain't afraid to test me mettle. Not like some I might name, who'd rather skulk around the battlements and brood about the ill-luck what's been dealt them."

"I must assume you are referring to me," he murmured with an ominous quiet that should have put her on her guard. "And what can you possibly know of it?"

"I know thee's been seen in the wee hours, draped all in black like 'ee be now. Staring out to sea, 'ee was, night after night, till they've named thy lookout Demon's Perch and swear 'ee's the devil bent on luring poor souls to their deaths below."

Brie winced at the harsh bark of his laughter.

"And you believe it?" he demanded with a cynical curl of the lip. "Yes, I can see the uncertainty in your eyes. But then, why should you not? Perhaps I am the devil."

Brie gave a snort of disgust.

"Thee'd like that," she retorted scathingly. "To have me shiverin' in me boots. But Brian Murdoch believes what he sees with his own eyes. Thee's a man, not a wraith. And a poor fool what should know better than to spend all his time feeling sorry for himself."

"Impertinent whelp!" She nearly backed before the

hard lash of anger in his voice. "Take a good look at me." With an effort she kept herself from staring at the gloved hand he held up before her. "Do you think it is pity I want? Do you think I do not know how they stared at me behind my back when I was in London? Or how I should be regarded by the local gentry here were I foolish enough to expose myself to them? I assure you I have had enough of pity to last a lifetime."

"Gammon!" Brie retorted, suddenly out of patience with him. " 'Tis all a fudge, and 'ee knows it. Does 'ee think I doesn't see that what ails 'ee bain't thy hand, but thy heart? Thee's like this ship — all empty inside and yearnin' for somethin' only the sea can give 'ee. Well, me, I'd rather take me chances in a stiff gale than wither up inside for the lack of trying."

Brie heard the sharp intake of his breath, saw the muscle leap along the hard line of his jaw. For the barest instant she thought he might strike her. Then suddenly he went inexplicably still.

"No, not the sea," he muttered, taking a step toward her.

Brie felt her limbs grow suddenly all trembly and weak as he loomed over her. For what seemed an eternity he held her with those black, piercing orbs that seemed capable of seeing through to her very soul. Then the moment passed and just as suddenly he released her, a shutter seeming to drop in place over the pale visage. Unwittingly, she shivered.

"You are cold." He made it sound like an accusation. "You must go below at once. No doubt the cabin boy will have something to suit in the way of dry clothing." Seeing her draw back, he smiled acerbically. "Are you afraid of me, Brian Murdoch?"

At once Brie's head came up, her chin defiant.

"No more'n I'd fear the devil, milord," she stated

boldly, though, inside, her stomach was queasy with butterflies. "I expect thee'd not murder me outright, unless 'ee was powerful mad. Nevertheless, I'd just as soon pass on thy hospitality."

"That," he answered smoothly, "is out of the question. After all, we have unfinished business to discuss, you and I. We had a pact, Brian Murdoch, and now I am afraid I must insist on the pleasure of your company."

Brie, well aware that she had never any choice in the matter, reluctantly allowed him to usher her through the cabin hatch and down the shadowed companionway.

Brie was conscious of vague surprise as they entered the Demon's private quarters. The cabin was neither spacious nor sumptuously arrayed with the trappings one might expect of a man reputed as wealthy as Malvern. Located in the stern of the ship, it was large enough to accommodate little more than a bed, which was more the size of a cot, a fine cherry wood secretary, the glassed shelves lined with books, a small table for dining and a pair of velvet-covered chairs. An exquisite wine chest, beautifully carved, and the gold leaf edging on the wall panels were the sole pretensions to wealth and refinement.

Still, she decided, observing him sling off his caped greatcoat and settle on the padded bench seat beneath the stern windows, the rather Spartan quarters suited him somehow. Indeed, limned against the restless bulge of the sea, his dark hair wet and clinging to his forehead, he seemed an inseparable part of his surroundings.

"Has no one ever told you it is bad manners to stare at your betters?"

At his amused drawl, Brie started from her protracted scrutiny.

"To my way of thinkin', it bain't no worse than what thee's done to me. At least it bain't no crime to stare, milord."

"I see, and taking in a parentless whelp and giving him employment is, I suppose."

" 'Tis, when 'tis done against a boy's will," retorted Brie. "An' who's t'say I haven't got employment of me own? Brian Murdoch looks after his own self well enough, thank 'ee."

"Oh, no doubt." Malvern's tone was singularly ironic. "And yet in the short time I have known you, you have placed yourself in peril of your life not once, but three times that I am aware of. It occurs to me that you, my maggoty young friend, stand in dire need of a man's supervision."

Brie's eyes widened in disbelief.

"An' 'ee thinks thee's the one to do it?" she demanded.

A faint smile twitched at the corners of the handsome lips.

"A hideous prospect, I agree," drawled his lordship. "However, I had more in mind giving you to Hartwell to tame. He has considerable experience dealing with hard cases like yourself."

Brie, having already had some prior experience with Malvern's coxswain, did not doubt it for a moment. Nevertheless, she refused to be intimidated.

"Pooh!" she retorted. "Thee can't bullock me, gov'nor. I bain't afraid of a slowtop like Jack Hartwell."

"Then you have, I fear, misjudged my cox'n. But be that as it may, you will serve me in the end." All at once he looked at her, his face singularly devoid of humor. "I intend to find my brother's murderers. And you are going to help me."

Brie felt as if the cabin were closing in on her.

"But I doesn't *know* anything, gov'nor," she said. "I

minds me own business and keeps my nose clean. Else I'd gone the way of Duncan a long time ago. Thee'd do well to follow my example. It doesn't pay to be overinquisitive, and not even Demon Drake hisself is safe from the vengeance of the flaskers."

A look of impatience swept the pale visage.

"I suggest," he murmured coldly, "that you concern yourself with your own probable fate should I decide to give you over to the excisemen. Somehow I doubt that either they or the likes of Kermit Lachlan and his ilk will deal as generously with you as I am prepared to do — should you decide to cooperate. A se'ennight should be sufficient time for you to make a few discreet inquiries. I suggest you begin by finding out what you can about a young blood hereabout. He is reputed a rogue and a gambler, and now rumor has it that he has been dabbling in the free trade of late. Perhaps you are already acquainted with him. His name is Collin Morgan."

Brie's face went deathly pale.

"C-Collin Morgan?" she stammered. "B-but he's thy intended's brother. Surely 'ee doesn't think *he's* one of the gentlemen what killed thy brother."

Malvern shrugged.

"It is naturally my hope that he is in no way involved," he said, his eyes unreadable beneath heavily drooping eyelids. "However, I find it exceedingly strange when a man known to be pockets to let turns up suddenly in possession of a purse full of gold. Morgan, it seems, has been spending rather too freely of late, a circumstance which has not gone unremarked by a certain officer of my acquaintance — a Lieutenant Wilcox, to be exact, of the coast guard. In short, I cannot but suspect that my future in-law is not only a smuggler, but a complete and utter fool as well."

Brie, who could not but wholeheartedly agree with his final assessment, felt suddenly sick to her stomach. Good God, how *could* Collin have been so lackwitted as to flaunt his ill-gotten gains before the world! Not only had he brought suspicion down upon himself, but he had dragged her into it as well. For if Brian Murdoch's true identity were uncovered now, would it not seem to Malvern and Lieutenant Wilcox that she herself was involved with the smugglers? Indeed, she would be hard put to explain what she had been doing in Smugglers' Cave disguised as a boy and bending over a gentleman's crop of goods.

"Now what is it to be, Brian Murdoch?" murmured the earl, jarring her back to the present. "Do you intend to help me, or do I turn you over to Lieutenant Wilcox tonight for questioning?"

"Thee doesn't leave me much of a choice," Brie uttered grudgingly. "I expects I'd rather take my chances with 'ee than the picaroons."

"An excellent decision, I've no doubt," applauded the earl. "Then it is agreed. We shall meet here again on Saturday next—shall we say at dusk?"

Brie stared at him askance.

"I doesn't get it," she said. "Does 'ee mean to free me? What if I just decides to make meself scarce? Is 'ee sayin' thee'll trust me?"

"Rather say I am confident that I can find you, should the need arise. Just as I did tonight. Bear in mind that I am a man of considerable influence. I daresay England is not big enough to hide you, should you be so foolhardy as to disappoint me."

Brie for once had no ready retort. Caught in the coil of her own making, in fact, she could only agree with him. In truth, she could see no way out of her dilemma, for should Brian Murdoch fail to appear, surely nothing would keep Malvern from going after his only other link to the smugglers—her brother, Collin Morgan!

As if made suddenly impatient with her silence, Malvern turned to glance out the stern windows.

"There appears to be a lull in the storm," he observed shortly. "It has stopped raining." Deliberately he looked at her again. "I suppose we should take our leave while we can. It should be safe enough now for you to make your way home."

Something in his tone struck Brie oddly. Strange, came the disjointed thought. If she did not know better, she could almost believe he was truly concerned for her welfare. In fact, the unsettling suspicion sprang to her mind that his sole purpose in bringing her here had been to keep her from daring the cliffs in the fury of the storm. But that was absurd, she told herself. Besides, he could have no way of knowing that her way led up the smugglers' trail to Gullan Carn—or could he?

Lifting her eyes to his, she became aware that Malvern was watching her, a faint, mocking light in his disturbing orbs. Hastily she gathered her wits about her.

"Well, then. If thee's no more need of me tonight." Nervously she shifted, her glance flickering toward the exit then back again to the nobleman.

For a moment longer Malvern held her. But at last taking pity on her, he rose and, retrieving the greatcoat from the bed on which he had left it, slung it carelessly around his shoulders. Then he turned and started toward her, and suddenly her mouth went dry at something she sensed in his slow, measured movements. Pride alone compelled her to stand her ground.

Nevertheless, her heart was pounding as he came at last to stand over her. He stared down at her, the black eyes glittery in the pale mask of his face.

"Repellent boy," he said at length. She could not stop herself from wincing as his hand came up to pluck a bedraggled lock of the wig from her forehead. "You are wet to the skin, and now it is too late to get you into dry clothing. You must give me your word you will go directly home. I should be greatly displeased to learn that Brian Murdoch had succumbed to a fatal inflammation of the lungs."

"And why should 'ee care, one way or t'other," Brie queried gruffly. "I bain't nothin' to thee."

"No," he agreed, the faint curve of his lips ironic. "But you are of some little worth to me alive." She nearly sagged with relief when at last he straightened and moved away from her. At the exit he paused, turning to glance back at her over his shoulder. "Dead, however, you are of no use to me at all. Now, if you are ready?" he murmured, gesturing toward the dark interior of the companionway.

Brie, ducking her head to avoid his eyes, stepped grudgingly past him and headed topside. Inexplicably, his answer had hurt her somehow. And yet what else should she have expected? After all, to him, she was only Brian Murdoch, a boy who might lead him to his brother's murderers. Heaven forbid that he should ever discover otherwise, she told herself firmly.

Nevertheless, she was conscious of a vague dissatisfaction with both him and herself as, moments later, she seated herself in the midsection of the little boat and took up the oars. Nor was the feeling lessened as she rowed in silence. Indeed, she was acutely aware of the still figure seated in the stern sheets.

His face was obscured in the deepening shadows of falling dusk, made gloomier still by the low-hanging clouds. Still, she could feel his eyes on her and she could sense a subtle strain about him. As if his arm were giving him pain, she thought, then instantly discarded the notion. No, it was more like something troubling on his mind, and somehow she was certain whatever it was, it had to do with her. Like a bowstring drawn too tightly, the tension steadily mounted.

When at length the prow finally struck, Brie hastened to leap over the side. With Malvern's aid, she dragged the boat ashore and stood panting a little from her exertions. Then, at last, she could not bear the silence longer.

"How *did* 'ee find me, gov'nor?" she blurted, voicing the thing that had been nagging at the back of her mind. "There wasn't nobody about when I took me *Mere-Magden* out. I made sure of that."

"Did you," came the answering drawl. "But then, you might have made equally certain that you would not escape the Demon's notice—if what you have told me is true."

"Thee was at thy perch! Ecod, I should have known!" Brie groaned. "The whole time thee was watching me."

"I confess my curiosity was piqued when first I beheld a skiff weather the headland. Only a fool, I told myself, or a man on a desperate mission would set a course for France with a storm brewing." He paused, and instinctively Brie braced herself. "I am still wondering. Perhaps you would care to tell me, Brian Murdoch. Did you find whatever it was you were looking for?"

Brie bridled at the accusation in his voice.

"I doesn't know what 'ee's talking about," she said, suddenly visualizing her afternoon's jaunt as he must have seen it. To one who did not know her better, her aimless wandering up and down the coast might indeed invite suspicion. It might even be construed as the antics of a smuggler dragging the sea bottom for a concealed crop of goods! "I wasn't lookin' for nothin'. was only sailin' for the sport of it. La, gov'nor, if I was creepin' for sunken casks, does 'ee think I'd be fool enough to do it in broad daylight?"

"I assure you I am not such a gudgeon," replied his lordship in chilling accents. "I suggest you keep in mind that I had you under my eye for some considerable time. Long enough, in fact, to lose sight of you. In the time you were gone, it would have been a simple matter to rendezvous with a vessel out of sight of land. Smuggling, you young fool, is one thing, but exchanging information with French agents is quite another. If that is what you have embroiled yourself in, you would do well to tell me now."

Brie stared at him in dawning horror. Then, as the enormity of what he had said sank home, horror gave way to mounting fury.

"Is that what thee thinks?" she demanded hotly. "That Brian Murdoch's a bloody traitor? I'd sooner croak than sell out to the murderin' frogs. An' if thee believes differently, why—why thee can just go to the devil. That's what I say, Captain Bloody Demon Drake."

Furiously she spun on her heel and started to stalk away, when steely fingers caught her wrist and yanked her ruthlessly about again.

"I did not give you leave to go," Malvern said, bringing his face to within inches of her own. "If what you have said is true, you have little to fear from me. But if you are lying, mark my words well. For reasons I do not care to expound, I am of the suspicion that someone of the gentility hereabout is selling information to the French. I think Duncan found out about it, but before he could report his discoveries to the authorities, he was murdered. If you—or any of your acquaintances—know anything of this man's identity, you would do well to divulge it now, before it is too late. Do I make myself clear?"

"Oh, aye," Brie bitterly retorted, her heart sick within her. " 'Ee's made thyself clear enough. Thee believes 'tis Collin Morgan what's sold his soul to the devil, and Brian Murdoch what thinks to cash in on it. But thee's wrong—about both of us."

"Perhaps. And perhaps Morgan's actions have already condemned him. Either way, he treads a treacherous path fraught with pitfalls. Make sure, my young friend, he does not take you down with him."

The warning in his words pierced Brie through. For an instant she stared speechlessly into the chiseled hardness of his face. Then at last, overcome with the need to be free of his unsettling presence, she spun on her heel and without a backward glance fled into the deepening night.

Chapter Eight

The trek home from Men-aber was accomplished without mishap, and Brie fortunately was able to slip into the house unseen. Hastily she changed her breeches for a gown before descending to face her grandfather, who, Fionna informed her in an ominous undertone, was awaiting her in the dining room.

Pausing with her hands on the sliding doors, she took a deep breath and then went in. She did not need more than a single glimpse at the commodore, standing, hands clasped behind his back, before the fireplace, to know the temper of his mood. He wore the forbidding aspect of a senior officer sitting in judgment at a court martial.

"Poor Gramfer!" she exclaimed, deciding in the circumstances that her best defense was to assume a bold front. "Are you terribly famished? You really should not have waited dinner for me, you know. I should have been perfectly contented with a tray in my room."

"That can be arranged," observed her irate grandparent, his gaze unrelenting beneath bristling eyebrows. "Though I doubt 'twas bread and water 'ee had in mind. Perhaps it would not be too much to expect an explanation for where thee's been all day? Just what the devil has thee been up to that 'ee couldn't see fit to let someone know where 'ee was goin'?"

"Oh, dear. I am properly in the briars, am I not. And you have every reason to be put out. It was thoughtless of me to go without a word to anyone. It is just that I had so wished to surprise you, and if it had not been that I was caught out in the middle of that plaguey storm, I should have, too," she declared, hating herself for having to deceive him. And yet what choice had she? It would hardly have done to tell him what had really happened, not with Collin under suspicion not only of being a smuggler, but a murderer and a traitor to his country as well! "The truth is, I went down to East Looe in the hopes of purchasing fresh lobster for your dinner. You know how you love it served in butter sauce, with just the right garnish. And—well—I did miss the springtide harvest."

She had spoken all in a rush, before he could get a word in edgewise, but now she stopped and, spreading wide her hands, gave him a rueful look.

"I am sorry, dearest Gramfer," she offered with sincere contrition, "for any anxiety my absence may have caused you. But it did seem best to wait out the storm in the inn at the crossroads. I pray I did not cause you any undue worry."

"Humph," he snorted, relief at having her safely home gradually subduing the more unsettling emotions to which he had been prey. "And doubtless 'ee thinks to be excused for thy dereliction of duty because it was done for my benefit, is that it?"

"I do not ask to be excused." Crossing the room to stand before him, she gazed up at him out of beguiling green eyes. "But perhaps you can find it in your heart to forgive me? Just a little?"

The sly little puss, thought the commodore, well aware that he had already lost the first round to her. And yet maybe, just maybe he could still turn the tide of battle. Noisily he cleared his throat.

"Ahem! Lobster, did 'ee say?" he queried gruffly.

"Aye," she replied, reaching up to straighten his indifferently tied neckcloth.

"*Fresh* lobster, minced and cooked in white wine with just a sprinkling of nutmeg?"

"Aye, and finished off with a butter sauce — just the way you like it," she added, giving the tidied knot a final pat.

The commodore's thick eyebrows lifted in his wrinkled brow.

"It sounds a meal fit for a king — or an earl as the case may be. 'Ee did fetch enough for Malvern to share in the feast?"

Instantly she drew back, her hands going to her hips as she favored him with a chary eye.

"I did not," she stated bluntly. "I am sorry, no doubt, but there was money enough to provide only for an intimate family affair. If 'tis lobster his lordship desires, I am afraid he shall have to look elsewhere."

"Nonsense, if 'tis to be a family affair, he might as well have Collin's portion, lest 'ee was meanin' to throw it away. As it happens, thy brother's off with Rory Gale to the Townsends'. A house party, he said, in the way of a come out for the youngest of that brood of females."

"A house party?" Brie echoed, her heart skipping a beat. Then a frown darkened her brow. "Gramfer, if this is some of *your* doing . . ."

"*My* doing?" boomed the commodore in patent disbelief. "Be 'ee saying that I persuaded the Townsends to give their daughter a come out for the sole purpose of making room for the earl at a dinner I knew nothing about?"

Obviously it was a preposterous notion, and yet Brigida could not help feeling she was being outmaneuvered somehow.

"But Collin said nothing to me of any such plans," she persisted. "Indeed, I cannot but wonder why I should not have been invited. And the earl, too, for that matter. Certainly, *he* at least would have been considered a feather in Mrs. Townsend's cap?"

"And who said 'ee wasn't invited?" the commodore rejoined with the air of a man who has been waiting for the moment to let go with a broadside. " 'Ee was. Unfortunately, 'ee was nowhere to be found, and, come to think of it, neither was the earl. Kind of makes a body wonder, don't it."

Brie, feeling the blood rise to her cheeks, hastily turned away.

"Not at all," she retorted. "Indeed, why should it? No doubt his lordship is free to come and go as he pleases."

"Aye, no doubt," agreed her grandfather drily. "But be that as it may, Collin waited as long as he dared in the hopes 'ee'd eventually show up. I expect he's going for the sake of Elsbeth, the chit's eldest sister. Always did have a soft spot for the lass, in spite of the fact that she never took. Five girls, and all wed, save for her and this last to make her curtsy in polite society. Was it me, I wouldn't look for him before Friday eve."

"I see," murmured Brie, her heart sinking. Oh, how like her brother to be gone just when she needed him the most!

The commodore, meanwhile, seeing that she was all in irons, brought his guns to bear for the coup de grace.

"Well, then, 'tis all settled," he stated with obvious satisfaction. "I'll send Neal over to Tal Carn first thing in the morning with an invitation for Malvern to join us for dinner." Rubbing his hands together in apparent anticipation of the event, he seated himself at the table. "Well, lass? Was 'ee intending to stand there all night? Me stomach tells me I've been made to wait long enough for me supper."

Fuming in impotence, Brie seated herself. But her appetite had suffered a sudden eclipse. Oh, he had turned the tables neatly on her, had he not. Malvern would come to dinner, and she would have no choice but to be civil. And to top it all off, Collin had gone off with Rory Gale for a se'ennight!

She did not like the sound of that. There was no telling into what mischief the squire's ne'er-do-well son might lead Collin in a week's time. She would be greatly surprised, in fact, if they ever made it to the Townsends' at Hessenford, a journey of some ten miles or so. Rory Gale's tastes, after all, hardly ran to schoolroom misses making their come outs. Something was afoot, she could feel it in her bones. And yet Collin had given his word. If only she had had the chance to warn him about the earl and his suspicions before he left!

Malvern! she thought with a sinking feeling in the pit of her stomach. In truth, she did not know which was worse: the possibility that her brother might be coaxed to make another smuggler's run with Rory Gale or the certainty that she would by this time tomorrow be entertaining the Earl of Malvern over dinner. Certainly neither prospect was all that alluring, she decided when, the meal finished at last and the leavings cleared away, she made her way upstairs to her bed.

The next day found Brie up early, overseeing the preparations for the proposed evening. She could only suppose it was some perversity in her character which compelled her to make certain everything would be perfect. As it was, she spent an hour going over the menu with Mrs. Guthrie and another thirty minutes instructing Fionna how to prepare the table. Then donning an apron and cap and rolling up her sleeves, she set about with the help of two girls from the village to rid the downstairs rooms of the last vestige of dust. It was not until late afternoon that she was finally able to turn her attention to the last and most troublesome of her tasks—the problem of her own appearance.

Collin had been right about one thing. Her wardrobe was sadly in need of refurbishing. At no time since the death of her parents had there been sufficient funds for a great many dresses and gowns, and the last two years she had sunk every penny into keeping Gullan Carn afloat. With the result that she possessed only a single gown that was even remotely suitable for receiving callers, and it, unhappily, had seen better days.

With a sigh, she went to her clothespress and pulled open the doors.

A low gasp escaped her lips at the surprise awaiting her within—not one, but three new dresses hung conspicuously in the forefront awaiting her inspection.

"But where did . . . ?" she began. A tentative hand reached out to caress a feathery light fabric. Then it came to her. "Collin!" she exclaimed, swept by a whole gamut of emotions, chief of which were anger at his apparent reckless flaunting of smugglers' gold and a wrenching at her heart for such thoughtfulness from a brother, who, in spite of his fondness for her, had never before seen fit to lavish her with presents.

Her first thought was to relegate the gowns to the back of the wardrobe until she could decide how best to dispose of them. She could hardly aid in her brother's downfall by displaying them before his chief accuser, after all; and yet some deeper instinct, purely feminine, caused her to hesitate. It could hardly hurt to look at them, just once, here, in the privacy of her own room, came the insidious thought. Her brother's motives, at least, had surely been above reproach. In which case, she practically owed it to him to examine the evidence of his generosity, did she not?

Half defiantly, Brie took out the first of the gowns and held it up to her in front of the looking glass.

The morning dress of sprig muslin, with a high waist and short puffed sleeves, brought a delighted grin to her lips. How different it was from the drab woolens she was accustomed to wearing! Why, it was so light, she would hardly know she had anything on, a circumstance which was bound not to go unnoticed by her dearest grandfather—*if,* that is, she were ever actually to put the dress on, she thought with a wry grin. And of course she would not.

With a sigh, she laid the gown across the bed and reached for the next. This one, a walking dress of emerald green, with long sleeves tapering to embroidered bands over the wrists, was even more exquisite than the first. There was a habit-shirt, worn over the bodice with the high neck fastened under the chin, and it was beautifully trimmed in swansdown. Never had she seen such a gown! And yet she was soon to discover that she had saved the best for last.

A mist momentarily clouded her vision as she held the lovely thing up. Quietly elegant in ivory satin with mother-of-pearl sewn into the bodice, it draped in soft folds from an empire waist to a short train at the back. The sleeves, puffed at the shoulders, were long, tapering delicately to the wrists and ending in a fine spray of spider-net lace. A faint blush tinged Brie's cheeks at sight of the décolletage. In the shape of a V, it appeared almost indecently low, and yet nothing would have induced her to change it. It would have been the very first evening dress she had ever owned, and it was absolutely perfect in every detail. Odd, she thought, for, indeed, it was almost as if it had been especially designed with her in mind.

That thought brought a perplexed frown to her brow. How in the world had Collin managed the thing? Such gowns could only have come from London or from an extremely talented seamstress familiar with the first stare of fashion. Short of Plymouth, she knew of no one noted for such quality of workmanship. Further, Collin was hardly in the petticoat line. Until now, she never would have guessed he possessed either the keen eye for detail or the knowledge of feminine attire which would enable him to order gowns so well suited to her in size and in color. But then, of course, he must have had someone to help him. Elsbeth Townsend, perhaps, or some other female of their acquaintance, she told herself and still was not totally satisfied.

And then it came to her. If anyone knew anything about the mysterious gowns, it would be Fionna, she thought as she rang for the maid servant.

It was not Fionna, however, who answered the bell, but one of the girls Brie had hired from the village for the day. Fionna, she was informed, was helping Mrs. Guthrie in the kitchen with the finishing touches and could not be spared at the moment.

"I see," answered Brie, hard put to conceal her irritation at the delay in having the troublesome matter of the gowns laid to rest.

Then, realizing how late the hour must be, all else fled from her mind but the need to hurry. Giving the girl instructions to bring water for her bath, she set about laying out the things she would need to complete her toilette.

It was while rummaging in the back of her wardrobe for her only pair of dress shoes that she came across the ivory satin sandals. Suffering a small wrench at her heartstrings, she straightened, the dainty examples of ladies' footwear clasped in her hands.

She knew without having to look that the sandals, which had belonged to her mother, perfectly matched the color of the new evening gown. For a moment, she stood staring down at them, thinking of the one and only time they had graced Gwyn Morgan's feet. She had worn them to a soiree at Squire Gale's at Wickham in celebration of the May Day. Brie, who had been allowed to stay up late to watch her mother dress for the gala event, had slipped the sandals on and been delighted to find they were nearly a fit.

"You are growing up," her mother had said, smiling at her in that special way she had had, as if they shared some delectable secret between them. "Before you know it, you will be donning your first ball gown. Oh, what a merry chase you will give your young swains! We shall have such fun, you and I, sharing your triumphs. I promise I am quite looking forward to it."

How young and vital she had looked then, as she took her daughter's hands and danced her about the room! Yet hardly a month later she had been dead—drowned in a sudden gale at sea. For the first time it came to Brigida to wonder if that had not been the real reason she had not accepted her aunt's invitation to make her come out in Plymouth. Her uncle had even offered to stand the nonsense of a modest investment in gowns. But Brigida had been too proud to accept charity, or at least that is what she had told herself at the time. But perhaps the money, or, rather, the lack of it, had been only an excuse, and her pride naught but a mask behind which to hide the hurt and anger she had still felt at the loss of her mother.

Overcome with the realization that if Gwyn Morgan could see her daughter now, she would be greatly disappointed, Brie uttered an anguished groan. Good God, could she in truth have been trying to punish her mother for having left her when she needed her the most? All at once her head came up to reveal a defiant sparkle in the sea-green depths of her eyes. She did not know the answer to that, but just this once she would be what her mama had envisioned for her and the devil with the consequences. She would wear the ivory silk gown and dazzle the odious Earl of Malvern!

Making short work of her bath, Brie donned her

underthings and settled before the fire to dry her hair.

Her coppery locks, worn short for convenience sake and possessed of a natural curl of their own, would have been the envy of many another female, who must spend each night in curling papers or hours wrestling with a curling iron. As it was, in little more than half an hour or so, Brigida was crowned with a mantle of soft, alluring curls. Giving them a final pat, she hurriedly thrust her feet into the ivory satin sandals and reached for the evening dress.

As she slipped the lovely thing over her head, the soft rustle of satin flowing down her slender length sent a little thrill coursing through her. Cool and smooth against her skin, it made her feel elegant, something she had never experienced before. And in truth, she hardly recognized the creature staring back at her from the looking glass.

The small head, clustering with curls, was held regally high. Eyes, the cool green of the sea, peered back at her—shadowy and deep, mysterious somehow. Unconsciously a hand rose to the soft swell of her breasts above the daring décolletage. An uncomfortable warmth pervaded her limbs at the thought that soon she would appear thus before a pair of black, glittery orbs. Then deliberately she uncovered herself.

The devil fly away with Malvern. She did not care what he thought of her. The hoydenish Brie Morgan was banished. Tonight she would be Brigida—a woman, provocative and cool, confident in her femininity.

Gathering up her ivory-sticked folding fan, she slipped the loop over her wrist and left the room.

The case clock was just striking five when Brigida stopped on the landing to look down into the great hall. As if on cue, the hollow clang of the brass knocker resounded through the house. Instantly her earlier resolve fled and she stood frozen to the spot. Her mouth dry and her limbs strangely shaky, she watched Fionna cross to the door and open it.

"Good eve, gov'nor," greeted the maid, neglecting in the usual Cornish fashion to use the more proper title for an English lord. Taking the earl's caped greatcoat and curly brimmed beaver, she ushered him into the hall.

Brigida's breath caught in her throat at sight of the slim, compelling figure. Except for the somberly gloved hand, he had foregone the usual funereal black for a waistcoat of white marcella and a snug-fitting coat of blue superfine. How well the cut accentuated the well-knit masculine shoulders! And the white kerseymere breeches tucked into the tops of shining brown Hessians! They seemed particularly designed to draw attention to the muscular thighs. Oh, but he was a fine figure of a man, thought Brigida, wishing he was less handsome by far. If the ladies in London had stared at him, it surely was no wonder!

At that point Fionna's plaintive voice perhaps fortunately interrupted the disturbing train of her thoughts.

"Miss Brigida bain't come down yet," said the maid servant to the earl. "But the commodore be awaitin' fer thee in the Rose Room, if 'ee'd be plaised t'follow me, sir."

The thought came to Brigida that it was not too late. She could still flee unseen upstairs to her room. And then what? Lock herself in and refuse to come down? She could not be so craven. Then Malvern turned, and it *was* too late.

She felt a shock wave shudder through her as his glance lifted to find her standing there—like a mindless idiot, she thought, resisting the urge to run her tongue over lips that were gone suddenly dry. Gathering her courage, she started down the stairs.

The dozen or so steps down to the hallway seemed to take an eternity, executed, as they were, under the penetrating gaze of the Demon of Malvern. Indeed, it seemed to Brie, intent on not tripping on the hem of her dress, that she had suddenly forgotten how to walk. But at last the thing was done.

"Welcome to Gullan Carn, milord," she murmured throatily and, wondering half hysterically if she had lost what few wits she had been blessed with, dropped into a curtsy. "It is kind of you to honor us with your presence."

"Not at all, Miss Morgan. I am never kind, and the honor of being here is all mine, I assure you." The earl's soft drawl resonated thrillingly in the quiet of the hall, and Brie was conscious of an answering flutter in the region of her heart. Nor was that all or the worst of it, she realized, as, taking the strong supple hand he held out to her, she experienced an unsettling tingle of nerve endings.

Blushing angrily at herself, Brie rose with unconscious grace to her feet and found Malvern observing her with unnerving intentness. Irritably, she wondered if he found some objection to her appearance.

"Ivory satin suits you admirably, Miss Morgan," he drawled, as if in answer to her thoughts. "I see my sister-in-law was quite right to insist on it. I trust the other gowns are equally satisfactory?"

Brie started.

"The other . . . !" she gasped. Then stricken with awful realization, she bit off what she had been about to say and turned hastily away. Her voice when she spoke was low and quivering. "Then I have you to thank for the additions to my wardrobe?"

She did not give him time to respond to the question. The answer, after all, was all too painfully obvious.

"Good God, what a fool I was," she blurted out, pacing a few steps away and then coming back again. "Collin would not know satin from fustian. Or an evening dress from sackcloth and ashes. How could I possibly have imagined the gowns came from him!"

"How, indeed?" murmured the earl, apparently much struck at the notion.

Brie gave him a withering look.

"I suppose you find all this terribly amusing, do you not?" she demanded, her magnificent eyes blazing.

"Not at all," Malvern corrected. "Perhaps you will pardon me if I admit I have not the least notion what you are in a huff about."

"Oh, have you not, indeed?" she uttered blisteringly. "I suppose it never occurred to you that I might wish to refuse your generosity, had I been made aware beforehand of its source."

"The thought did occur to me," he blithely admitted. "However, since I did send them by way of one of my footmen, whose livery, as it happens, should have left little doubt as to his employer's identity, I naturally assumed you would realize from whence the gowns came. Tell me, is it your intention to rush immediately upstairs and rectify the error?" he inquired with suspicious blandness.

Angrily Brie bit her lip. That was exactly what she had contemplated doing. And how utterly impossible he had just rendered any such notion! Silently she cursed the fate that had placed her in such an untenable position. Oh, why had no one seen fit to inform her of the circumstances surrounding the delivery of the gowns! she fumed, and knew at once the culprit was most probably her dearest grandsire. Naturally *he* would have been perfectly aware of how she would receive any gift from Malvern.

Perhaps unfortunately she chose just then to glance up into that worthy's countenance. Something — a gleam of amusement in the dark, compelling orbs or the faint twitch at the corners of the mouth — awakened in her her normally keen sense of the absurd. Unwittingly, she choked on a bubble of laughter.

"Oh," she gasped, her eyes brimful of wry humor. "You really are quite odious. You must know I can do no such thing. Not without being made to appear hopelessly childish."

"Quite so," he agreed smoothly. "In which case I suggest we forget the entire matter." Impaling her with his eyes, he extended a strong, shapely hand. "Truce?" he queried, with only the faintest hint of irony. "For the balance of the evening at the very least?"

Brie stared at him, little trusting what appeared a less forbidding side of the earl and yet drawn in spite of herself.

"Very well, your lordship," she answered, her head nevertheless high as she took the proffered member. "A truce it is, so long as you understand my mind remains firm on this matter of our marriage."

"I never thought otherwise, I assure you," he said and, holding her eyes, lightly saluted her knuckles with his lips.

"Yes, well, just so long as you do understand," Brie retorted, not sure at all, and, blushing, pulled her hand free.

Dinner that night was not at all the strained affair she had anticipated. Malvern, she was soon to discover, could be both charming and wholly engaging when he put himself out to be. Eighteen years spent in the King's Navy had provided him with an extensive store of seafaring tales from which to draw, and while he might be reticent when it came to talking about himself, he was not averse to relating those stories of a less personal nature. But more importantly, he was a good listener as well. For every anecdote he shared with them, he managed to elicit two from the commodore.

Nor was Brie proof against his subtle charm. Before she knew what she was about, she was telling in humorous detail any number of her girlhood adventures and misadventures with her brother, as well as her hopes and dreams for Gullan Carn. It was only much later that she realized just how adroitly he had drawn her out, inducing her to reveal much more of herself than she had ever intended.

As for Malvern, he continued to remain something of an enigma for Brie, who was finding that she rather liked this relaxed, unassuming man. Indeed, she was having difficulty reconciling the image of the cold, unassailable earl with this new, more personable nobleman when the commodore laid his napkin on the table.

"Brigida, my girl, 'ee's outdone thyself," he said, shoving back his chair. "Inform Mrs. Guthrie, will 'ee, that everything was prepared to perfection. And now I must ask you both to excuse me. I'm afraid I'm not so young as I once was. After such a meal as this has been, I feel uncommonly ready for me bed."

Brie stared daggers at her deceitful grandparent. The commodore's ploy to leave her alone with the earl was not only too transparent by far, it was blatantly underhanded.

"But the evening is young yet, Gramfer," she protested. "No doubt his lordship would be pleased to join you in an afterdinner wine. I shall simply withdraw to the Rose Room."

"Nonsense. Malvern did not come to see me. Play him a tune on the pianoforte. Or, better yet, there's a moon out tonight. Take his lordship out for a stroll in the rose garden. As for me, I'm turning in."

Brie's heart sank at this unforeseen turn of events. In impotent fury she watched the commodore bid his guest a gruff farewell and retire, leaving her alone with the earl. Feeling vaguely foolish and more than a little uneasy, she searched vainly for something to fill in the gaping silence. It was Malvern, however, who performed that service.

"Do you indeed play, Miss Morgan?" politely queried his lordship. Brie glanced up in vexation, only to be taken off guard by the warm glimmer of amusement in the dark, sleepy eyes.

An irrepressible dimple peeped out at the corner of her mouth.

"Intolerably, milord," she replied frankly. "I suggest we should do better in the rose garden."

Outside, the air was chill, and Brie was grateful she had stopped long enough to fling a wrap around her shoulders. Acutely conscious of the man at her side, she stepped off the flagstone verandah and wandered aimlessly among the budding roses.

"This was my mother's favorite retreat," she said, inhaling the perfumed fragrance of the breeze wafting inland from the sea. "She had a passion for working among the flowers, an interest we did not perfectly share. I fear the garden has suffered in her absence."

"And where do your interests run, if neither to music nor horticulture? Perhaps, like many of your contemporaries, you entertain a fondness for horses?"

"No, never." Brigida laughed. "I am afraid I should have been a sad disappointment to my fraternal grandfather, the squire. He was used to keep a stableful of prime bloods, I am told, which he did not scruple to race for ridiculously high stakes. No doubt that was the beginning of our present financial difficulties. No. I confess to but a single passion and have even cursed the fates that determined my gender. Had I been born a boy, milord, I, like you, should have chosen the sea for my vocation."

"Then I must be grateful to those very same fates that made you what you are," murmured the earl, his face unreadable in the shadows cast by the moonlight. "You would seem to be unaware of it, but you, Miss Morgan, are a remarkably lovely woman. In my humble opinion, it would be a shame had the world been denied such beauty."

"No doubt I should be flattered, milord," responded Brie, grateful for the darkness, which hid her blush. "I, however, place little value on my looks. Indeed, I should gladly exchange them for the freedom to be able to do and be whatever I might wish. You cannot know how I have envied you—I, who, bound to the land by gender and convention, have been nurtured on tales of seafaring men. I come by it honestly, after all—my passion for the sea. I am descended, both on my mother's and my father's side, of a long line of Cornish sailors."

"As am I," observed his lordship, his voice unmistakably cynical. "The walls of Tal Carn are lined with portraits of Cornish admirals, smugglers, and a smattering of pirates. And yet this freedom, which means so much to you—I suggest to you that it is largely an illusion. Do you think because I am a man I am any less bound by what the world expects of me than are you?"

He was thinking of his disfigured body, she knew, the scars and the tortured limb, which in his own eyes and in those of many of his kind would somehow render him something less than the whole man he used to be. Unexpectedly, she found herself cursing the admiralty, which, in depriving him of his command, had robbed him of that which largely had made him what he was. Damion Drake was a proud man, a warrior, a Cornishman with the sea in his blood. How galling for such a one to be barred from what he knew and loved best!

"Perhaps," she murmured, leaning her back against the gnarled trunk of a weathered oak. "And yet, what can you possibly know what it is to be a woman? Do you know the anguish of a seafarer's wife, who must watch her man go to sea? Or the endless days and nights—nay, the months, even years, of waiting for his return—*if* he returns? That was my mother's lot, and *her* mother's and grandmother's before her. If freedom is an illusion, it is yet parceled out, with men allotted a far greater portion than that which is granted to women. Can you blame me for wishing for what you, as a man, take for granted?"

Malvern's eyes glinted coldly in the pale mask of his face.

"The sea," he drawled cynically, "is an unforgiving mistress, intolerant of the fools who succumb to her allure. You are better off tending your sheep, Miss Morgan."

"And you, milord?" she came back at him, driven by curiosity and something else she did not quite fathom. "Are you better off tending your estates? Had you it to do over again, would you have resisted her allure?"

Her heart skipped a beat as he suddenly loomed over her.

"No, Miss Morgan," he said. Leaning his hand against the tree beside her head, he rendered her peculiarly powerless either to move or protest. "I should undoubtedly have done just as I did." For a moment longer he held her his unwitting prisoner with eyes that searched her face. Then, with mesmerizing deliberation, he lowered his head toward hers. "More the fool I," he muttered grimly and covered her mouth with his.

Chapter Nine

At the touch of his lips against hers, Brie quivered and stiffened. Indeed, she had the oddest sensation that a lightning bolt had just shot through her body, leaving her tingling from the top of her head to the tips of her toes. And yet it was a gentle kiss, inquisitive rather than demanding. Dazed and disarmed, she felt herself melting to its warmth so that she hardly realized when his arm embraced her waist and pulled her to him or when his caress changed, deepened, until it seemed to draw on her very soul. She was even unmindful of the fact that her own traitorous limbs had, as of their own accord, crept slowly up his shoulders and now clung tightly about his neck. She knew only that he had broached something deep inside her, a yearning, perhaps, like a slow smoldering, which she had never before known existed within her and which now leaped forth in flames.

She returned his kiss with a sweet, innocent abandon. And when he released her, she suffered a sharp pang of regret. Slowly her eyelids fluttered open, and she stared dazedly into the Demon's orbs, brilliant and black in the moonlight.

Malvern, who had been as surprised as she by the melting sweetness of her response, lifted his head to gaze at her with a sort of baffled wonder. His breath ragged in his throat and his eyes dark with barely controlled passion, he took note of her flushed cheeks, of her eyes, dusky with the emotion he had aroused in her, yet bewildered, vulnerable, like a child's. A faint smile touched his lips. She was all fire and innocence, was the remarkable Miss Morgan.

"I am afraid you will have to give up this dream of yours to go to sea," he remarked, his smile curiously askew. Reaching up with his gloved hand, he gently brushed a stray lock of hair from her cheek. "You, my love, are very much a woman. Admit it. You enjoyed this little interlude every bit as much as did I."

He had spoken without thinking. It was a mistake, he instantly realized. Recalled to a bewildering sense of herself in his arms, she covered her confusion with a swift blaze of anger.

"H-how dare you!" she gasped and was appalled to hear her own voice, tremulous with lingering emotion, breathless. Furiously she blushed. "I am *not* your love, and I shall thank you to unhand me. At once, sir!"

He obliged her, spreading wide his hands at either side of her. How young he looked, she thought abstractedly, seeing the hard lines about his mouth vanish as his lips curved in a grin of amusement. Only then did *she* realize that she yet clung to him!

Mortified, she retrieved her arms and turned hastily away, but not before the earl glimpsed the anguish in her face. Instantly the smile faded. Frowning, he stepped toward her.

"Brigida—!" he said, a hand going to her arm.

"Don't!" The single utterance seemed torn from her throat. Malvern, ruefully aware that he had rushed his fences, cursed himself for a fool and let his hand drop.

Brie pressed trembling hands to her cheeks, hot with more than embarrassment. Good Lord, what was happening to her? she thought distraughtly and wished that she might drop dead on the spot. Indeed, he was a devil, was Damion Drake, to make her so forget herself. She had behaved shamelessly—nay, wantonly! In truth she did not know herself, she realized, and certainly she dared no longer trust herself—not alone with the Demon of Malvern.

"Brigida—,"

"I do not recall granting you leave to use my given name, milord. Indeed, I-I think perhaps you should leave now," she said stiffly, without turning to look at him. Thus she did not see the finely molded lips thin to a chiseled hardness, or the bitter self-derision in the look he bent upon her. Almost immediately, the mask fell in place again.

"Yes, perhaps I should," he answered, his eyes never leaving the straight-backed figure of the girl. "However little I might wish to." His glance shifted to the moon, already riding low on the horizon. His mouth curled cynically. "The dark of the night is nearly upon us, after all. It is time the Demon was at his perch."

Brie experienced an odd wrench at the irony in his tone. Still, she said nothing. She was too shaken, too uncertain of herself. The silence stretched, until she thought she must scream. Then at last she heard what sounded like a sigh pass Malvern's lips.

"I shall thank you for a very pleasant evening

then, Miss Morgan," he drawled with cold formality. "No need to see me out. I can find my own way."

Brie heard him turn and start toward the house, presumably to retrieve his greatcoat and curly brimmed beaver. And then the significance of what he had said sank home. He meant to lie in wait for the return of the smugglers, just as he had done the night he surprised her in the cave, just as he no doubt had been doing every night in hopes of finding his brother's slayers. And what if this time he came upon them — alone, with no one to help him! He, too, might be murdered! Unaccountably, she trembled at the thought. And then another possibility, almost as unnerving, struck her. Good God, what if he found the smugglers, and Collin was with them?

"No, wait!" The words were out of her mouth before she thought. She had turned, and as Malvern stopped and looked back at her, she had the insane urge to giggle. She had acted on impulse, thinking vaguely to detain him lest he return to Tal Carn and discover her brother with the smugglers slinging the casks. It was the one thing she had not thought of before, the thing that had troubled her, but that she had not been able to put her finger on, when she elicited the promise from Collin — that one night they would have to return to the cave to retrieve the smuggled brandy!

The earl's voice startled her out of her reverie.

"Yes, Miss Morgan? Was there something you wanted?"

Desperately she searched her mind for something to say.

"Yes. I-I . . ." She glimpsed the dark eyebrows draw together in a frown of suspicion. Blushing, she stopped and, nervously wringing her hands, turned and walked a pace. "A-about the gowns," she blurted, grasping at straws. "I-I suppose I should thank you." Straightening her shoulders, she turned at last to look at him. "Indeed, I—I probably owe you an apology for the boorish manner in which I acted. It was . . . in spite of what I may have said before . . . not that I did not mean it, because I quite assure you that I did—about not wishing to marry you, that is, or anyone for that matter—but still I cannot but be cognizant of the fact that truly it was thoughtful of you to—to . . . well, to go to all the trouble of—of . . ."

"Not at all, Miss Morgan," broke in the earl, delivering her from her hopelessly convoluted sentence with wry amusement. "As it happens, it was my sister-in-law who suggested the idea. It was something she found distressing in the extreme—trying to appear the part of the Countess of Malvern with the scarcity of fabrics in the wilds of Cornwall, and of seamstresses capable of turning out dresses suitable to a lady of refinement. The truth is, I fear poor Cordelia was never quite comfortable in her role as chatelaine of my brother's house."

No, nor should I be, thought Brigida, tempted to tell him just *how* difficult it had been for Cordelia, wed to a man like Duncan. But something, what seemed his tactfulness, perhaps, kept her from it. Cordelia, after all, must have made him perfectly aware that it was lack of funds, not seamstresses, which prevented Brie Morgan from dressing in the style of a future Countess of Malvern. For why else should he have presented her with what had every appearance of being a bridal trousseau? That was something he should more naturally have expected

Collin, as head of her father's house, to provide for her.

"You—you have been to Torpoint to see Cordelia?" she said instead, a little surprised that he had apparently gone out of his way to see his brother's widow. From all accounts he and Duncan had not exactly been close, even as boys together.

"No, not to Torpoint. She has taken a house in Brighton for the season. She and her sisters. I called on her there to see how she goes on."

"Cordelia in Brighton?" exclaimed Brie, startled at such a notion. "It is not possible, surely."

A smile, faintly reminiscent, touched his lips.

"Oh, but I assure you it is. She is hardly a pauper, after all. And apparently she has decided it is time she enjoyed life just a little. In her own quiet way, she has become quite an accepted member of the established set."

Brie stared at him in disbelief. The thought of Cordelia in Brighton was astonishing enough, but to picture her making forays into polite society was almost beyond the bounds of imagination. Cordelia Drake had ever presented the image of one painfully shy and retiring. But then, until recently, she had never known what it was not to live in the shadow of a domineering man—first her father and then her husband, the one a tyrant and the other a veritable Tartar, she grimly reflected.

"I'm glad," she said simply. "And it was she who helped you order the dresses? Yes, of course. It had to be. In spite of—of everything, she always displayed excellent taste in clothes." Summoning a smile, which felt stiff on her lips, she lifted her eyes to Malvern's. "It *was* kind of you to go to all the trouble and expense. But you must see that I cannot accept such gifts."

"On the contrary, Miss Morgan. I do not see it at all."

"I beg you will not pretend ignorance, milord," Brie replied with an impatient gesture of the hand. "You must know I should be sunk beneath reproach were I to accept such gifts from a man I do not intend to marry. I shall have the others sent over to you as soon as possible. As for this one—since, regrettably, I have already worn it and thus made its return impracticable, perhaps you would be so kind as to tell me what you paid for it. I shall naturally see that you are reimbursed."

"Do not be absurd." She nearly winced at the hint of steel in his voice. "I haven't the least notion what I paid for it, and if I did, it would not signify. The gowns are yours to do with as you will."

"But I have told you I cannot accept them."

Her breath caught at the leap of anger in his eyes.

"Indeed, you have made yourself quite plain," he uttered coldly. "And now I shall be equally plain. You will keep the dresses, much as it pains you. And as for the proprieties, I pray you will not concern yourself. Before I am done, you will be my wife. Of that you may be certain."

"And I tell you I won't!" she retorted, her face flushed with resentment at his high-handed manner. "Indeed, I cannot imagine why you persist in a suit which can so little profit you. Far from liking you, I find you are arrogant—and loathsomely overbearing. I cannot feel anything for you, milord, and nothing you do or say can possibly change that."

"Nothing? Can you be so sure, Miss Morgan?" he queried, suddenly dangerous. Brie backed as he strode purposefully toward her, like a man-of-war bearing down on some hapless prey. She gasped as she came up hard against the weathered oak and found she could go no farther.

"Do not come any nearer, I warn you. I-I swear I shall scream if you dare to lay a hand on me."

"Shall you?" he uttered mockingly and, clasping her hard about the waist, yanked her to him. Brie stood, rigid, in his embrace, her eyes fixed with horrified fascination on his, as, deliberately, they searched her face. "Shall you indeed," he muttered thickly and covered her mouth with his.

His lips, cruelly demanding this time, jarred Brigida to her senses. Pressing her hands against his chest, she pushed with all her might—to no avail. He was too strong for her. And then, suddenly, she had ceased to struggle. Good God, this could not be happening to her, flitted feverishly through her mind, just before she was engulfed by a delirious flood of sensations. With a sigh she gave in to them.

When, what seemed an eternity later, he released her, she felt shaken and weak. As from a distance, she heard Malvern expel a shuddering breath and opened her eyes to him. The pale countenance appeared carved from marble, but the eyes glittered with a feverish intensity—nay, a hunger, which he quickly masked.

Shaken to the core by an answering hunger within herself, she hastily lowered her eyelids.

Good God, she thought, stricken with the terrible truth. She loved him, had loved him from the very first moment she had laid eyes on him. But how could this be? He was overbearing, toplofty, and impossibly arrogant, was he not? Aye, and totally heartless, even ruthless, when he was crossed. He was a law unto himself, demanding the absolute obedience of those beneath him, capable, even, of coercing women and children to his will. And yet still he had somehow conquered her heart. She knew it with a certainty that left her mind reeling.

She started at the touch of his hand beneath her chin, forcing her head up to look at him. At sight of her face, a harsh bark of laughter seemed forced from him.

"In future, my love," he drawled, insufferably mocking, "I should be careful what I said if I were you. You see, I never could resist a challenge."

Stunned at his callousness and rendered mute by her bewildering discovery, she reacted out of instinct. With the palm of her hand, she struck him.

In awed fascination she watched the quick leap of anger transform to cynical amusement.

"Brava, Miss Morgan," he murmured. "It would seem Demon Drake has found a worthy match in his promised bride."

"Oh, how detestable you are!" she cried, tearing herself free of his arms. "If my brother were here, he would call you out for the reprehensible manner in which you have treated me."

"No doubt," he answered mockingly. "And where, I cannot but wonder, is this elusive brother of yours? He would seem to spend remarkably little time attending to his rightful business."

Brie's chin lifted in angry disdain, though, inside, her heart fluttered with sudden fear.

"Where he is is nothing of your concern, milord," she retorted haughtily. "As it happens, he has gone to Hessenford. To a house party at the Townsends'. We do not expect him back for a se'ennight or more."

"But how very convenient. And the Townsends, I

must suppose, would be willing to vouch for his presence?"

"Since it is the truth, I am quite sure they would. Though why they should have to, I cannot imagine."

"No, naturally you cannot," he countered, his tone singularly ironic. Brie's eyes flashed green sparks of resentment.

"Just what are you trying to imply, milord?" she demanded frostily. "That my brother has *need* of someone to establish his whereabouts?"

"No doubt you would be better prepared than I to answer that, Miss Morgan," he countered, his eyes beneath drooping eyelids assuming a patently bored expression. "I was not aware that I was implying anything."

"Oh, how perfectly insufferable you are!" she exclaimed. "You know very well that you were."

"On the contrary. I was merely evincing a certain curiosity as to why your brother seems never to be around. He is your father's heir, after all. As such, he would naturally have a say in how his sister's future is to be settled. Thus far, however, he would seem to demonstrate a remarkable lack of interest in your affairs. Perhaps he has something of a more pressing nature to occupy him?"

She glared at him, well aware that he was baiting her and yet mindful of the danger of giving into her hasty temper. No doubt he was in hopes she would let slip something that would link Collin with the smugglers, she thought, and was conscious of a dull ache somewhere in the vicinity of her breast that he could use her so.

"No doubt I am sorry to disappoint you, milord," she said, suddenly wanting only to be free of his loathsome presence. "However, in spite of what you may think, my brother, I assure you, is involved in nothing more questionable than renewing an old acquaintance. Perhaps you know her—a Miss Elsbeth Townsend? There used to be something of an understanding between them, and I am in hopes there will be again. Now, if you have exhausted your curiosity, perhaps you would be good enough to leave me. I find I have developed a splitting headache."

A disconcerting frown knit his eyebrows. She winced as he reached out a finger to smooth the furrow between her brows.

"Yes," he murmured disturbingly. "I see you are decidedly out of sorts, a circumstance for which I must naturally take the blame. It seems you have an uncomfortable knack for bringing out the worst in me, Miss Morgan."

"No, have I indeed, milord?" she queried acidly. "And consequently I must be held accountable for your boorish behavior, is that it?"

A wry gleam lit the incomprehensible black orbs.

"Not at all, Miss Morgan. I accept full responsibility for my actions. I should even go so far as to apologize for having taken undue advantage of you—so long as you do not expect me to regret what came of it. That I could never do, since on the contrary, I enjoyed it immensely."

"Well, I did not enjoy it. If anything, it has only convinced me more firmly than ever that we should not suit. It is, in fact, my sincerest hope that I shall never have to lay eyes on you again, milord. For you, sir, are no gentleman."

"And you, Miss Morgan, are a hypocrite and a liar."

"I-I beg your pardon? H-How dare you—!"

"I dare because, unlike you, I make no pretense of

what I want. I want you, Miss Morgan—for my wife. And I fully intend to have you." A sardonic smile curled his lip at her gasp of outrage. Then, hatefully cool, he continued. "Regrettably, I am called away for a few days on business. But I shall be back, Miss Morgan. And then we shall lay our plans for the wedding. I suggest you reconcile yourself to the inevitable."

For an instant longer he held her with those hateful, mocking eyes. Then, bowing ironically at the waist, he turned and left her.

Brie stared after him, rendered mute with unspeakable loathing and a host of other emotions, none of which she could possibly have defined at the moment. A challenge, she thought. That was all she meant to him. And, God help her, he had won! She nearly writhed with the terrible knowledge that she not only had given in to his embrace, but that, far worse, she had rendered up her heart to him as well, when all at once her head came up, her eyes flashing with a fierce determination.

Impulsively, she ran after him. Passing quickly through the Rose Room, she burst into the hall, only to find it was deserted, save for Fionna.

"Miss Brie!" exclaimed the woman, alarmed at the sight of her wild-eyed young mistress. "What is it?"

Ignoring the maid's outburst, Brie flung past her to the door. But already she was too late. Malvern was gone, the sound of his horse's hooves receding rapidly in the distance.

"Oh!" she cried, beside herself with rage. Then, "It meant nothing! Do you hear me?" she flung after the retreating figure. "*You* mean nothing to me. I shan't marry you. Not ever. I should rather die than marry you!"

She was on the verge of tears, torn between an inexplicable hurt and anger, when moments later Fionna came out to find her and fetch her in. How dared he use her so? He was heartless and vile, and if she had been fool enough to fall in love with him, it mattered not. She would find some way to eradicate him from her heart. Indeed, she would rather cut out that traitorous organ than allow it to remain possessed of the Demon of Malvern.

Understandably, the next few days were hardly conducive to Brie's peace of mind. Barred from seeking release from her troubles aboard her beloved *Mere-Magden* and denied access to her brother by his absence, she assayed to immerse herself in numerous household tasks, drudgery which in the norm she would have found onerous in the extreme. In truth she hardly knew herself anymore. One moment she would be attacking with dogged determination a particularly stubborn stain in the Aubusson carpet, and the next she would find herself staring dreamily into the distance, the scrub brush, dripping soap and water, clasped with apparent fondness to her bosom. Even more unsettling, however, were her startlingly swift changes of mood. She never knew when she might burst suddenly into song and even give into the impulse to waltz about the room with a feather duster for a partner, only to find herself the next instant succumbing to a fit of the vapors over something so innocuous as having mislaid her basket of thread and sewing needles. Desperate for a measure of respite from her plaguey thoughts, she drove herself to a point of exhaustion each day, only to fall in her bed and lie awake long into the night, too bone-weary to sleep. Clearly she was working herself toward a state of utter collapse. And while mending old linens, cleaning out cupboards, and ridding the old house of the least hint of cobwebs and dust did serve to numb her brain, she yet could not banish from it the memory of all that had passed that fateful night in the rose garden.

So this was what it was to be hopelessly in love, she thought sardonically to herself one morning as she dragged her weary body out of bed. Listlessly she crossed to the window and stared out at the Cornish hills burgeoning with new spring flowers. For the first time in her young life, she was oblivious to their beauty or to the cheerful cacophony of birdsong. For her the sun, dazzling in an uncluttered sky, held no appeal. Nor did the breathless flight of the sea gulls, swooping and soaring high above the cliffs. She felt lifeless and dull and wondered secretly if she were losing her mind.

A plague on men, and on one man in particular! she thought crossly to herself. For indeed she could not doubt that she owed all the present upheaval in her life to the odious Earl of Malvern. Nor did it help in the least that at times it had come to her quite clearly that the anguish she was suffering was totally unnecessary. It was only pride, she told herself, and her overweaning need for independence which kept her from grasping at a happiness she thus far could only imperfectly comprehend.

The truth was she was afraid. For almost as long as she could remember, she had relied on herself, on her own strength and determination, to keep Gullan Carn from falling to rack and ruin, to keep her family from disintegrating. She had set goals for herself and had worked tirelessly to achieve them against all odds, and now that she was on the point of seeing everything for which she had labored realized, she was being asked to fling it all away. It was as if everything she had done counted suddenly for nothing, indeed, as if her whole life up until that moment had been rendered utterly pointless. And if she gave in to it, gave in to this stranger who, having dropped out of the blue into her life, had irrevocably disrupted it, might she not find that she had lost herself forever? To be Brigida Morgan was something she understood. To become Brigida Drake, the Countess of Malvern, was filled with uncertainties.

And yet, she thought, leaning her forehead against the leaded windowpane, might it not be that life with the enigmatic Earl of Malvern promised a deal more than she could ever imagine? Inevitably her thoughts turned, as they had over and over again the last few days, to that night of moonlight and madness.

Never had Brie experienced anything remotely resembling those stolen kisses, her very first from a man other than a near relative. Even now the mere thought of them was enough to suffuse her body with a delicious tingling warmth. A long, gusty sigh broke from her depths, and unconsciously she hugged her arms about her, as she conjured up the image of strong, masculine features, a lock of raven hair falling carelessly over a manly forehead, and eyes, black, brilliant, and piercing. Silently she cursed. He had bewitched her with those eyes, and with lips that set her blood on fire.

"The devil take him!" she uttered out loud, made suddenly aware of where her thoughts had taken her. Irritably, she flung away from the window and threw herself fretfully across the bed. It was neither his lips nor his eyes that hàd made her love him. They had only been agents in awakening her to her unwanted state. She had loved him long before that night in the rose garden.

When, then, had this mysterious alchemy of her soul taken place? she wondered. When had Damion Drake wormed his way into her heart? Perhaps it was preordained, like the cursed marriage contract drawn up between their fathers. From earliest childhood, she had been nurtured on tales about the heroic young naval officer. He had been everywhere, done everything she could only dream about doing. The Far East, the China Sea, the West Indies — he had seen them all. At fifteen he had fought Barbary pirates and at twenty-one had had a part in the Glorious First of June. At twenty-two he was in command of his own ship in the Caribbean when the British had taken Pondicherry, St. Pierre, and Miquelon from the French. He had been with Nelson's fleet at the Battle of the Nile! And then what must he do, but stumble on the rearguard of the French and Spanish fleet making for Cadiz.

Brie had hardly known what she felt when word reached Cornwall that Drake had sunk a Spanish frigate and disabled a three-decker before his own ship, battered almost beyond recognition, had been swept with fire. Excitement, attendant with cold shivers at his reckless daring, dread fascination for his cold-blooded nerve, curiosity? Aye, she thought, all of these and more — pride in what he had accomplished. For, in spite of his wounds, he had yet managed to lead his men on to the decks of the disabled French man-of-war and captured her, even as his own vessel had sunk to the bottom. Her imagination already captivated by the heroic figure of this and countless other adventures, was it any wonder that her heart should have been so easily captured by the man himself?

Then why, she asked herself, did she fight it so? He wanted her. He had made that abundantly clear, had even gone so far as to declare he would have her whether she willed it or not. Oh, *why* did she not simply accept his offer of marriage and any possibility of happiness that might go with it? She knew the answer to that at once. It was *because* he had declared he would have her, decreed it as if she had no say in the matter. And even more reprehensible, he had made it quite clear that he did not even want her for herself, but simply because she would not have him!

Had he not told Brian Murdoch that he considered his promised bride to be without countenance or polish? Aye, he had. And had he not further stated that since he had found no one among the marriageable females to interest him that Brigida Morgan should do as well as any other? Oh, indeed, he had. And once they were married, did he not fully intend to relegate her to the nursery to care for his children while he pursued his pleasures elsewhere? Brie's eyes flashed green sparks at the detestable memory. He had, and that was the unkindest cut of all! But still that had not been enough, for he had further sunk himself beneath contempt when, having surprised her into betraying herself with his loathsome kisses, he had deliberately humiliated her. He had called her a challenge! Good God, as if she were an enemy ship to be conquered! And once conquered, easily forgotten, she thought, bolting upright on the bed.

What a fool she had been to suffer a fit of the

doldrums over something that did not merit even a single unquiet moment. Doubtless this thing she had mistaken for love was only a momentary aberration, rather like a megrim or a stomach upset, which required only a certain determination and fortitude to get through. Yes, that must be it. Why, if she were to meet his lordship face-to-face this very morning, she no doubt would discover she was grown quite impervious to his devastating presence. And certainly she had no intention of gratifying his masculine ego by allowing herself to go into a sharp decline over a couple of insignificant kisses. Made buoyant by such reasoning, she even went so far as to wish the earl would indeed show himself that she might demonstrate how little it should effect her.

Then rising, she began to dress herself, humming as she did so.

The sudden tattoo on the door, followed by Fionna's frantic entrance, caught Brie with her head buried in the folds of her gown.

"Miss Brie! Somethin' terrible's happened," panted the woman, going to help her mistress. " 'Tis Master Collin. Covered all over in blood, he is and looks t'be half dead on his feet. Cook nearly swooned at the sight of 'im!"

In the grip of sudden, terrible fear, Brie nearly ripped the gown in her efforts to pull it down over her head.

"Hurry, Fionna," she gasped. "Where is he now? Has the commodore seen Collin? Fionna, answer me! Does Grandfather know?"

"He don't know nothin'," answered the harried maidservant, struggling with the fastenings at the back of Brie's dress. "Hold still, Miss Brie, if 'ee wants me to get these buttons for 'ee. And 'ee needn't get all in a huff over the old gentleman. He bain't come down yet for his breakfast. I were ordered to come ahead to warn 'ee. They be bringin' Master Collin upstairs right this minute. . . . Miss Brie, wait! 'Ee can't let 'im see thee like that!"

Brie, however, was already through the doorway.

"Oh!" she gasped, nearly colliding with a grim-faced masculine figure, who was half supporting her brother down the hall. "Good God. It's you!"

"Quite so, Miss Morgan," drawled the Demon of Malvern, coming to a halt. A bemused smile softened the hard lines of the chiseled countenance as he took in the enchanting picture of womanhood, barefooted and her hair a disheveled mass of coppery curls. "No doubt you will pardon me for having called at so unfashionable an hour. But as you see, there were certain extenuating circumstances which demanded it."

Brie, stricken with confusion at the warmth in Malvern's eyes, felt frozen to the spot. Indeed, it was not till he reminded her of the "extenuating circumstances" that had brought him there that at last she was able to wrench her gaze from him to the other man, weaving drunkenly on his feet.

She felt her senses reel at sight of him, his head bound in a hastily contrived bandage stained with blood and his face pale as death.

"Collin," she gasped.

Chapter Ten

"Easy, Brie girl," she heard Collin exclaim, followed by a particularly eloquent hiccup. "Not sho bad azh looksh. Malvern only nicked me. Even sho, 'tis a bleshed miracle I'm here at all. Shwear an oath, his lordship'sh bloody devil with a shword."

"Malvern?" gasped Brie weakly, her bewildered glance flickering from one to the other of the two men. "*You* did this to him? But why? Good God, Collin, what folly have you been up to?"

"Afraid I've made a dreadful muddle of thingsh'," confessed her brother, assaying a lopsided grin. "An' now there'zh th' bloody devil to pay."

Brie's glance narrowed sharply on her sibling's face. Collin, she suddenly realized, was three sheets to the wind, and, further, it appeared that he had recently taken a plunge into deep water—literally. His clothes, mud-stained and sodden, clung to him, and his hair was plastered to his forehead. What in heaven's name! she thought. And then the enormity of his declaration hit her. In a sudden dawning sense of outrage she turned on the earl, who was watching the interesting panoply of emotions cross her face with sardonic amusement.

"Good God," she blurted, "how dared you raise

your sword against him! You—you bloody monster! Was not the insult you did me enough to satisfy you, but you must try and kill my brother, too?"

Considerably taken aback to find his sister suddenly transformed into an avenging angel, Collin stared at Brie in befuddlement.

"Killed?" he uttered thickly. "What 'ee shaying, Brie girl? Ain't nowhere near being dead, assure 'ee."

He might as well have been baying at the moon for all the attention either of the other two paid him.

The warmth vanished from Malvern's eyes to be replaced by a cynical hardness.

"No doubt you are in the right of it, Miss Morgan," he murmured coldly. "I trust, however, that this conversation can wait until we have my hapless victim more comfortably settled? Perhaps you would even be good enough to direct me to where you want him."

Brie, thus pointedly reminded that they still stood in the hallway and that, further, her brother only managed to remain on his feet because the "bloody monster" supported his arm across a lean muscular shoulder, bit her tongue to keep from delivering his lordship a blistering retort.

It was at that juncture that the scandalized Fionna chose to make her presence known.

"Now, Miss Brie," she exclaimed. " 'Ee can't parade around like 'ee was no better'n some hussy. I'll show his lordship where to go whilst 'ee make thyself more presentable."

"Oh, not now, Fionna, I beg you," Brie snapped peevishly. "I trust his lordship is not totally unfamiliar with the sight of a lady's bare feet."

"Not totally," agreed the earl, taking time to assess the merits of those presently in question.

"A-hem!" was Fionna's notable comment. "Nevertheless, I'll not budge an inch till 'ee's properly covered," she insisted, holding out a pair of worn house slippers to her difficult young mistress. "Thee's a lady now, an' 'tis past time 'ee was actin' like one."

"Oh, very well, Fionna!" Ruefully aware that Malvern must be enjoying her discomfort immensely, she shoved her feet into the disreputable-looking red satin mules. "And now you will be pleased to fetch hot water and a roll of lint to Master Collin's rooms. At once, Fionna!"

Muttering disgruntledly to herself something about the queer ways of the quality, the maidservant did as she had been bidden, while Brie returned her attention to the patently amused earl.

"This way, milord," she continued in tones meant to freeze the villain's soul. "Two doors down from mine, an' you please."

His lordship bowed his head in polite formality.

"After you, Miss Morgan. I may be a boor and a monster, but I have not yet forgot my manners."

"Have you not?" queried Brie, favoring him with a toss of her coppery curls. "No doubt 'twas only a momentary lapse, then, when you forced yourself on me. And was it a duel between 'gentlemen' when you sought to murder my brother?"

"No, no, 'ee's got it all wrong," objected the victim of mayhem, ponderously shaking his head. "Told 'ee was only a scratch." Coming to an abrupt halt, he peered with bleary eyes at the nobleman. "Shtill, might have been better had 'ee just killed me outright, m'lord, and had done with it. Better for all concerned."

"The notion, I must confess, gains merit with each passing moment," his lordship observed, apparently giving the matter his careful consideration. "However, I confess I have a peculiar aversion to snuffing a man's life before I have had opportunity to fortify myself with my morning cup of coffee. Therefore, I suggest we proceed as before. No doubt you, too, will think better of so desperate a measure once you have had opportunity to sleep on the matter."

"Dunno. 'Tis a damnable toil I've got meshelf in, thanksh to your bloody lordship." With exaggerated deliberation, he turned his gaze on his sister, who stood, waiting, her hands on her hips and her eyebrows lifted in an expression of incredulity. "There's worshe things than dyin', if 'ee knows what I mean."

Upon which, to Brie's growing indignation, the earl followed suit and turned his measuring glance on her, too.

"Oh, but I do know," he agreed with infuriating gravity, which did nothing to hide the sardonic gleam of amusement in his eye. "Indeed, I am all sympathy."

"Knew 'ee would be, gov'nor. Figgered 'ee for a right 'un the moment I laid eyesh on 'ee."

"Oh, hush, Collin!" snapped his sister, who had not the least notion of what they were talking about. "You are alive and you should be grateful. And any trouble you have wrought for yourself is your own fault. Do you hear me?"

A comical grimace twisted at her brother's lips.

"Oh, I hear thee well enough," he said wryly.

"As must anyone else with an ear to listen," contributed his lordship. "I suggest, Miss Morgan, it were better if the commodore remained ignorant of your brother's infirmity."

Brie, who could not but see the wisdom of such advice, was nevertheless sorely tempted to dispute it.

It was only with an effort that she curbed both her temper and her tongue till they had got the reeling Collin safely in his room.

"Put him in the chair by the window," she ordered testily, as she closed the door behind them. "We must get those wet things off him before he catches a chill, and then we'll see to the wound. No doubt we may be thankful for once that his skull is as hard as good Cornish granite."

"Perhaps it would be better, Miss Morgan, were you to allow your maid to assist me in the disrobing," suggested the earl blandly as he watched Brie cross purposefully to her brother.

Instantly Brie impaled him with huge limpid eyes.

"You are not suggesting, milord," she queried dulcetly, "that it would be improper for me to minister to my brother's needs? If you are, then I think you should know that this is not the first time I have been called upon to give like service. This is not London, your lordship, but Cornwall. Some of us cannot afford to be simpering ladies of fashion where doctors are scarce as hen's teeth."

A discerning man, Malvern read a great deal more between the lines than Brie had intended to reveal.

"As you wish, Miss Morgan," he drawled, his gaze peculiarly steely as it came to rest on the sprawling figure of her elder brother, who for no apparent reason had burst forth into what might be construed as a song. "It would seem that I have forgot a great many things about my homeland, and that, indeed, I have a great deal to learn about at least one Cornish woman."

Brie, intent on ridding her brother of his ruined jacket, was saved from having to comment on that disconcerting admission by Fionna's timely arrival.

"Here I be, Miss Brie," she announced, with the breathless air of one pursued. "But I'd best not be stayin'. The old gentleman's below a hollerin' for his breakfast. 'Twas all I could do to slip by him without bein' seen. I'm afraid 'ee an' his lordship'll have to do for Master Collin without me."

"By all means, Fionna. Do whatever you can to keep the commodore occupied," said her mistress, who, ably aided by his lordship, was in the process of divesting the patient of his ruined coat and waistcoat. "We shall be down directly."

As the maidservant left them, Brie was too occupied with the tasks at hand to consider the fact that for all practical purposes she was alone with the infamous Malvern. Collin was displaying a playful tendency, which she knew from experience would soon progress to the pugnacious, and, if he lasted so long, to the lachrymose. This final stage was usually the prelude to winking out entirely. In short, at present, he was making an utter nuisance of himself.

Lunging unexpectedly to his feet, he fairly knocked Brie to the floor, and, declaring he was in need of a libation, lurched for the door.

Malvern was there before him.

"I think perhaps you should reconsider, old boy," drawled the earl, casually propping a shoulder against the oaken barrier. "You are not at all well, you know. In fact, you appear to be perilously close to falling flat on your face."

"Not sho," objected the younger man. Shoving his nose to within inches of the earl's, he grinned belligerently. "Feel fine enough, 'old boy,' to draw your cork if you don't move out of my way."

"You may try, of course," Malvern conceded, "but I heartily advise against it. You are in no state to match me in a game of fisticuffs."

Brie groaned and rolled her eyes ceilingward. The earl could have said nothing which was more certain of rousing her brother's fighting temper.

"Well, then, if tizh a mill 'ee's after . . ." Grinning hugely, Collin drew back his fist and swung.

What happened next occurred with such blinding swiftness that Brie was never certain afterward exactly what she had witnessed. One moment the earl was lounging easily against the door and the next he had Collin stretched face down on the floor, his arm pinned neatly in the hollow of his back.

"There now, I did warn you," drawled his lordship. "Henceforth you will be a good lad, will you not, and cease to give your sister any trouble."

"Aw, gov'nor," groaned a chastened Collin Morgan. " 'Ee needn't rub it in. Never meant to make a cake of meshelf."

"One never does," Malvern observed drily and, rising, helped the other man to his feet.

A short time later, Brie bent over her patient, who, withdrawn now and sullen, offered no resistance as she removed the soiled bandage and with fingers that trembled, cleansed the caked blood from above his left temple. A sigh of relief broke from her lips at sight of the slender gash. True, it had bled profusely, as scalp wounds were wont to do, but clearly it was more painful than serious. Indeed, the scar, once the wound had healed, would be negligible and easily concealed beneath his hair. Apparently, she thought grimly, the Demon of Malvern had a light touch indeed.

"There," she said at last, as she finished binding her patient's head in a fresh bandage. "It may be tender for a day or two, but I think you are not like to die of your folly. Nevertheless, you are exceedingly fortunate that you did not lose what few brains you were blessed with. One can only hope you have learned some sort of lesson from all of this, Collin Morgan."

Collin's glance was exceedingly wry.

"Funny. Eggzactly what *he* said—when he wrapped me head in his cursed scarf."

"When *he* wrapped it . . . !" Snatching the blood-stained cloth from the table on which she had laid it, Brie stared at the expensive silk fabric. She should have realized at once that it was his. Indeed, no doubt she would have done, had she not been thinking only of Collin's wound. It was not, after all, the sort of neckcloth that her brother affected.

Raising puzzled eyes to the brooding figure standing at the window, one booted foot propped on the window seat and his back to the room, she was conscious of a queasy sensation in the pit of her stomach. What a curious man he was to be sure, she thought, one moment to be intent on slaying a man and the next to be ministering to his wounds. And then, too, he had been put to a deal of trouble to bring his victim home. For the first time it occurred to her that she may have misjudged the earl's motives.

"I think," she said, "it is time someone told me what happened."

It seemed to Brie, watching him, that a tremor shook the slender frame. Then deliberately Malvern straightened and turned to look at her; his face maddeningly unreadable.

"I believe," he drawled, insufferably cool, "I shall leave that to your brother to explain."

Incredulously, Brie watched him stride past her to

the door.

"Wait! You cannot simply walk out like this," she blurted. "With not a word, no—no explanation—nothing. Where—where are you going?"

Malvern's smile was ironical.

"I am going home, Miss Morgan," he answered. "To a hot bath, breakfast, and bed. Oh, you needn't look so downpin. I have every intention of returning. This evening, shall we say—around five, if it is convenient. Somehow I am certain we shall have a great deal to discuss."

In the next moment he had opened the door and was gone.

"C-o-l-l-i-n?" Brie crooned in an ominous voice and pivoted to face her brother.

"Now, now, Brie girl," exclaimed the rogue, who not only had had time to sober somewhat, but was beginning to develop a bone-splitting headache. "There's no need to go off half-cocked."

"Then suppose you explain what it is that Malvern and I shall have to discuss. Your imminent departure to the penal colonies, no doubt? Shall you be going alone, I wonder, or should I, too, begin packing?"

"You may indeed be packing before the week is through," replied her brother, dropping his head gloomily into his hands, "but not, I think, to go to the penal colonies."

Truly alarmed now, Brie came around to stare at his bowed figure with searching eyes.

"Malvern surprised you and—and the others in Smugglers' Cave, slinging the casks, is that it?"

"Well, no, not exactly," Collin hedged and shifted his weight uncomfortably. "The goods were already well away when his lordship made his unfortunate appearance." He lifted his head to look at her. "There was no evidence to link me to the flaskers, Brie, if that's what 'ee's worried about."

Brie stared at him blankly.

"But then, I don't understand. Why *did* Malvern attack you, if not for smuggling?"

"For murder most foul," Collin announced, and had the temerity to grin in what seemed, considering the nature of his startling declaration, a wholly reprehensible manner. "It seems his lordship caught me in the act of doing away with a certain young lad of the lower orders. You knew the victim rather well, I believe. Y'see, 'twas your very own Brian Murdoch."

"Good God," his sister breathed, sinking weakly down on the edge of the bed. "I suppose if I am to understand any of this, you had better start at the beginning."

It soon transpired that Collin and Rory Gale had indeed not only set out for Hessenford, but had even reached the Townsends — not, however, the same day they had departed.

"We waited in the tavern down at the crossroads," Collin complacently informed her, "till the storm broke. A fine piece of luck, that. No sooner had the sun set than it was dark as the bottom of a barrel, a circumstance that we didn't hesitate to take advantage of. The excisemen weren't like to expect us to go after the crop in the middle of a gale, but we did. And what's more, we managed the thing without loss of a single cask."

"No doubt you are to be congratulated," Brie observed acidly. "Not only did you avoid the excisemen, but the Demon as well."

"Exactly so," said her brother, grinning without an ounce of remorse. "After the business was done, we made straight for Hessenford."

"And had a jolly good time with Elsbeth Townsend, I suppose, while I was left to entertain the Earl of Malvern over lobster," Brie bitterly surmised.

"Aw, and surely 'twas not so bad as all that?" Collin disclaimed. "He doesn't seem such a bad sort, when 'ee get to know him. Why don't 'ee try and give him a fair shake, Brie? 'Ee might even discover 'ee deal extremely well together." Upon which Brie's sorely tried temper snapped.

"Sometimes, Collin Morgan," she declared, springing to her feet and pacing angrily before him, "I could wish our parents had had only girls. Have you any notion of the anxieties I have suffered, wondering what new devilry Rory Gale was leading you to, terrified that one night I might open the door to the excisemen come to inform me you were being held under lock and key—or worse, that you were dead? You sit there and pat yourself on the back for having pulled the wool over their eyes, and yet you fling money around like a drunken sailor. With the result that Malvern is not the only one who holds you and your activities in suspicion. You've managed to alert the coast guard as well. Collin, how could you be so witless? Has it occurred to you even once to ask yourself why it was that Malvern was not on hand to discover you that first night?"

"No, why should it?" Collin replied sullenly. "It was a miserable night. No doubt his lordship was safely ensconced in his castle. 'Twould've been the sensible thing."

"Well, as it happens, you are way off the mark. Far from being in his castle, he was on his yacht, and he was not alone. Unhappily, Brian Murdoch was with him."

It all came out then, how she had been discovered

by the earl in the inlet and then been persuaded to accompany him aboard his vessel, and most of what came afterward.

"He is on to you, Collin," she said, coming to the end of her tale, "and 'tis all your fault for flinging smugglers' gold indiscriminately about. I have been utterly distracted with worrying about how I shall face him again as Brian Murdoch. And what I shall tell him about you when the time comes. And if that were not enough to occupy me, I must worry as well about what idiotic thing you will be up to next. Indeed, if it were not for Gramfer and what must inevitably happen to Gullan Carn were it left to you to run, I should be half tempted to wed him simply to be rid of you and your witless pranks."

If she had meant to intimidate him by threatening to abandon him to his inevitable fate, she soon found she had misjudged her man. On the contrary, he seemed, if anything, immensely relieved.

"Then 'tis settled, Brie darlin'," he declared, noticeably brightening. "Naturally 'ee mustn't give me or the place another thought. No doubt we shall rub on well enough. Oh, not that we shan't miss you, for of course we shall. But what sort of brother would I be did I stand in the way of seeing me only sister happily settled?"

"What sort indeed?" echoed Brie, considerably taken aback by his reaction. Then instantly her eyes narrowed in suspicion.

"You seem uncommonly pleased at the thought of being rid of me," she ventured speculatively. "Or is it something else, I wonder. Something you have not told me yet. You have said the earl caught you in the act of doing away with Brian Murdoch, and yet we both know that there is no such lad. Or, if you will, that I am he. I, however, am far from being dead. What, then, should have led his lordship to so erroneous a conclusion?"

She knew the answer to the last question almost as soon as she voiced it.

"The clothes I used for my disguise!" she exclaimed. "They are missing from my wardrobe. *You* took them. Before you left for Hessenford. You must have done. And then what did you do? Leave them in the cave when you went for the casks — to make it look as if the smugglers had done away with what would supposedly be an informer? That is it, is it not? Only something happened. What, Collin? What kept you from carrying out your idiotic scheme?"

"It wasn't idiotic," sullenly objected Collin. "It was brilliant. Only I never got the chance to do it that first night. Rory stuck to me the whole time. So last night on the way back from Hessenford — after Rory and I parted at the crossroads inn — I went to the grottoes instead of coming home."

"And that is when the earl discovered you."

"He must have been at his blasted perch and spied the light from me lantern. Came out of nowhere, he did — like some bloody ghost. Gives me the shivers even yet when I think about it."

"Aye," murmured Brie, thinking of her own similar first encounter with the earl. "He has a way about him, when he's of a mind to put the fear of the devil in one. Still, it seems rather odd that he should have tried it on one he supposed was a hardened felon. Unless — Collin, is it possible he knew all the time who you were?"

"No, not at first. The lantern was at me back. It was impossible that he got a good look at me. Not till later, when he nearly cut off me ear with his sword.

Then, 'Hellsfire!' he yelled. 'You're Collin Morgan. I've seen your likeness among the portraits at Gullan Carn. What the bloody hell are you doing here?' " A shudder shook him. "Lord, Brie, 'ee should have seen him."

"Thanks, but that is one sight I should rather be spared, I think. Tell me what led up to the swordplay. What did you do to provoke him?"

Collin uttered a short bark of laughter.

"Not much, just tried to hold him off with a gun. When he came upon me, I was bent over the fissure where we'd sunk the casks. Had me back to him, trying to make it look as if Brian Murdoch's things'd been wedged beneath the rocks and then washed loose with the tide. I wanted to make sure he found them, but without its lookin' as if they'd been planted. The next thing I knew, I felt the cold point of steel between my shoulder blades.

" 'I fear, my friend, you are too late,' says he. 'The goods have already been retrieved.' I had my pistol on the ground beside me, and I figured it was worth a try."

"Naturally," interposed Brie grimly. "You had been drinking, had you not? You think you are invincible when you are in your cups, Collin. You know you do."

A wry grin twisted at her brother's lips.

"Aye, 'tis a failing I have. One that nearly proved the death of me last night." A look of bafflement tinged with reluctant admiration flickered in his eyes. "He knocked the gun from my hand before I knew what happened. And then what does he do, but stand back and let me draw my sword. The stories they tell about him are all true, Brie. Even in my cups I'm handier than most with a blade, but I've never seen his like. He could have put a period to my existence any number of times, but instead he played with me till I was fair ready to drop from exhaustion. That's when he put his mark on me. Wouldn't 've been so bad," he added with a wry grimace of disgust, "if I hadn't tumbled like a blooming idiot into the fissure and had to be hauled out again. Made a damned corker of myself."

But Brie, who had gone from hot to cold during his narration, was not listening. She stared at him with an inexplicable feeling of foreboding.

"He had some purpose in what he did. He always has some purpose behind everything he does. There is something you are not telling me." She had been reasoning out loud, trying to put all the pieces together, trying to put her finger on the thing she sensed but did not yet understand. And then it hit her. "You said he accused you of murdering Brian Murdoch, which means he saw the clothes and fell for your little ploy. Why, then, did he not turn you over to the law? Why, Collin, did he go to the trouble to bring you home?"

She did not need to hear his answer. She knew immediately from the look on his face what it was.

"He means to keep it to himself, does he not," she said in a hard little voice. "He offered you your freedom in exchange for my hand in marriage, didn't he? *Didn't* he, Collin?"

"Aye! He did," Collin groaned. "I told 'ee, didn't I, that I'd made a terrible muddle of things."

"Aye," answered Brie, feeling suddenly sick inside. "And unless we tell him the truth of it, I shall undoubtedly be the one to pay the piper."

Chapter Eleven

Brigida stole a look out of the corner of her eye at the earl. He rode silently beside her, his face an impregnable mask, and she might not have been there for all the notice he paid her, she thought with a trace of something suspiciously like pique. He had not spoken more than half a dozen sentences to her since they had left Gullan Carn. But then, if she were to be perfectly honest with herself, she had not been the most congenial of companions. As a matter of fact, she had been grateful to be left alone while she struggled to grasp the enormity of what she had done, for she had just wed the Demon of Malvern.

The private ceremony, which had taken place in the chapel in the green at two o'clock that very afternoon, seemed the product of a fantastic dream. The lovely creature in ivory satin and lace had seemed a stranger, the endless walk down the aisle on her brother's arm, a vague unreality. Only Malvern, unassailable and compelling as ever, his obsidian eyes boring holes through her as he watched her approach, had assumed a significance larger than reality. In a dark blue coat and dove gray pantaloons, the pallor of his face in striking contrast to the blue-black of his hair, he had loomed as inevitable as the web of circumstances that had brought her there to him.

Of the ceremony she remembered little, or of the marriage feast that had come after, attended only by the immediate family—and the earl's cousin, of course, who had stood up for him. Devin Drake, she thought, wondering what it was about Malvern's kinsman that vaguely bothered her. He presented a pleasing enough aspect, after all, displaying an easy charm that put her in mind somewhat of her scapegrace elder brother. And yet, there was a subtle difference she could not quite pin down.

Suddenly she sighed. Oh, what did it matter? No doubt it was only that everything had been colored by her own muddled feelings concerning Malvern and the manner in which he had forced her into marrying him. An angry blush tinged her cheeks at the memory of the day he had brought Collin home from Smugglers' Cave. Had it in truth been only ten days ago? It seemed like a lifetime since he had returned to Gullarn Carn to receive her answer to his loathsome proposition.

He had been distant and cold as only he knew how to be, and the plea that she had rehearsed for his tolerance in the matter of her brother had remained, unspoken, on her lips. Oh, if only he had shown some spark of human warmth, some hint of a forgiving nature! But he had been all flint and steel, and her earlier resolve to confess all to him and fling both her and Collin on his mercy had died a precipitate death. She would not lower herself to beg, nor had she dared to put her brother's fate to the Demon's touch. She had rather barter her soul to the devil!

The earl's voice and his hand, covering hers unexpectedly on the reins, startled her out of her unpleasant reverie.

"No doubt you will forgive me, my dear, for intruding on your privacy," he drawled carelessly. "However, I feel I must warn you. Sable Dawn may be a gentle lady, but she is not lacking in spirit. If you persist in yanking the bit, she is very likely to dump you."

"I-I beg your pardon?" stammered Brie, blinking. "What did you say?"

A glimmer of something like amusement flickered behind the hooded gaze.

"The reins," he said. "It is better to keep a light touch."

A blush suffused her cheeks as it came to her that while thinking of the earl and the loathsome manner in which he had treated her, her fingers must have clenched upon the lines. Even more discomfiting, however, was the bitter certainty that he was aware of it, too. Indeed, he seemed to have the uncanny knack for knowing at any given time exactly what was going through her mind.

Unconsciously lifting her head, she stared straight ahead.

"You are right, of course, milord," she answered. "Indeed, I cannot imagine what came over me."

"The incomprehensible quirks of fate, no doubt," he remarked drily and released her hand.

Brie's head came around with a jerk.

"If it was fate that has brought us to where we are, then you, sir, would seem to have had an uncommon hand in it. Are you always so certain to have things turn out the way you want them?"

The cynical curl of his lip would seem to belie his heavy-lidded look of boredom.

"I might have been fool enough to believe so — once," he replied. "I have since learned better. Indeed, I have never been less certain than now of the final outcome, I assure you. So much, you see, depends on you, and there is nothing, you will agree, so unpredictable as a woman."

"You will forgive me if I do *not* agree," retorted Brie. "On the contrary, I fear I must take exception to so blatant a generality. Women are neither more nor less unpredictable than men. You, I find odiously incomprehensible."

"Do you?" The inquisitive arch of a single, arrogant eyebrow brought a reluctant burble of laughter to her lips. Indeed, she had the distinct impression that he was roasting her. "Odd, but I should have thought I had from the first made myself crystal clear. What, exactly, would you wish to know that I have not already told you?"

Brie stared at him in dumbfoundment.

"Everything!" she exclaimed. "Why, if you believed my brother capable of so heinous a crime as murder, you did not feel compelled to turn him in. Why you should go so far, instead, as not only to save him, but to incriminate yourself as well. Your—your insistence on this marriage, which you cannot possibly want. What is it, milord, that you expect from me?"

"Nothing." He shrugged. "Except what you are willing to give, I assure you. And in return, my promise that I shall not overly interfere with your freedom. As for the rest, suffice it to say that it simply did not suit my purpose to have your brother marched to the gallows. So long as he behaves himself in future, he has nothing to fear from me."

"No doubt I should be gratified," retorted Brie bitterly, "if it were not your 'purpose,' sir, which confounds me."

"As to that, you need not concern yourself," he answered in such a way as left no doubt that she would get nothing further from him on that particular subject.

Hurt by his brusqueness, Brie hastily lowered her eyes. Not, however, before the earl had glimpsed the troubled frown in their depths. With a sigh, he relented ever so slightly.

"You are my wife now, my dear. I should hope that in time you might learn to trust me. You may believe me, Brigida, when I say I should never willingly do anything to hurt you."

They had been walking their mounts along the track that led through a wood thick with live oak, sycamore, and ash, but now Brie pulled her mare to a halt. Turning her head, she gave him a long, probing look.

"And if I were to say I believed you, milord?" she queried soberly. "What then? Would you in turn come to trust me? Would you believe *me* when I say my brother is incapable of murder?"

He appeared to hesitate, but almost immediately the cynical mask dropped in place, effectually shutting her off from his innermost thoughts.

"I should never dispute your word, madam," he drawled, insufferably cool. "The evidence, however, would seem to suggest otherwise."

"Yes, of course," she said stiffly, feeling her heart go leaden inside her. "The evidence." Lifting the reins, she set her mount once more in motion.

So that was that, she thought, oppressed at the seeming hopelessness of her situation. What did it matter that he had apparently wanted her enough to force her to the altar? Surely nothing good could come from a marriage devoid either of trust or affection. And what if, whispered a small insidious voice, he might be brought, in time, to care for her, if only a little? A disturbing warmth invaded her limbs at the thought, and suddenly she realized she yearned with her whole heart to have him look at her just once with tenderness, just once to have him hold her in his arms and . . . But, no. She must not think such thoughts. It was impossible that he should ever love her, so long as the lies lay, like an insurmountable barrier, between them. Oh, God, what was she to do? The very thought of having him always near and yet distant and cold, a stranger, rent her heart in two. In truth, she did not see how she could bear it.

A plague on Collin Morgan and his misguided meddling in her affairs! she groaned inwardly, and without remorse consigned her brother to the devil. He had got them into a fine kettle of fish, and while the only way out was to tell Malvern the truth, she knew that she could not bring herself to do it. Not so long as it meant Collin might be implicated in Duncan's death or, far worse, that he might be found to have been involved with traitors to his country!

And then it hit her—Malvern's "purpose" in allowing Collin to go free. With Brian Murdoch gone, Malvern had had to preserve his only remaining link to the smugglers. Good God, he still believed her brother might lead him to those responsible for Duncan's murder, and Collin could hardly do that if he had already been sent to the gallows!

Suddenly, as she began to grasp the full magnitude of her dilemma, she almost reeled in the saddle. What a fool she had been to think for one moment that Malvern might truly want her. The truth was that he was using her, just as he had meant to use Brian Murdoch, and her only hope of disentangling herself from the web of lies she had woven was to discover for herself who the real culprits were.

Lost in her less than rewarding thoughts, Brigida was suddenly startled to discover they had emerged from the wood. With an involuntary sense of awe, she stared out over the broad park with its green, sweeping lawns, to the graceful summerhouse nestled in a spinney of ancient oaks and set on an island in the midst of an ornamental lake, and then, beyond—to the great house perched on the cliffs of Tal Carn.

All her life, she had lived in the shadow of Malvern Castle, had viewed it, mysterious and brooding in the distance, as she sailed her skiff in the bay or searched for eels along the shoreline at the base of the cliffs. In her daydreams she had tried to visualize it the way others had described it—the circular keep and buttressed walls, the great hall, added to and modernized in the Tudor era to reflect the style of the times, and all the succeeding additions made by later generations in the form of wings and open courts—but, seeing it like this, ancient and sprawling, its battlemented walls and twin towers glinting in the sunlight, she realized she had never come even close to the reality. It was a deal grander and far more daunting than she could possibly have imagined.

"Malvern," she intoned, thinking of the long line of earls who had occupied and preserved the ancient pile.

"It means 'bare hill' in Celtic," remarked the earl, watching the play of emotion on her face. "The first Earl of Malvern was so named by William the Conqueror, who ordered a fortress to be raised here in his defense. It has stood ever since—a lone sentinel overlooking the sea."

Something in his tone made her look at him.

"Strange," she murmured. "All those years at sea, and yet—. You love it, do you not. That vast pile of stone."

A faintly quizzical expression glinted briefly in his eyes.

"You are a sentimentalist, are you not," he quipped, making light of it. Then he turned and let his gaze rest on his ancestral home, and suddenly he was no longer smiling. "There were times, usually when it seemed I might never come here again, that I would picture it as it was the last time I saw it. I could see it in my mind's eye as clearly as if I had left it only yesterday." He shrugged. "Perhaps it is only that a sailor must have someplace to come back to." He looked at her. "Some*one*, if he is lucky."

"And you never did? Is that why you stayed away?"

Malvern's sudden laugh rang harshly in the glade.

"But you are mistaken, surely," he drawled meaningfully. "There was someone. My promised bride."

She frowned dampeningly, refusing to be baited.

"I do wish you will be serious, milord. A child, or even a schoolroom miss, would hardly have offered any inducement to one such as you."

He smiled, apparently amused at her perspicuity.

"You are right, of course. Even so, you must not imagine that I was some tragic figure, exiled at an early age from my home and family. When my father was finally brought to grant me leave to pursue a career in the King's Navy, I went gladly, without regrets. I consider myself fortunate that in all those years, I never once found myself without a ship."

"Until now," said Brie, forcing herself to look at him. "No doubt you will forgive me for wondering if Malvern Castle, for all its wealth and noble heritage, is enough to make up for that forfeiture."

She saw the spasmodic leap of muscle along the lean line of his jaw. Then he smiled in that way he had that never failed to set her teeth on edge.

"But how not?" he answered cynically. "No doubt it shall amuse me to play the country squire. And if it should pall after a time, there is always London."

Lifting the reins, he inclined his head in the direction of the great house, waiting in the distance.

"And, now, if you are ready?"

Brie stared at the lean profile. In his face, she could read nothing. He was Malvern—impenetrable, cool, and maddeningly elusive.

Angrily, she clapped heels to her mount and set off down the slope, impatient to have the loathsome journey brought at last to an end.

Apparently someone had been posted to report the arrival of the earl and his new countess, for the entire staff was waiting outside to greet them as they cantered through the gatehouse and up to the great Tudor mansion. Overwhelmed by the sheer number of retainers who lined the drive, Brie had the insane urge to turn her mount and flee. She was chatelaine of Malvern Castle, and they would naturally look to her for their orders. She did not see how she could possibly learn to command so many.

"Do not let yourself be daunted by them, milady," advised a low-pitched voice at her elbow. "Except for Griffith, the butler, they are an unexceptional lot. You will find they are all eagerness to make you feel welcome at Malvern."

Startled, Brigida glanced down into the bespectacled blue eyes and thin, rather intense face of a young man who apparently was waiting to help her to dismount. He wore a ditto suit of brown drab, which, while well cut and neat, lacked the dash of a gentleman about town. He was, she judged, a younger son of gentility who must work for his living.

"James Pembroke, milady," he supplied in response to her inquisitive arch of an eyebrow. "The earl's private secretary and your servant, ma'am."

"Yes, of course. I believe I have heard mention of you." Leaning her hands on his shoulders, she allowed him to lift her down from the saddle. "And thank you for the advice. No doubt I shall be pleased to keep it well in mind."

She was, nevertheless, grateful for Malvern's commanding presence at her side as she was led toward the first in that long line of retainers. Assuming a composure she was far from feeling, she waited for his lordship to present to her Griffith, the butler—stone-faced and formidable as ever she remembered him.

"M'lady," he intoned, threatening to break his stays as he bent rigidly at the waist. "As head of the household staff, it must naturally be my pleasure to bid you welcome. Should any question arise concerning the manner in which things are done at Malvern, I trust you will feel free to apply to me."

"But how very good of you," murmured Brie, who was not so naive as to mistake the point of that carefully rehearsed speech. It obviously had been meant to intimidate her. Apparently his lordship's exceedingly superior servant meant to make sure she did not try to interfere in matters of the household. All at once she felt herself go deadly calm. Griffith, she decided, needed taking down a peg.

"You may be sure I shall avail myself of your kind offer," she said pleasantly. "And since I shall wish to familiarize myself with the house as soon as possible, you may begin by turning the keys over to me for that purpose—shall we say—first thing in the morning?

Naturally you will be the first to be informed what changes, if any, are to be made." Having made her point, she smiled frankly. "Meantime, I shall look forward to collaborating with you on matters concerning the household. I have no doubt we shall get along famously."

Griffith, looking as if he had been dipped into starch and summarily pressed, inclined his head stiffly.

"As you wish, milady. It is naturally my desire to serve you in anyway I am able."

Brie was almost certain she heard a muffled snort from the rank and file as, satisfied, she tucked her hand once more in the crook of Malvern's arm.

"You amaze me, my dear," murmured that worthy, leading her toward the next in line. "You handled yourself just as might be expected of a Countess of Malvern. I do fear, however, that in Griffith you may have made a formidable enemy."

Brie, conscious of an unwitting thrill of pleasure at his vote of approval, gave a small toss of the head.

"Better to have him as an enemy than a petty tyrant," she whispered back.

When at last the thing was done and Brigida found herself being ushered into the great hall, she felt drained and more than a little dazed by the wearing events of the day. With all her heart she wished nothing more than to be allowed some time to herself. In fact, she would like nothing better than to retire to a quiet room someplace and curl up in a soft, warm bed to sleep the sleep of exhaustion.

No sooner had that thought crossed her mind than she felt her cheeks grow suddenly warm. Tonight was her wedding night. It was exceedingly unlikely that she would be spending it alone.

Feeling suddenly ridiculously shy, she glanced up to find Malvern watching her from beneath heavily drooping eyelids. Confused at the intensity of his gaze, she was grateful when Mrs. Alcott, the housekeeper, bustled forward.

"Now then, m'lord, I expect you and her ladyship'll be wantin' to freshen up after your ride," she said with the familiarity of one who had spent her life serving the inhabitants of Malvern. "I trust you'll find everything has been arranged as you requested."

"I am sure of it, Mrs. Alcott," replied the earl. "And now," he added, turning back to Brie, "I'm afraid I must ask you to excuse me, my dear. It seems James has some matters of business to discuss. If there is anything you need, you have only to ask Mrs. Alcott."

"Yes, of course. Please do not concern yourself," she hastily assured him. "I shall be perfectly all right."

For an instant it seemed he would say something more. Then apparently he changed his mind. Turning his head, he addressed his next remarks to the housekeeper.

"Mrs. Alcott, if you would be so kind as to show her ladyship to her rooms. And see that a tray is brought to her. Unless, of course, my dear, you think you would prefer dining downstairs?"

"Well, as to that, I must confess I am feeling rather weary..."

"Yes, I thought as much," he smoothly interjected and, holding her with his eyes, raised her hand to his lips. "You go ahead with Mrs. Alcott. I shall be along directly to see how you go on."

Vaguely confused by such unlooked-for thoughtfulness, she merely nodded before turning to follow the housekeeper up the curving staircase.

"Such a fine man, soft-spoken and gentle in his manner," Mrs. Alcott grunted as she trudged up the stairs, a hand heavy on the banister rail. "Not like some who've stood in his shoes. Even as a young lad, he was kind and thoughtful of others. But then, he always did have more of the way of his mother about 'im. I expect it was sending him away the way he did, in anger, that broke his father's heart and led to his early grave. Had it been up to him, he'd never have let him go. But there was no holding Master Damion once he had his heart set on the King's Navy."

Brie looked at her in surprise.

"But I thought . . ."

"You thought he was sent away in disgrace. Aye, I've heard the tales told of 'im. Demon Drake, they call 'im. An' belike he came by it, fair an' honest, for a more fearless lad, I never knew. Nor a fiercer one to fight, when he was pushed to it. Many's the time I had to patch 'im up after he'd had a go with his brother, an' him no more than half the size of Duncan. It fair broke my heart, it did, when I saw what the French'd done to 'im."

"Indeed? You would seem to entertain a great fondness for his lordship, Mrs. Alcott. He is fortunate to command such loyalty from those in his employ."

The older woman colored slightly, coming to an awareness, perhaps, that she had been letting her tongue wag a little too freely.

"Yes, well, be that as it may, milady," she said, arriving a trifle breathlessly at the top of the stairs, "we couldn't, any of us, be happier that his lordship has brought his bride home to Malvern. It isn't good for a man to be so much alone as his lordship has been these past weeks. Maybe now there'll be the ring of merriment in these old halls, just like it was used to be in the old days."

They had come to a carved door as they spoke, and now Mrs. Alcott reached for the door handle.

"Here we are, milady." Opening the door, she stood aside to let the young countess precede her into a room made bright with Oriental butterflies hand-painted on silk wallpaper. Yellow caffoy-upholstered wing chairs and a pale green brocade settee were ranged before an Adams fireplace in white marble, and on the floor was a flowered Wilton carpet. Brie crossed to touch a Minton figurine on the mantelpiece. Everything had been done in perfect taste, even to the freshly cut roses arranged in a vase on the small satinwood table.

"The late earl's father had the rooms done over for his lady wife shortly before she died. No one's used them since, Duncan and Lady Cordelia preferring the newer, west wing the way they did. No sooner had his lordship arrived home than he ordered them refurbished—the old master bedroom and his mama's. Belike he had his bride in mind when he had it done. I hope you will be comfortable here, milady."

"I am certain I shall be, Mrs. Alcott," Brie answered, pulling off her black kid gloves and smiling. "Thank you."

"Yes, well, I'll be going now—to see to your dinner. And doubtless you'll be wanting hot water for a bath." A sudden frown creased her brow as if something had only then occurred to her. "His lordship never mentioned if you'd be needing someone in the way of an abigail. If you'd like, I could send someone up?"

"No, that will not be necessary." She suffered a small pang as it came to her that she would like nothing better than to have Fionna there with her. But she had not liked to take her away from Mrs. Guthrie and the commodore. They would be shorthanded enough at Gullan Carn now that she was gone. "I am quite capable of taking care of myself for now. Perhaps later I shall find someone."

Looking doubtful, Mrs. Alcott nodded and after admonishing her to ring should she require anything further, quietly let herself out.

It was done, thought Brigida distractedly, as she found herself alone at last. Damion Esterbridge John Phillip Drake, Earl of Malvern, was her husband, and she was chatelaine of the great house perched atop Tal Carn.

With a stunned sense of disbelief, she wandered through the double doors into the bedchamber and stopped to stare at her reflection in an ormolu looking glass. At Gullan Carn she had been too preoccupied to notice, but now she decided wryly that the riding habit of green silk, cut *a la militaire* and trimmed in gold braid, suited her admirably, as did the rather absurd black beaver hat with the ostrich feather dyed to match the dress. In truth, from the top of her head to the tips of her black kid half boots laced in green, she looked every bit the Countess of Malvern. And still she could not believe that she was indeed wed to the earl.

Her eyes strayed about the spacious room, to the poster bed on a high dais, the canopy seemingly draped in pale pink roses, to the matching camlet curtains, the plush Wilton carpet, the exquisite gold dressing table adorned with cut crystal bottles of perfumes and toiletries. She crossed to the double doors of the wardrobe and opened them wide. A gasp burst from her lips at sight of the exquisite things hanging within—everything from frocks and gowns to lovely peignoirs and silky nightgowns—an entire bridal trousseau. His lordship had spared nothing in creating the perfect setting for his new bride. Almost she was tempted to pinch herself to make certain she was not dreaming.

Instead, she sighed and reached up to pull out the ivory hat pin that held the black beaver in place. Then removing the hat as well, she laid it on the dressing table. In spite of her luxurious surroundings, she somehow did not feel very much like a bride on her wedding day.

She felt even less so when, an hour later, she had finished her bath and sat down to the intimate dinner with covers, perhaps mistakenly, laid for two. Another hour passed and she had picked desultorily at the fresh oysters, minced crab, paper-thin slices of ham, chilled asparagus, freshly baked bread, tangy cheese, and sweetmeats and jellies, and still the earl had not deigned to show himself. Whimsically, she poured herself a glass of champagne from the bottle that had accompanied what had most certainly been intended as a nuptial repast. It seemed almost indecent somehow, she reflected ironically, that she was about to experience her very first sip of champagne alone. It was, after all, her wedding night, and champagne was the wine of lovers.

Experimentally, she tasted of it. A frown puckered her lovely brow at the unfamiliar bite. Then lifting the glass in a silent toast, she drained it.

Feeling vaguely absurd and perhaps just a little melancholy in a cream-colored silk nightgown and matching peignoir trimmed in swansdown, she poured herself another glass of wine and crossed to the window to stand staring out at the sea bathed in moonlight.

He would not come, she decided, and even went so far as to tell herself that that was the way she wanted it. That she might be more than a little hurt and possibly piqued, she firmly refused to contemplate. What had she expected, after all? It was to be a marriage of convenience.

Defiantly she downed her drink at a single long pull and went back to the table to pour yet another.

She rather liked the way the bubbles tickled her nostrils, she decided, when moments later she finished that one, too. She picked up the bottle and was vaguely surprised to discover it was nearly empty. Ah, well, it would be a shame to waste it, would it not? she thought to herself and, upending the bottle, poured the rest of its contents into the glass.

Her breath caught at the low rap on the door between the master bedroom and hers. Nearly spilling her champagne, she turned.

Malvern, she thought, and had suddenly to reach out to the table to steady herself. No doubt it was the effects of the wine stealing over her, she decided, which imbued her with a wondrous feeling of lightheadedness. Resolutely she squared her shoulders and graciously granted his lordship leave to enter.

It occurred to her that his appearance was not quite what she had expected. Minus his coat and waistcoat, his white silk shirt open at the neck and looking a trifle rumpled, he presented more the picture of a man who had spent the past hour or two fortifying himself with brandy. Still, she could not help but note the ripple of muscle beneath the thin fabric of his shirt or that the buff unmentionables tucked into the tops of shining Hessians accentuated his slim-hipped masculine build to perfection. Never had he appeared so breathtakingly handsome. Nor so arrogantly aloof, she thought, her head lifting in instinctive defiance.

"Milord," she murmured, and without spilling a single drop of wine, sank into a deep curtsy no less graceful for its subtle hint of irony. "The champagne is delightful, and you really must try some of the minced crab. I recommend both very highly. Forgive me for dining without you, but, you see, I had decided to give you up."

The faint curl of his lip was sardonically amused as deliberately he bent his head to salute her knuckles.

"Not at all — 'milady,' " he drawled with cool significance. Then straightening, he looked at her, the obsidian eyes beneath heavily drooping eyelids unreadable as ever. "I am sorry I was detained. Indeed, I shan't bother you long. I wished only to discover if everything is satisfactory. The rooms are to your liking?"

"Why, yes, thank you. Indeed, how could they not be." She made a sweeping gesture with the hand that held the wineglass. "They are lovely, everything a lady could possibly wish."

"Every lady, but one, I shouldn't wonder," he commented in acerbic tones.

Brie eyed him doubtfully.

"I beg your pardon? I'm afraid I haven't the least notion what you are talking about."

Without warning, Malvern reached up to frame the side of her face with his hand.

"You do that so well," he murmured, his gaze strangely rueful. "You almost make me believe you." Then, at the frown in her eyes, he laughed and moved away to stare out the window overlooking the sea. After a moment he turned back to her. "There are forty other rooms that you might choose from, if these failed to suit, but somehow I think none would appeal to you quite so well as the one you left behind at Gullan Carn. You will no doubt excuse me if I find that singularly ironic."

Brie's eyes flashed green sparks of resentment. Good God, he blamed her for their predicament! Naturally, she would prefer her old, comfortable existence at Gullan Carn. And why should she not? At least there she had been wanted!

"But you are mistaken, milord," she declared, reacting out of a perversity of character which demanded she prove him wrong. From somewhere she summoned a brittle laugh. "I find that I like my new situation very well. And how not? Is it not every woman's dream to find herself dressed in fine silk and sipping champagne, while an army of servants waits to gratify her smallest desire? Yesterday I was a nobody worrying about something so mundane as a flock of sheep. Today I find myself a countess." Deliberately she raised her glass. "Let's drink to her, shall we? To Brigida Drake, the new chatelaine of Malvern Castle." Throwing back her head she drained the glass. She would have dashed it against the fireplace had not Malvern caught her wrist in a grip of steel and stopped her.

"How quickly marriage would seem to transform a woman," he observed in a steely voice, but the eyes probing hers held a curiously baffled expression. "The Brigida Morgan I knew would never have sold herself for anything so insignificant as a fortune or a title. Or was she all a carefully contrived sham? Forgive me, Countess, if I find little to resemble her in this new persona of my wife."

Angrily Brie stiffened, the multiple implied meanings of his speech abominably clear.

"No doubt it is the clothes," she retorted icily and

tried unsuccessfully to pull her hand free. "Such finery, after all, is hardly the usual attire of one who but a short time ago might have been mistaken for a field hand."

The sudden leap of his eyes should have warned her.

"You are wrong, surely." His glance moved deliberately over her face, pausing to linger suggestively on her lips. "Only a blind man could be such a fool. No matter what the attire, you are far too lovely, my dear, for a field hand."

"Am I?" she countered bitterly. "And have I the look of a murderer? Or at the very least the accomplice of such a one? Tell me, milord, will you sleep soundly knowing I am beneath your roof?"

Malvern's laugh rang harshly in the room.

"Deceitful little wretch," he uttered grimly. "I may not sleep soundly, but I shall at least be snug — with you in my bed beside me!"

Brie, made suddenly aware of her peril, felt her face go deathly pale.

"But of course, milord," she answered, forcing herself to stand perfectly still in his grasp. "I am your wife. You made sure of that. The least I can do is oblige you."

Malvern's grip tightened on her wrist so that she had to bite her lip to keep from crying out. For an instant she thought he must surely strike her. Then just as suddenly he released her.

"Damn it, Brigida, I—!" He did not finish it, but turned away instead, as if he could no longer bear the sight of her.

Brie swayed, feeling dizzy and more than a little sick to her stomach. She did not know what had come over her. Too much wine, perhaps, or the bitter knowledge that for her there could be no turning back. She had given up everything for a marriage she had neither wanted nor asked for, and he had dared to mock her for it.

"I am aware I have given you very little reason to trust me," Malvern said after a moment. "But could you but find it in your heart to try, I am convinced we could do better than this."

Brie swallowed, searching in vain for something to say and yet knowing she dared tell him nothing—not so long as her brother's life was at stake. With a feeling of impotence, she saw the muscles of his back ripple beneath the snug-fitting fabric of his shirt.

"Quite so," he murmured coldly and, straightening his shoulders, came around to face her once again. "Go to bed, Brigida. You needn't worry that I shall trouble you again tonight. Perhaps in the morning things will look differently to you."

"Y-yes, in the morning." Brie's hand lifted distractedly to her forehead. She was finding it strangely difficult to concentrate. If only the room would stop its odious spinning. If only he would leave her before she disgraced herself utterly before him!

As from a distance, she saw Malvern's glance narrow sharply on her face, saw him start suddenly toward her. Then with a groan, she felt her knees buckling beneath her. The next instant, a lean arm caught her about the waist and dragged her ruthlessly against an unrelenting chest.

Her head swimming, she forced open her eyes to find herself staring up at the earl, grim-faced with concern.

She sighed, too weary to protest, and, finding it quite natural in the circumstances, flung an arm about his neck. " 'Tis all your fault I've made a mull of things," she confided as she let her cheek sink against his chest. "Never wanted t'be a countess. Was doing just fine on my own, building up the flock. Put everything into the sheep—even Mama's diamonds. Would have made it, too, if you hadn't interfered."

Suddenly her eyes flew open. "You won't tell the commodore? Promise you won't? He doesn't know how close we came to losing everything. Please, he'd never forgive me if he knew what I've done to save Gullan Carn."

A wry smile twisted at Malvern's lips. She appeared so frantic, indeed, so adorably young and vulnerable with her guard down.

"Softly, child," he murmured. "You have my word."

Satisfied, she exhaled a long breath and relaxed once more against the chest placed so conveniently for that purpose. But almost immediately she frowned, troubled by a new thought. "It isn't right, you know," she uttered gravely, peering up at him out of pensive eyes. "Shouldn't have to drink champagne alone on a person's wedding night."

Slowly her eyelids drifted closed so that she did not see the grimness leave his face to be replaced by a look of bemused enlightenment. Bending down, Malvern caught her over his shoulder and lifted her.

"Quite so, my dear," he murmured softly and carried her to her bed.

Chapter Twelve

Brigida frowned, disturbed by the incessant rustle of movement somewhere nearby, and flipped irritably over on to her stomach. Abruptly the noise ceased. Thank heavens, she thought. No sooner, however, had she let her muscles go lax than a firm step sounded.

"Miss Brie? Miss Brie, 'tis nearly noon. There's folks been asking about 'ee."

"Go *away*, Fionna," she groaned and burrowed her head more deeply into the soft mound of pillows. "Tell Grandfather I won't be coming down for breakfast."

"Whatever 'ee say, Miss Brie. Thee's a fine lady now, and I expect 'ee can sleep till the cows come home if 'ee wants to." Brie went suddenly stiff in the bed. Then bolting upright, she stared incredulously at the grinning face of her former servant, standing, hands on hips, looking down at her. Satisfied, Fionna continued drily, "An' as for Mrs. Alcott and old stoneface, the butler—why, they can just go on waitin' for their orders."

"Fionna!" Brie gasped. "Whatever are you doing here? Good God, there's nothing amiss at Gullan Carn? The commodore and Collin—?"

"Now, now. They're fine, Miss Brie," Fionna hastened to assure her. " 'Ee doesn't need to be goin' and borrowin' trouble. Me cousin Mavis was ever so plaised to take me place at Gullan Carn. She's a good girl, and eager for the work. So when his lordship sent a man over to fetch me first thing this morning, I just threw me things together and come on."

"Oh, Fionna, I am so glad. Indeed, I could not be happier. You cannot think how wonderful it is to see a familiar face."

"I expect that's what his lordship had in mind when he come up with the notion," remarked the maidservant knowingly. "Now, what be 'ee doin' still abed, lass? There's a new life awaitin' 'ee outside those doors. 'Tis time 'ee was seein' to it."

Aye, thought Brie ruefully, as she allowed Fionna to shoo her from her bed. A new life, and she had made a fine beginning, had she not. She felt a sudden ache in the region of her heart almost as acute as the one throbbing in her head. Though her memories of the previous night were somewhat foggy, she recalled enough to know that she had behaved very badly. She had, in fact, most assuredly sunk herself beneath contempt in the eyes of the earl. And still he had thought to send for Fionna.

Why? she wondered suddenly. Indeed, why was he constantly stepping in and out of character—one moment to behave toward her with such arrogance that she was quite certain she had never met anyone more detestable and the next to do something so extraordinarily thoughtful? Perhaps he had a conscience after all and thought by this to make amends for uprooting her from her previously ordered existence. Or maybe, and far more likely, he simply derived some perverse enjoyment from keeping her perpetually off balance. Oh, the devil! she fumed, for, whatever his reasons, the fact remained that she now found herself in the unenviable position of being in his debt, and after she had made an utter fool of herself imbibing too freely of what she firmly believed must be the devil's own brew. Champagne, she groaned, clutching her throbbing head in her hands. Good God, she did not know how she was ever to face Malvern again.

Thus it was that Brie, emerging from her rooms an hour later, was no little relieved to learn she had been granted a brief reprieve from the dreaded encounter. His lordship had departed earlier that morning.

"He said to tell you he was gone to Plymouth on business," Mrs. Alcott informed her. "I fear he did not say when to expect him back. Perhaps you would care to break your fast, milady? I daresay you'll find the turbot to your liking. Or perhaps the kidneys and eggs. I'd be glad to show you to the breakfast room."

Brie, feeling her stomach turn at the mere mention of food, assayed a rather feeble smile.

"Oh. Well, perhaps some toast and hot coffee, Mrs. Alcott. I am really not very hungry. And afterward, if it is convenient, I should be grateful if you would take me on a tour of the house."

Since Mrs. Alcott was more than willing to oblige her, it was not long before Brie was immersed in taking over the reins of Malvern Castle. She spent the remainder of the morning going over menus with the cook and the afternoon acquainting herself with the major portion of the house that was in use.

She had addressed herself to the ground floor, containing the great hall, the buttery, pantry, and, below, the kitchens, and was leaving the family chapel with the intention of exploring the upstairs when Mrs. Alcott was called away. Preferring not to elicit the aid of Griffith, who, other than relinquishing his keys, had not participated in her orientation, she proceeded on alone up the circular staircase.

It was hardly any wonder if his lordship were given over to fits of melancholia, she decided, as she cupped her hand about the flame of her candle to keep it from going out. Dark and dreary, Malvern Castle exuded more the atmosphere of a mausoleum than a great house of nobility and would soon have thrown even the heartiest of souls into a gloom. Obviously, her first order of business was to render the interior more cheerful. She had begun downstairs by ordering the drapes to be opened, an act, which, she doubted not, would greatly displease Griffith. It was at his insistence, Mrs. Alcott informed her, that they were always kept closed to prevent the sun from fading the antique tapestried furniture and Oriental rugs.

"Yes, well, no doubt Griffith is to be applauded for his diligence," she had remarked with only the slightest hint of irony. "And while due care will be given to preserving such fine pieces, a house is meant to be lived in. Anything which cannot withstand the light of day we will simply move to a part of the house which is little used." If nothing else, she had added to herself, it would serve as a good excuse to store in a dark place some of the more unsightly heirlooms — the stuffed boar's head over the mantel, for example, or the particularly hideous tapestry of a ferocious dragon on the point of devouring a hapless wretch. One of the earlier Earls of Malvern, no doubt, who had suffered an unfortunate reversal in battle, she mused, dimpling naughtily.

Then instantly her thoughts returned to her burgeoning plans for the house. It was time new drapes were hung, she reflected, and it certainly would not hurt to redo some of the furniture with lighter fabrics, more pleasing to the eye. No doubt there were some who found a great deal to be desired in red damask and heavy brocades, but she was not one of them. Camlet, dimity, or caffoy fabrics in cool shades of green along with pale rose or ivory were more soothing to her way of thinking. She had already ordered that flowers, freshly cut each day from the gardens, should be always present in the rooms most frequented by the family and any guests that might happen to call. She would see to it as well that various potted plants should be introduced as soon as possible. A house needed living things, and this one perhaps more so than others.

Preoccupied with devising a mental checklist of things to be done, she came to the stone apse at the top of the stair and paused to consider which way she should proceed next. The wing that held her rooms and those of the earl was to the left, which meant that the newer addition, that which Duncan had favored, must surely lie in the opposite direction. On a whim, she took the stairs on the right.

The "newer," west wing probably dated back to no more than three-quarters of a century or so, she noted drily, as the way led her eventually to an open gallery. Leaning a hand on the iron-work balustrade supported on ornate C-scrolls, she found herself poised a full story above a magnificent ballroom. Along the length of the far wall glassed French doors opened on to a flagstone terrace and admitted a muted glow of sunlight through thin white curtains. On the ceiling and walls plump plaster-work cherubs sported amid a profusion of lions' heads, shell shapes, grotesque fish heads, and swirls of fruit-laden foliage. Apparently Malvern's great grandfather had made the Grand Tour in his youth. The French influence was unmistakable. Indeed, she would be willing to wager that the furniture draped in holland covers would be *Louis Quinze* to match the decor.

Curious to see if she was right, she started toward the staircase that descended into the ballroom.

The sound of a door closing somewhere below, followed by footsteps, halted her in midstride. Hardly knowing what prompted her, Brie hastily doused her light and backed away from the balustrade into the shadows.

"Yes, this is better. We should be able to speak uninterrupted in here," echoed eerily through the empty ballroom. "Now, what was so important that you would risk showing yourself at Malvern?"

"Plenty. I just came from Gullan Carn."

Brie only just managed to stifle a gasp. While the first voice was vaguely familiar, it was so distorted by echoes that she could not place it. The latter, however, she could never mistake. She had heard it too often before. It was Rory!

"So. You came from Gullan Carn. What of it? You will pardon me if I find little in that to inspire alarm."

"Perhaps not, but I thought you might be interested to know a Lieutenant Wilcox of the guard was there to see the commodore. And it wasn't a social visit. He was asking a lot of questions about Collin."

"Indeed? And was the lieutenant able to learn anything of significance?"

"Hardly. The old man threw him out as soon as he guessed what Wilcox was getting at. But you may be sure the commodore'll have plenty to say to Collin when next he sees him."

"So let him. That is hardly any concern to us. The worst that can happen is that the two of them will have a falling out. You, quite naturally, will sympathize with Morgan — praise him for asserting his independence. He is, after all, the head of his father's house." The man's laugh, expressive of contempt, caused Brie to clench her hands into fists. "No doubt such an estrangement can only prove of greater profit to us in future."

"But it is no longer safe, I tell you! Malvern is already suspicious. Not a night goes by that he isn't prowling somewhere about. And now you tell me his new bride thinks to renovate the bloody castle. I don't like it, Bram, What if she stumbles on to the—?"

The hair at the nape of Brie's neck rose at the sudden hiss of warning.

"Quiet, you fool! I told you never to mention that name out loud. One never knows who might be listening."

"The devil you say. No one ever comes to this part of the house. You said so yourself. No, I think you're just stalling. The truth is that you botched things when you decided to do away with Duncan. At worst, he was a blustering fool, but Demon Drake's another matter altogether. I say it's time we got out, while we still can."

Brie froze where she was.

"And so we shall—soon, my friend," came the answer, in a voice that sent chills down her spine. Good God, the man who had killed Duncan was there in the hall below her, and she had only to peer over the balustrade to see who he was. Her heart in her throat, she started to inch forward.

"I have only just received word to expect one more run in a week's time," she heard him say.

"A week! But they're asking the impossible. Or maybe you didn't hear me when I said Malvern has been sniffing around. He and that blasted Wilcox. They're already on to Collin and some of the others."

Hardly daring to breathe, Brie strained to see over the iron rail. Below her, Rory Gale appeared, pacing agitatedly. He had on a brown riding coat and buff unmentionables, and his blond curls, brushed in the windswept, looked unwontedly disheveled, as if he had just been running his fingers through them. Of the other man, she could see nothing. Apparently he stood directly beneath her, concealed in the overhang of the gallery.

"I tell you I want my money now," Gale exclaimed, wheeling to face Duncan's murderer. "As soon as things die down, I'm taking a place in London. It's the only reason I ever let you drag me into this in the first place—for the money and what it will buy me—my one chance to get away from here and live in the style I was meant to. And I don't intend to see it all thrown away for nothing."

"But I assure you you have nothing to fear. Thanks to your foolish young friend Morgan, there is every reason to suppose we shall never even fall under suspicion."

"Collin? But he would never agree to be a part of this. I fail to see how he can be of any possible use to us."

"But it's quite simple, really. Due to his careless excesses, he has already attracted a deal of unwanted attention. We have only to make certain he is disposed of in such a manner as to leave no doubt he is behind everything. Meantime, it will be your job to make sure he has plenty of pocket money—and that he freely indulges his weakness for the gaming tables. That should not be too difficult, surely. Especially now that his sister is no longer on hand to keep him on a tight rein."

Brie, who realized all too well how easy it would be,

took an involuntary step forward. Oh, *why* did not the blackguard show himself?

Her heart stood still at the sudden creak of the floorboard beneath her foot. Indeed, she had hardly wit enough to step back before Gale could catch sight of her.

"What was that?" he exclaimed, trying to pierce the shadows above him. "Did you hear something? It sounded like it came from up there."

Her back pressed to the wall, Brie held her breath.

"I fear your nerves are on edge, my friend," remarked his companion after a moment. "I am sure it was nothing. You know these old houses. They are full of noises."

"Yes, I suppose you're right." Even so, Rory's laugh sounded nervous and more than a little strained. "For a moment I fancied the bloody Demon was up there listening to every word we said."

"Nonsense. You must not let your imagination run away with you. Malvern, I assure you, is nowhere near. I myself saw him depart for Plymouth this morning. And now I think it is time you took your leave as well. If I need you, I shall get word to you in the usual way."

Once more there was the sound of a door being opened and shut, and then an uneasy silence fell over the room. Weak with relief, Brie sagged against the wall, one hand pressed to her pounding heart.

She could not believe what she had heard. The man who had killed Duncan was someone in the castle! And Rory Gale — the blackhearted scoundrel — had betrayed her brother. Quick upon that thought came the realization that a considerable time had elapsed since she had left Mrs. Alcott. Any moment someone might come looking for her, and it would not do to be discovered here. The man who had killed Duncan would hardly scruple at doing away with her if he even suspected she had overheard the two of them talking.

Picking up her skirts, she turned and fled heedlessly back the way she had come. She did not see the figure of a man emerge out of the shadows directly in front of her until it was too late. A strangled cry broke from her lips as she found herself pinned to a hard, masculine chest.

"Let . . . go!" she panted, breaking into a struggle. "Let go, or I swear I shall scream."

"I fear that would be of little use, my dear, since it is highly unlikely anyone would hear you."

At once Brie ceased to struggle.

"Oh!" she exclaimed, going limp with relief. "Thank God. It's you."

"No doubt I should be gratified at so touching a greeting," remarked the earl in ironic amusement. "Tell me, is it your usual practice to rush headlong down murky corridors without even the aid of a candle?"

Brie, suddenly acutely aware of the earl's arm clasped snugly about her waist, straightened and pulled self-consciously away.

"I had a candle, milord," she answered as steadily as she could. "Unfortunately, a draught blew it out. It is here—somewhere. I-I must have dropped it when I stumbled into you."

"Yes, well, never mind that. I am more interested at present in learning what brought you flinging into my arms. I do not mean to pry, my dear, but if something occurred to frighten you, I should quite naturally wish to know."

"Oh, but it was nothing," Brie evaded, wishing he would let the matter rest. "I should much rather just forget it."

"No doubt, and yet I fear I really must insist. Tell me, Brigida, what happened back there."

There was that in his tone which left no doubt in Brie's mind that he would not let it go until he had some sort of answer. And yet what was she to tell him — that she had overheard an unknown man admit to killing Duncan and that, further, he and Rory Gale intended to make a scapegoat of Collin? It would sound too farfetched by half, coming from her. No, she must have proof to back up her claim, for had not Malvern already made it quite plain that without evidence her word was worth nothing?

"Oh, very well," she said at last, "if you insist. It — it was a mouse, milord."

"A mouse," he repeated as if he had not heard her aright.

"Yes, a mouse," she insisted demurely. "Oh, you may very well laugh. Indeed, it is the absurdest thing. But I assure you, there is nothing I detest more than rodents. No sooner had my candle gone out than I felt something run across my feet. I-I'm afraid I must have panicked."

"I see," he said. She could feel his eyes on her, as if they could bore holes through the shadows, and something more — his disappointment. She was glad when at last he moved away from her to gaze out over the empty ballroom.

"If you intend to explore, my dear," he remarked coldly after a while, "I suggest in future you take a servant with you. This is an ancient holding and some parts of it contain hidden perils. Indeed, I must ask your promise you will not enter what remains of the original structures. For your own safety, Brigida. Will you give it?"

Brie frowned, instantly suspicious. She had seen nothing to suggest the structures were unsound. Then Malvern had turned and was looking at her.

"Well, my dear?" he prodded when she still did not answer.

"Oh, I suppose, if you think it is necessary. But I confess I am more than a little disappointed. If you must know, I had quite looked forward to making the acquaintance of the ghosts of Malvern."

A wry smile twitched at the corners of the earl's lips. No fool, he was perfectly aware of the element of vagueness in her reply. No doubt his headstrong young bride would head straight for the oldest part of the castle no sooner than his back was turned, and that was something he wished at all costs to avoid. Still, there was more than one way to achieve a desired goal. If she were kept too busy, for example, to indulge her proclivity for landing herself in danger . . .

On a sudden thought, he leaned a hand on the balustrade rail and looked down on the ballroom steeped in shadows. Yes, he mused, it might serve. With any luck it could take a week, perhaps even two, for his impetuous countess to make all the preparations— enough time, surely, for him to finish the business he had begun. Then he would be free at last to devote himself to matters of a more intimate nature. His thoughts turned to the slender girl who had married him against her will, to the way she had felt in his arms just a few moments before. Two weeks, he decided grimly, could seem a bloody eternity.

Behind him, Brie shifted nervously, wondering what was going through the earl's mind. The silence was preying on her nerves, and she wanted nothing more than to be away from there. Oh, why had he to come upon her at that particular moment and why here? Indeed, she wondered suddenly, what was he doing at Malvern at all when by all rights he should have been miles away on the road to Plymouth?

"I hope your business was not of a pressing nature, milord," she ventured at last, to break the silence if nothing else. "I was led to believe I should not expect you till quite late."

"I beg your pardon?"

"Your business in Plymouth, milord. I cannot but wonder what could have called you back so unexpectedly—before you had time to reach your destination. I do hope you did not suffer some mishap on the road?"

He shrugged dismissingly.

"No, nothing. I simply changed my mind. What business could be more important, after all, than attending my lovely bride?"

"What indeed, milord," retorted Brie in exceedingly dry tones.

A smile twitched at the corners of the earl's lips. If he did not know better, he would think she had been disappointed to find him gone when she awakened that morning.

"A pity your first impression of the west wing should be shrouded in gloom," he remarked, deliberately changing the subject. "By all rights you should have seen it as it was meant to be—as it was in my father's day. It is hard to believe, is it not, that this was used to be a festive house. And yet there was a time when Malvern was noted for its hospitality. My mother, it seems, was fond not only of music and gaiety, but of people. She liked having them around." Her breath caught as he turned to look at her. "I think it is time we had the holland covers removed and the chandeliers restored to their former brilliance. Perhaps it is not too late to return Malvern to at least a semblance of that more gracious era."

"I-I beg your pardon, milord?" stammered Brie. "Are you saying you intend to open up the ballroom? But why?"

"But I should have thought it was obvious," he drawled in cynical amusement. "The Earl of Malvern has taken a countess. He would be a poor sort indeed did he not present her to his neighbors. And what better way than to give a ball in her honor?"

Brie stared at him in stunned disbelief.

"A ball? You cannot be serious!"

"On the contrary, I have never been more serious. And why should I not."

"Why not indeed?" exclaimed Brie bitterly. "Good God. Have you any notion what such a thing would involve? Well, I, I assure you, have not the least notion, for, far from having ever given one, I have never even been to one. If it is your intention to demonstrate how little worthy I am to fill the exalted station to which you have raised me, then rest assured you could have found no better way."

She had begun to pace in her agitation, but now the earl stepped forward and, clasping her wrist in a strong grip, pulled her to him.

"Come now, Brigida," he uttered impatiently. "Can you truly believe I should intentionally plot to ruin you? Can you think so little of yourself?"

"Yes!" she cried, and then, "No. Oh, I don't *know* what I think. Except that I should surely disgrace you, milord. Oh, don't you see? I am not like other females of your acquaintance. All my life I have looked after the commodore and Collin and — and Gullan Carn. There was never time for parties. Truly,

I should not know where to begin."

"Then it is time you found out, and who better to help you than Lady Cordelia. No doubt you will be pleased to learn I have sent for her. She should, in fact, arrive no later than day after tomorrow."

"Lady Cordelia, here? But why?"

"Even the Countess of Malvern is in need of someone to serve in the capacity of sponsor when she has yet to make her come out. Had my mother lived, it would have fallen to her to be your mentor. In her stead, it is my hope that Lady Cordelia might fill that office. Now and later, in Town. Oh, you need not look so surprised. Surely you must have anticipated we should remove to the town house for the Season, if not this year than certainly in time for the next?"

"No, how could I? I—I was not aware we had a residence in London," stammered Brie, stunned and more than a little bewildered by this new turn of events. "But it changes nothing. I have no wish to go to London or make my come out in society. I know nothing of such things. Oh, why did you not listen to me? I tried to tell you I am no fit countess for you. And now you and the whole world will be made to see it."

"And I tell you you could not be more wrong." A protest on her lips, she started to turn away, but Malvern pulled her back again. "No, listen to me. You are young, Brigida, and beautiful. Rather than disgrace me, you will make me the envy of every man present. Nor need you think that you will not be accepted by the female contingent. They cannot but account you as something of an original, a beauty of the first water with unexceptional manners. So you see, all your fears are quite groundless. Unless—" Suddenly he stopped, his eyes hardening to glittering points. "But of course. Good God, what a bloody fool I've been."

Releasing her, he turned and leaned his hand on the banister.

"Milord?" queried Brie uncertainly.

"Strange that I should have forgotten." Brie winced at the bitter self-mockery in his laugh. "You would naturally feel repugnance at the thought of being subjected to the stares of sympathy. The whispers and clucking tongues. But no matter. It will prove to your benefit, I have no doubt. What better foil for untouched beauty and innocence, after all, than to have the Demon of Malvern at your side? And so you see, my dear, all your fears may indeed be laid to rest."

For an instant Brie stood, speechless with disbelief at where his logic had led him. Then suddenly she was shaking with anger.

"How *dare* you!" she exclaimed witheringly. "You may think what you will of yourself, but do not deign to dictate what my thoughts should be. You have not the least notion what they are. You, sir, are arrogant and high-handed, and—and I am quite sure I have never met anyone more ill-tempered or pigheaded. But the fact remains that any woman would be proud to be seen in your company. Apparently only you would think otherwise. Indeed, had I not heard the accounts of your valor in battle, I might begin to suspect you of cowardice. For why else should you choose to hide behind an infirmity, which, though it is undeniably severe, might yet with a little determination be made better?"

"Be made better?" pronounced the earl in chilling accents. "What can you possibly know of it? Are you a physician?"

"No, but I am possessed of a deal of common sense,

which tells me that where there is pain, there is yet life." Carried on a sudden impulse, she stepped near him and with a boldness that later she would marvel at, took his maimed hand in both of hers. She felt him stiffen at her touch, but wonder of wonders, he did not pull away as gently she worked the glove off.

Even in the uncertain light, she could see the scars, the skin puckered and livid, the fingers curled in upon themselves. She felt a lump rise in her throat and for a terrible moment thought she would betray herself. Then she swallowed and, deliberately lifting the tortured limb to her cheek, raised her eyes to his.

"Have you ever noticed, milord," she said, holding him spellbound with those enormous orbs, "how a clerk who spends his days hunched over his books draws gradually in upon himself? Or how stoop-shouldered and stiff becomes the laborer bent always over his shovel? Is not the body molded according to its use? And if a limb is not used, but allowed to remain forever bent, does that not become its tutored shape?"

"Perhaps," he uttered, his voice, rigid with control, in sharp contrast to the smoldering fire in his eyes.

"Your touch is warm to my cheek," she continued and marveled at herself as she rubbed her face brazenly against his hand. "Surely you must feel it, too?" A heady thrill shot through her as she felt his tortured fingers clench over hers.

"What do *you* think, Countess?" Malvern growled, bending over her with a fierceness that took her breath away. "I am a cripple, but I am hardly dead."

"No, you are not dead," she answered with what steadiness she could. "And neither are the nerves and sinews in your hand. Oh, do you not see? I cannot but believe that at least a measure of strength and suppleness can be rewon. If you are but willing to try, milord."

She glimpsed the leap of muscle along the hard line of his jaw. And then strong, supple fingers wove themselves through her hair at the back of her head.

"And if I am," he whispered huskily, his face close to hers, "shall I have you to give me the inspiration I require?"

Brigida, mesmerized by the black glitter of his eyes, from somewhere found the wit to answer him.

"And how not?" she said simply. "I am your wife, milord. I should naturally wish to be of whatever help I can."

Behind them the echo of hurried steps sounded, coming toward them along the gallery. Brie heard them hesitate and then stop. Still the earl held her, his eyes never once leaving hers. At last a smile, strangely enigmatic, flickered in the pallor of his face.

"Yes," he said and, straightening, flicked her lightly beneath the chin with his forefinger. "You are my wife. And nothing can ever change that."

Brie blushed in confusion, uncertain as to his meaning. Then Malvern had turned away.

"Well, Hartwell?" he drawled, lifting an inquisitive eyebrow at the big coxswain, waiting uncertainly a few paces away.

"Beggin' your pardon, Cap'n—er—m'lord. I didn't know ye was with her ladyship. I expect what I got to say can wait for later."

"Never mind, Hartwell," said Brie, coming forward. "I was just leaving to find Mrs. Alcott. It would seem she and I have a great deal to discuss." Lifting her head, she turned her gaze deliberately to Malvern. "You see, Hartwell, his lordship and I have decided to give a ball."

Chapter Thirteen

After leaving Malvern with Hartwell on the gallery, Brigida fled to her room. She was grateful to find Fionna was not within. She needed a few moments alone to collect herself. Flinging herself on the bed, she waited for her heart to cease its pounding.

She closed her eyes, and she could see him — Malvern, bending over her, his obsidian eyes burning holes through her. Indeed, the image seemed etched in her mind. Clutching a pillow to her breast, she rolled over on to her back and stared blindly up at the rose-patterned canopy.

She could not believe she had had the audacity to do what she had done. And yet she knew she did not regret it. In spite of everything, it had been her heart that had compelled her to it, not her head. And what if Hartwell had not come when he had? she wondered, her pulse beginning to race again. Would Malvern have kissed her? Might it be that she would not be here alone had the coxswain not interrupted when he had?

Suddenly the roguish dimple peeped forth as she realized she would have liked nothing better than to have Malvern there with her. The truth was she wished with all her heart to be his wife in the truest sense of the word. She would find a way to make him love her, she vowed—once she had uncovered the identity of the man in the ballroom and cleared her brother's name.

She shivered at the thought that a murderer was somewhere within the castle walls. Who was he? she wondered. Surely not someone of the lower orders. His manner of speech would seem to rule that out. And yet he was someone of the accepted household, someone well acquainted with the house and its occupants. Two names sprang readily to mind—Devin Drake, the earl's cousin, and James Pembroke, his private secretary. And, yes, one other—Griffith, the butler. Him, she might readily believe capable of murder. He, at least, seemed cold-blooded enough.

One thing was for certain. She needed to learn more about the three, and she could hardly do that barricaded in her room away from everyone. All at once it came to her that the ball his lordship had determined upon might suit her purposes very well. What better excuse to seek out the men with whom she wished a better acquaintance than to elicit their aid in the grandiose entertainment? And while she was at it, she might as well invite Collin to come and stay for a time. It would be good to have someone around whom she could trust, someone to talk to, if nothing else. But more importantly, it would remove him from Rory's unsavory sphere of influence until she could figure out how to convince him his oldest friend was not to be trusted.

The next instant she had left her bed and, pausing only long enough to run a comb through her curls and to smooth the wrinkles from her dress, she went in search of Mrs. Alcott.

She found her in the great hall, supervising the

removal of the boar's head from above the mantel, and wasted little time in informing her of the proposed ball.

The housekeeper, to Brie's relief, was not in the least put out at the prospect of opening the house at rather short notice to a great many guests. On the contrary, she declared, hitching up her sleeves, it would doubtless do the staff a deal of good to be jolted out of their complacency.

"Don't you worry, milady. There are still those at Malvern who remember what it was like in the old days. Not like *some* I might mention if I were of a mind to," she added, casting a meaningful eye in the direction of the butler's private sanctum, located behind one end of the circular staircase.

Brie felt her heart skip a beat.

"But surely you cannot mean Griffith?" she queried, careful to school her features to reveal only polite interest. "It was my belief that he was a longtime retainer at Malvern."

"Oh, no. Not him, milady. Why, he isn't even Cornish bred. Master Duncan hired him sight unseen from an agency in London when old Driscoll was put out to pasture. It couldn't 've been more than six months before they found Duncan washed ashore, God rest his soul."

"I see," murmured Brie, wondering what should have necessitated the man's removal from London to the wilds of Cornwall. Surely it could not have been a matter of preference. After all, for one such as Griffith, such a move could only be seen in the light of forced exile from the very hub of civilization. "Well, at any rate, I trust Griffith is not inexperienced in dealing with large entertainments. I depend on you both to carry the thing off. And the first order of business is to prepare rooms for some visitors. You will no doubt be pleased to learn his lordship has informed me that we may expect Lady Cordelia to arrive in the next day or two. And, further, I have decided to invite my brother to come for an indeterminate stay. At the very least until after the ball. I have no doubt I shall make good use of him in the succeeding days."

"Collin at Malvern?" obtruded a masculine voice from the front entryway. "But what a capital idea. Just what we need to liven things up around here." Brie, dismissing the housekeeper with a nod, turned to behold the earl's cousin striding toward her.

Dressed in a drab riding coat, which could only have been cut by a tailor of the first water, buff unmentionables, made fashionably tight to accentuate muscular thighs, and shining brown Hessians, Devin Drake presented the image of a town beau somewhere in his middle to late twenties. His hair, cut in the Brutus, was brown, as were his eyes, and his features, regular and reasonably handsome, if somewhat dissolute, were possessed of a sardonic tendency. He was the only son of Damion's father's younger brother, who had met an untimely demise by his own hand after an unfortunate spell at the gaming tables, and he was next in line to inherit.

"Then you approve, Mr. Drake?" Brie queried with a false lightness. The villain she had overheard in the ballroom would naturally prefer to have Collin flinging money away at the gaming tables. "Am I to understand that you find the country somewhat less than stimulating?"

"I find the country, my dear girl, an intolerable bore and would vastly prefer never to set foot farther from London than an occasional visit to Newmarket.

Unfortunately, when one hasn't a feather to fly with, there would seem little point in cavilling over what cannot be helped. Ergo, I take what pleasure I can from my enforced period of rustication."

"You surprise me, sir," retorted Brie guilelessly. "Somehow I should never have suspected you to be a man of forbearance."

An appreciative gleam flickered in his eye at her subtle hint of irony.

"Nor am I," he conceded. "Only practical. My turn of bad luck cannot last forever, after all. Your presence at Malvern would seem proof of that."

Brie cocked an incredulous eyebrow at the gentleman.

"*My* presence. You will pardon me if I fail to see what the one can possibly have to do with the other."

"Surely it is obvious," he said smoothly. Gracefully he saluted her knuckles, then, lifting his head, he gazed up at her with undisguised admiration. "It has been some time since a woman as beautiful as you graced these halls. How could I count myself other than fortunate?"

He certainly was not lacking in brass, mused Brie wryly. How dared he think he might set up a flirtation with his cousin's bride of less than two days, and under the earl's very own roof as well! Obviously he was an unprincipled rake and a womanizer, but was he a murderer?

"I think," she answered, firmly pulling her hand free, "that you have indeed been too long away from your London pursuits. In which case you will no doubt be glad to learn there is to be a ball at Malvern."

An expression of profound surprise crossed the handsome features.

"Obviously you wield a deal more influence over my cousin than I had hitherto thought possible. A ball indeed. You are to be congratulated, my dear countess. Malvern playing the host to the local gentry was the last thing I should ever have anticipated."

Brie gave him a wide look out of cool green eyes.

"Truly? But why, Mr. Drake? He is the Earl of Malvern. Surely it would be thought extremely odd should my husband *not* take on the responsibilities of his station."

"Oh, you'll get no argument from me. I have done what I could to woo my cousin from this house. Hitherto, however, he has proven quite unshakable in his determination to remain a recluse. And who could blame him? After all that he has suffered, I am afraid I, too, might be tempted to shun the curious attentions of my neighbors."

Brie's eyebrow swept up in her brow at what she perceived as unctuousness on his part.

"You say that as if there were some shame in his being the object of curiosity," she observed in a deceptively mild tone. "And yet, why should his neighbors not be inquisitive? He is a hero, and he is a son of Cornwall. Quite naturally they would wish to see him. I'm afraid, sir, that if that is the sort of persuasion you have used with the earl, then it can be little wonder that it has failed."

For an instant she was sure she glimpsed a flash of anger behind the suave mask of his face. Then almost immediately he was smiling again, ruefully this time.

"You are right, of course," he said. "I simply never looked at it in quite that way before. You see, I am scarcely acquainted with my cousin, never having met him till a matter of a few months ago. I'm afraid I did not consider it my place to stick my nose in where it so obviously was not wanted."

It was Brie's turn to feel chagrin. Naturally, in such circumstances he would be reticent to interfere in his cousin's affairs. And how much more so if his livelihood depended on the earl's good will?

"I beg your pardon, Mr. Drake—"

"Devin. Please. After all, we are related now. And we are, I trust, going to be good friends."

Brie hesitated, feeling a vague irritation at the smooth manner in which he had turned the tables on her.

"Oh, very well. Devin, then," she answered, giving a grudging laugh. "And I do beg your pardon if I appeared to jump to conclusions."

"Not at all. You are refreshingly honest. And a veritable tigress when it comes to the defense of your husband. I believe I begin to envy my cousin."

Brie felt an uncomfortable wash of blood to her cheeks at the way he looked at her then. Not that it was lacking either in sincerity or warmth, because it was not. It was, in fact, just the sort of look she might have wished from Malvern. However, it came not from Malvern, but from his cousin, and, as she had no previous experience dealing with the advances of practiced rakes, she was perhaps understandably flustered.

She certainly was not prepared for the sound of a light, thrilling step directly behind her. Turning, she flushed even deeper at sight of the earl observing her with gimlet eyes from the foot of the stairway.

"M-milord," she exclaimed and was further chagrined to hear the breathless catch in her voice. Angry at herself as well as the smiling rogue who was the cause of her discomposure, she dropped into a curtsy.

"Ah, Damion, old boy," murmured Devin Drake, patently amused at the turn of events. Taking out an exquisite enameled snuffbox, he flicked open the lid and helped himself to a pinch of the stuff. "This is a surprise. It was my understanding you were off to Plymouth."

The earl's sleepy glance shifted from his wife to his cousin. Brie shivered, feeling the clash of two wills like a palpable thing. Devin Drake was the taller and more powerfully built of the two, and yet Malvern, she sensed somehow, was infinitely the more dangerous.

"And so I was," the earl answered in his inimitable, soft drawl. Leisurely he advanced into the room. "As it happens, I was saved from having to go so far by a chance meeting on the road." Coming to Brigida, he stopped. "The man I had meant to see was already on his way here."

"But how fortunate," remarked Devin. "The road to Plymouth is beastly this time of year. And how much more pleasant to be here in the company of your lovely young bride."

"Exactly so," said the earl, reaching up to touch the back of his hand lightly to Brie's cheek. For a moment he held her with dark, unfathomable eyes. Then turning, he released her. "I see you have already begun making changes, my dear," he observed, his gaze going to the empty space over the mantel.

"Indeed, milord. I-I thought one of the antique mirrors, or a painting, perhaps, would lend a more cheerful aspect. I hope you do not mind."

Malvern shrugged. "No, why should I? The house is yours to do with as you will."

Inexplicably hurt at his cold indifference, Brie

brought her head up.

"I see," she crooned, a dangerous glint in her seagreen eyes. "Then if I am to have carte blanche, you will not object if I order new drapes to be made up for the hall and certain of the other rooms. Several of the chambers could do with new wall coverings as well, and some of the furniture should be refurbished, perhaps even replaced, before we invite guests in."

She was well aware what she was suggesting would cost a great deal of money. However, if she had expected to get a rise from him, she was to be disappointed.

"You will of course do as you see fit," he replied without the flicker of an eyelid. "Order whatever you wish. I have already instructed James to set aside funds for your quarterly allowance. You need only apply to him for whatever further sums you require."

Brie gritted her teeth in vexation. How dared he choose such a moment to inform her of his arrangements with Pembroke! She noted the faint twitch at the corners of the handsome lips and realized he must have been perfectly aware she could not refuse his generosity with his cousin looking on. Obviously she had played right into his hands!

And then Devin decided to complicate matters further.

"If you intend to do so much in such short order," he cut in smoothly, "you will undoubtedly need the help of someone familiar with the area. Someone who knows where you might find fabrics and artisans capable of doing all that you require. I should be pleased to offer you my services in such an undertaking."

"But how very *kind* in you, sir," Brie lilted.

"Yes, no doubt," murmured the earl.

Unaccountably, Brie felt the blood rise to her cheeks.

"Not at all." Devin smiled. It would mean, after all, that he would find himself a great deal in the company of his cousin's enchanting new wife. "And now that that is settled, I must beg you both will excuse me. Regrettably I am promised elsewhere this evening. Milady," he intoned, gallantly saluting her hand before making his leisurely departure.

No sooner had the heavy oak door shut behind the rogue than Brie turned flashing eyes on the earl.

"I suppose you have no intention of telling me what that was all about," she said bitterly.

A single imperious eyebrow shot upward in the pallid brow.

"I beg your pardon," drawled his lordship, his face unreadable behind a mask of ennui. "I fear I haven't the least notion what you are talking about."

"Oh, haven't you indeed," she countered, clenching her hands into fists at her side. "Well, I, sir, have not spent all my life around men without learning a thing or two about them. And I could not but see that Devin Drake is no friend to you. On the contrary, I think he would delight in making trouble if he could. When you walked in on us, you—you thought that I—that we—were—were—well, that he—"

"—was setting up one of his well-known flirtations?" supplied the earl. "And that you, being the green girl that you are, were caught at something of a disadvantage?"

"Yes. I mean, no!" Immediately she got hold of herself. "I mean, sir," she said crossly, "I am *not* a green girl. I knew perfectly well what your cousin

213

was about."

"Did you. And no doubt you have found yourself confronted with any number of practiced rakes at Gullan Carn. Having been reared all your life among men, as it were."

A reluctant bubble of laughter rose to her lips at the sight of his bland look.

"What a gammon. You know very well that I have not," she retorted with mock indignation. "Oh, it is all your fault, bursting in on us like that. I was doing quite well on my own until you complicated matters."

"I beg to differ, my dear," murmured his lordship, leaning one elbow on top of the mantelpiece. "I did not 'burst' in. I came downstairs thinking I might find you here."

"And of course you did, just in time to catch your cousin paying marked attention to me." Brie favored him with a small moue of vexation. "I begin to wonder, milord, how it is that you are forever popping up out of nowhere when you are least expected."

A faint smile twitched at the corners of the handsome lips.

"No doubt I am drawn," he mused whimsically. "Rather like a bee to honey."

"Yes, no doubt," Brie acerbically retorted. "Well?" she demanded, arching delicate eyebrows. "You have found me. Was there something in particular that you wanted?"

"It is only a small business matter — some papers to be signed. It will not require more than a few moments of your time should you care to accompany me to the study."

Brie, conscious of vague disappointment that it was for business only that he had sought her out, placed her hand on the arm he offered.

"But of course, milord. If you wish it," she answered and allowed him to lead her to the stairs.

"My cousin can be quite charming, I believe," ventured the earl after a long moment as they made their way up the staircase. "And unfortunately there is little enough at Malvern to divert a young and beautiful woman."

Coming to the head of the stairs, he turned and gazed speculatively down into her face.

"I do not mean to interfere in your affais, *enfant*," he said. "It would perhaps be better, however, did you not find yourself too much alone in his company."

"Why? Because he is dangerous?" she queried archly. "Oh, yes, a child could sense that in him. Nevertheless, I assure you I am quite capable of taking care of myself."

A hint of steel flashed in the gimlet eyes.

"You, my green girl, haven't the least notion what a man like Devin is capable of. If you did, you would not be so damnably sure of yourself."

"Indeed? And yet I do not suppose you intend telling me just what he *is* capable of? No? I did not think so. In which case, I fear I have no choice but to find out for myself."

Brie, noting the leap of muscle along the firm line of his jaw, was swept with a delicious sense that she was flirting with a more immediate peril than any offered by his lordship's cousin.

"If you so little trust him, milord," she added, pursuing what she conceived as her advantage, "then I cannot but wonder why you do not send him away. Surely one of your other houses would suit him just as well."

215

"Perhaps." His lip curled cynically. "And yet he is my closest living relative. For the time being it amuses me to have him here."

"Amuses you!" Brie stared at him in disbelief. Indeed, she experienced a sudden sinking feeling in the pit of her stomach as it came to her that her virtue might not be the only thing in peril. If Devin were indeed the man she had overheard in the ballroom, then he might very well be planning to put a period to the earl's existence.

As if she could contain herself in no other way, she wheeled and walked a pace, then came back again. "I do not understand you, milord. If the man poses some danger for you . . ."

He did not let her finish, but, drawing near, silenced her with a finger pressed lightly to her lips.

"Softly, my love," he murmured. "You almost make me believe you would care if something happened to me."

"Care? Why should I care? You are only my wedded husband. As it happens, I entertain a certain distaste for being made a widow before I have had a chance to enjoy the dubious advantages of being your countess."

"Now you *are* letting your imagination run away with you."

"Am I? How can you be so sure, when you yourself hardly know him? Duncan is dead, and Devin Drake is your heir. Perhaps he has ambitions to be more."

Reaching up, he cupped the side of her face with his lean, strong hand. "And I assure you you are jumping to conclusions. I never said he was a threat to me. But you are another matter altogether. You would not be the first woman my cousin has ruined, and now that you are no longer single, you are fair game for one such as he."

Brie, feeling herself drowning in the black intensity of his eyes, swallowed.

"And yet it is true, is it not," she managed a trifle huskily, "that you have only recently made his acquaintance?"

With a small sigh of exasperation at her persistence, Malvern let his hand drop to his side.

"Yes, it is true enough." Opening the door at the center of the stone apse, he let her into a broad corridor lined with portraits. Coming to a likeness of two youths posed in an attitude of familial devotion with their father and mother, the earl paused. Brie did not have to be told that she was viewing a portrait of his father and uncle. The similarities between Devin and the younger of the two boys was unmistakable.

"Devin's father and mine had a falling out long before my birth." Malvern's smile was ironic. "Until I returned to Cornwall and discovered him here, I never knew of Devin's existence. But it does not signify. I know him well enough." Turning, he looked at Brigida. "Only leave my cousin to me and do not bother your head about him—except to keep him at arm's length—and we shall all rub along well enough, I've no doubt."

Brie frowned, unconvinced. Still, a single glance at the earl's uncompromising expression made it quite plain further argument was pointless in the extreme.

"Yes, no doubt," she answered in a troubled voice as she turned to accompany him the rest of the way to the study.

The study, Brie soon discovered, was more in the way of a library, with rows of book-filled shelves, ceiling high, lining three of the walls. The fourth was filled with a Gothic fireplace in which a fire crackled. An oversized oak desk, leather-upholstered chairs, and a long couch, which might have been used as a daybed, gave the room a masculine aura, while rich Oriental rugs, covering a hardwood floor, lent it an air of warmth and comfort. Brie, noting the sextant in its velvet-lined box on the desk amid various rolled maps and charts, decided the room suited his lordship.

She started as Malvern came suddenly to loom over her, some sheets of paper in his hands. Taking them from him, she arched an inquisitive eyebrow.

"The Marriage Settlements," he replied in answer to her unasked question. "They require your signature. Read them first if you like."

Brie colored, embarrassed and suddenly angry. Straightening to her full five feet in height, she lifted her chin in stubborn defiance.

"I should prefer not to sign them at all, milord," she stated, staring straight before her. "It was not for your money that I have married you."

A look of impatience flashed across the chiseled countenance.

"I am well aware of why you married me, Brigida. This, however, is a mere formality—one with which you will comply."

"And if I refuse?"

"Then you would be behaving in a singularly childish manner. Would you have it said that Malvern failed to provide for his wife?"

At last she looked at him, a curiously wounded

expression in her eyes.

"Is it any worse than having it said that Brigida Morgan has married Malvern for his title and his fortune?"

Malvern's lips thinned to a grim line.

"You are a green girl indeed, my dear," he drawled coldly, "if you think for one moment the world would judge you harshly for such a marriage. On the contrary, it will be regarded as *un fait accompli*. But you do as you wish. I have other matters to attend."

Turning on his heel, he strode quickly past her.

Brie winced as the hard click of the door handle sounded loudly in the uneasy quiet. The next instant he had gone, shutting the door firmly behind him.

For a long moment Brie stood where she was. When at last she appeared to shake herself out of her abstraction, she gazed darkly at the pile of papers.

"Oh, the devil!" she muttered, and, taking an ink pen from its stand on the earl's desk, signed the loathsome documents.

Having received a message that the earl would be gone from the house that evening, Brie dined alone in her room and went early to bed. But sleep did not claim her. She had too much on her mind. Having exhausted herself, tossing and turning in the great bed, she at last rose to prowl restlessly about the darkened room until at last she found herself at the bay window. Settling on the window seat, she clasped her knees to her breast, and stared out at the bay, silvery in the moonlight.

Out of the corner of her eye she caught sight of something—a flash of movement or a flicker of light—and she straightened, suddenly alert.

From the jut of the window, set in the corner of the east wing, she had a clear view of the oldest part of the house in which resided the great hall—and, above it, the tower rooms, which, save for the study, she had been forbidden to explore. So, she thought with a sudden prickling of nerve endings, the structure was unsound, was it. And yet someone had dared to venture within, for from the turret window a light flashed on and off. Obviously whoever it was was using a dark lantern of the sort employed by mariners to communicate between ships at night.

All at once, her heart began to pound. It was a signal of some sort. It had to be! But to whom? Eagerly she turned to stare out across the bay. Her breath caught as she glimpsed an answering beacon, faint, but unmistakable, in the distance. Good God, it came from Gullan Carn!

She reeled with the first, swift instant of realization. But quickly she recovered herself. Her pulse racing, she looked once more to the tower window. Dark now and empty, it irresistibly beckoned. Hastily she thrust her arms through the sleeves of her dressing robe and, lighting a candle, slipped out into the hall.

It could not have been more than a few minutes past midnight, she decided—she vaguely remembered hearing the hollow chime of the hall clock shortly before she spotted the lantern—and the house was eerily quiet. Shivering a little in the chill air, she stole quickly along the hall to the stairs and then down to the stone apse. Moments later, she was making her way past the study. At the far end of the picture gallery, she came to a door and could go no further.

"The devil!" she exclaimed, giving the closed padlock a disgusted tug.

Suddenly weary and nearly chilled to the bone, she turned at last to retrace her steps to her rooms in the east wing. Dousing the light, she crawled into bed to lie staring into the darkness.

Less than ten minutes had elapsed since she had first seen the light. To have made his escape unseen before her arrival, the mysterious prowler must surely have had wings to fly! Unless, she thought, her pulse quickening, there was some other way into the tower.

From out of nowhere a thread of memory came back to her — Rory Gale raving something about her renovating the castle. He had been afraid she might discover something. What? And Malvern. Why should he have forbidden her to enter the turret? No doubt he was hiding something, too. A secret passage, perhaps, one like the earl's private stairway to Smugglers' Cave?

Excitedly she bolted upright in the bed. Yes, why not? she thought. Malvern himself had admitted to having smugglers and a smattering of pirates among his ancestors. They would have found it advantageous to keep their comings and goings secret and to have someplace in which to cache their store of pilfered or smuggled goods. No doubt that had been the purpose for excavating a passage to Smugglers' Cave. Indeed, there might be any number of secret passages honeycombing the original structures.

Suddenly she looked forward to Cordelia's arrival with a deal more anticipation than she had previously entertained. Her predecessor had lived in the castle for better than a decade. Surely she would know if there were any hidden corridors at Malvern.

At last Brie lay back against her pillows once

more. She could do nothing more tonight and the morrow promised to be an extremely busy day. She needed what little sleep was left to her.

Her last thoughts before she succumbed to weariness were of black piercing eyes and a promise she had made. She had planned to send a footman to Gullan Carn with the invitation for her brother, but perhaps it would be better if she went herself. It would give her a chance to speak with Malcolm. The old man, besides being a marvel with sheep, was something of a master craftsman. Indeed, he could make practically anything if once given an idea.

Chapter Fourteen

The days following events in the west wing seemed to mark a turning point in Brigida's relationship with the earl. As if by tacit agreement, no more mention was made between them of Collin or smugglers or Duncan's murderers. Nor did they bait one another as they had before. On the contrary, although she detected an aloofness in him, an impenetrable reserve that both vexed and hurt her somehow, his lordship yet treated her with kindness and consideration whenever he was near, which, had she stopped to think about it, was surprisingly often. Indeed, in spite of the fact that most of her waking hours were occupied with preparations for the coming ball, she might look up at any given moment to find Malvern standing in a doorway observing her from afar or, again, in the garden, striding toward her to take a basket of freshly cut flowers from her hand. On such occasions he might linger, engaging her in conversation for several minutes at a time, or sometimes, if circumstances permitted, even longer. With the result that she soon came to look forward to his sudden, unexpected appearances and to miss them if for some reason he failed to materialize.

He did not, however, come again to her bedroom.

Nor did he make any further demands on her of an intimate nature. Brie, torn at first between relief and disappointment, was thankfully too busy to dwell overmuch on it. For the time being, at least, she was contented to leave things between them as they were.

Lady Cordelia's arrival at the end of Brie's first week at Tal Carn created a sensation among the inhabitants of the castle. Dressed to the nines in a rose-pink cambric frock and a Spanish vest, her brown hair cropped fashionably short and brushed *a la Titus,* she carried herself with a quiet confidence quite unlike her former self. She was almost regally tall, and, with the exception of arresting gray eyes, was possessed of plain, somewhat angular features. In truth, Cordelia Drake was no beauty, but she displayed an elegance in style which more than made up for what she lacked in looks.

As soon as the former mistress of the castle had run the gauntlet of greetings from the staff, Brie took it upon herself to show her to her rooms. No sooner had they closed the door to what was to serve as Cordelia's sitting room, than the older woman breathed an audible sigh of relief.

"I confess," she confided, reaching up to remove her cottage hat of plaited straw, "to being quite overwhelmed at such a warm welcome. Indeed, I was not at all certain how I should feel upon coming here again, but now that I *am* here, I find myself strangely detached from the painful memories of this house. Rather as if I had only dreamed them." She laughed, a pleasingly melodious sound. "No doubt it has a great deal to do with the changes you have wrought. From what little I have seen, I should say they are nothing short of miraculous."

"But I have done nothing yet of any consequence,"

Brie started to protest, thinking of the thousand and one things that had yet to be accomplished.

"Oh, but you have." Turning at last to Brigida, Cordelia gathered the younger woman's hands in both of her own. "I am not blind, Brigida. I can see clearly what you have done. You have infused life into this ancient pile, and that is something that I was never able to do. You cannot imagine, my dear, with what pleasure I received the news of your marriage. I had believed for a long time that you were everything I could have wished for Malvern, and now I know I was quite right. The evidence is all around me."

"You—you are very kind," Brie answered, her smile a trifle off center.

A flicker of something like amusement shone in the discerning gray eyes.

"You are surprised," she said.

Brie, who had never had more than a passing acquaintance with Lady Cordelia and who believed the same might be said of Malvern and his sister-in-law, could not deny it.

"Well, a little, perhaps. I am not exactly in the usual style of females with whom one might associate a man like Malvern."

"No, which is *why* I should have chosen such a match, had it been up to me. Malvern himself, after all, is hardly in the usual style. When I first met him, he was hardly more than a boy. Yet he had already been in command of his own ship for four years and was well on the way to earning a reputation for himself as a man of resourcefulness and daring."

Brie started in surprise.

"You knew him back then?" she blurted without

stopping to think. "But I was not aware that until a few months ago he was ever in Cornwall."

A shadow, like pain, flickered in the fine eyes. Turning away, Cordelia walked to the window to stand looking out. "It was in London, some weeks after I—lost the baby. Duncan had taken me to see a physician, and Damion by chance was just arrived back in England after having taken part in the Battle of the Nile."

Brie bit her lip, chagrined at where her impetuous tongue had led her.

"Cordelia," she exclaimed miserably. "Forgive me. I-I didn't know."

"No, of course you did not. Indeed, how could you." Coming around again to face her young hostess, the older woman smiled. "At any rate, it was all a very long time ago."

Not *so* very long ago, thought Brie, sorry to have dredged up unhappy memories. Only seven years had elapsed since the Battle of the Nile. Malvern must have been about four and twenty.

"What was he like?" she asked, compelled by a curiosity that would not be denied.

Cordelia smiled strangely.

"Kind," she answered. "Patient, understanding, gentle even. Everything, in short, that Duncan was not. He took me places—strolling in Hyde Park, shopping in Bond Street. To the theatre to see Sarah Siddons as Lady MacBeth. Oh, I did enjoy that. And the opera. I believe I was almost in love with him by the time he received his orders. Certainly he had rescued me from the oppression into which I had been sunk. For that I shall be eternally grateful to him."

Brie stared at her, wondering if this was the same

man who had abducted Brian Murdoch and ruthlessly had blackmailed her into marrying him.

"And yet how much more difficult to come back to Tal Carn after that. To a man like Duncan," she murmured, thinking out loud. No sooner were the words out than she blushed furiously. "I-I beg your pardon. I should not have said that."

"And yet it is no more than the truth." Cordelia's gaze mirrored an odd mixture of bitterness and pity. "Poor Duncan. I was, I am afraid, a sad trial to him. In addition to being plain and painfully inept socially, I could not even bear him the heir he so desperately wanted. The extremely generous dowry with which my father had purchased a husband for his eldest daughter was perhaps the greatest irony of all. Shortly after our marriage, the earl met his untimely demise, and the fortune and title went to Duncan. Had he waited only a few weeks, it would have been unnecessary for him to take a wife for whom he could never feel anything but contempt."

"Then he was a fool. And while I must regret the circumstances that precipitated it, I am yet glad that you are free of him," Brie declared emphatically, though it seemed a vice had clamped down hard on her vitals. Their situations, after all, were not so very different. Malvern, no less than Duncan, had, for whatever reasons, felt compelled to take a wife not of his own choosing. How long, she wondered bleakly, would it be before he came to detest her as thoroughly as Duncan had evidently detested Lady Cordelia?

Cordelia, regarding the girl with a great deal of discernment, stifled a smile.

"As no less am I," she admitted freely. "Indeed, I find I am inordinately pleased with myself. Since having left Tal Carn, I have embarked on a whole new existence. Not only have I decided never again to be intimidated by what life has to offer, but I am firmly resolved to embrace it. I am, as a matter of fact, to be married in a few months' time to a man, who for some inexplicable reason swears an undying affection for me."

Brie, after the first stunned moment, found the wits to wish the other woman happy and to demand the details of the impending event. The gentleman, for so he was, was a widower with two young children in need of a mother. A clergyman possessed of a more than comfortable living, he had little need of her fortune, which was to remain her own.

"We shall set up housekeeping in Coldeen, a short distance from Brighton. And you must promise me you will bring Malvern to come and see us."

Brie agreed after only a slight hesitation. After all, she could hardly speak for Malvern. Then, suggesting Cordelia might wish some time to rest before dinner, she started to excuse herself.

"Nonsense, my dear," spoke up her ladyship. "I am not so tired that I should not prefer to enjoy a comfortable coze with my hostess. Sit down, child, and tell me everything—all about the wedding and Malvern. And about Gullan Carn. How is the commodore? And Collin, is he still leading the girls a merry chase?"

"Indeed, yes." Brie laughed and glanced away to hide the fleeting shadow in her eyes. Collin had left Gullan Carn shortly after the wedding and had not been heard from since. "I begin to believe my brother will never settle down to a home and family. And as for Grandfather, he is as crusty as ever."

"You have always been very close, I believe. You

must miss them both very much."

"Yes, well, fortunately I have been kept too busy to grow homesick. And, after all, they are not so very far away that I cannot go for a visit as soon as things have settled down a bit. At present I have enough to do just learning how to be chatelaine of this house."

In spite of her best efforts, her voice was perhaps just a trifle too bright. She nearly started when Lady Cordelia leaned suddenly forward to place a hand on her arm.

"I do not mean to pry, Brigida," she said quietly. "But I get the distinct impression something is troubling you. Is it anything to do with the earl?"

Brie stared at her. Strange, but she had the oddest feeling that she could tell Lady Cordelia anything, rather as if she had known her all her life.

"It has everything to do with the earl," Brie admitted at last, following her instincts. Coming to her feet, she began to move restlessly about the room. "He is obsessed with the idea of finding Duncan's murderers. Did you know that? Or that he is pitting himself against the 'gentlemen,' who no doubt were responsible for his brother's death? It is a frightfully dangerous game he is playing. I am afraid for him, Cordelia. Afraid that he will end up like so many others who have considered themselves beyond the reach of the flaskers."

"Oh, my dear," exclaimed Lady Cordelia. "Indeed, I had no idea. But surely there is somone who can do something—talk some sense into him."

"No, I fear not. He is the most pigheaded, obstinate man I have ever met. And yet perhaps there *is* something *you* can do."

Brie hesitated, wondering if she had done the

right thing in revealing so much to a near stranger.

"Yes?" prodded the older woman, her gaze expectant on Brigida. "Pray tell me what it is. You must know I would do anything within my power to help."

"Very well then. I will tell you, but you must promise to keep everything I have said to yourself. I have witnessed strange goings-on in this house. Overheard things that were not meant for my ears. The first night I was here I saw someone with a dark lantern making signals from the tower. But when I tried to discover who it was, I found the door to the stairwell locked. I can only think there is some other way to the tower, if only I could find it."

"But of course. There is the secret stair. Unfortunately I cannot say where it is to be found, but I know it leads to the turret. And, if I am not mistaken, it is joined at some point by a hidden passage, which emerges somewhere beyond the outer wall—on the side overlooking the sea. I myself have never been in either, and I only know of them from something Duncan once mentioned in passing. But how can this possibly help Malvern? I should be greatly surprised if he did not already know of their existence."

"Oh, you may be sure of it," Brie said with such a fierce glint in her eye that Lady Cordelia was momentarily taken aback. "For if you must know, he has positively forbidden me to explore in the oldest part of the house."

"And quite understandably so," agreed Cordelia, thoroughly alarmed at what she quite accurately perceived as Brigida's meddlesome look. "They are extremely old and very likely hazardous. You will *heed* his warning, child, and make no attempt to find them?"

Lady Cordelia appeared so sincerely distressed at the notion that Brie felt compelled to reassure her.

"Oh, you needn't worry," she said lightly. "I am far too busy to be prowling around looking for secret stairways. Which reminds me. I still have a great many things to see to before dinner. I pray you will excuse me. If there is anything you need, you know you have only to ring."

She was already at the door and out before Lady Cordelia could draw breath to protest or to question how knowledge of the secret stair could possibly help Malvern. Disappointed that Cordelia could not reveal the entrance to the stairway, Brie directed her footsteps downstairs to see how the task of restoring the ballroom to its former splendor was progressing.

No sooner had she reached the stone apse than Griffith called out to her from the hall below.

"Milady. I beg your pardon, but there has been a disturbance belowstairs. An elderly man of questionable appearance, obviously of the lower orders. He insists he will not leave until he has seen you. Shall I have one of the footmen escort him from the premises?"

Brie's heart skipped a beat.

"You will do no such thing, Griffith. Have him brought at once to me in the conservatory. Oh, and, Griffith. You will of course treat him with the courtesy due an invited guest in this house, will you not?"

She could feel the man's disapproval behind the careful impassivity of his face. "As you wish, milady," he intoned, bending stiffly at the waist.

As soon as he had vanished around the corner, Brie gathered up her skirts and fairly flew down the stairs. Eagerly she made her way to the conservatory, which overlooked an enclosed garden at the back of the house. She was standing with her back to the door, her gaze fixed, but unseeing, on the freshly budding roses outside, when Griffith escorted her visitor into her presence.

Turning, she favored the butler with a cool nod.

"Thank you, Griffith," she said dismissingly. "That will be all."

No sooner had the butler withdrawn, however, than she had dropped all pretence of the grand lady. In an instant the old, roguish dimple had peeped forth and she was crossing to greet her caller with unaffected eagerness.

"Malcolm," she exclaimed. "I never thought to hear from you so soon. Did you do it? Pray tell me you have got it with you."

The keen blue eyes exhibited a decided twinkle.

"I have it here, Miss Brie, or I'd not've come all this way."

Dinner that night was an unusually merry affair. It was the first evening since Brie's arrival at Tal Carn that the entire company was present around the dining table, and everyone seemed in a mood to make the most of it. Malvern, striking in a cutaway coat of blue superfine over a white marcella waistcoat and dove gray pantaloons, was clearly disposed to be as engaging as he had been that fateful night at Gullan Carn. With an effortlessness of manner, he set them all their ease, even going so far as to entertain them with any number of *on dits* about persons of note with whom he had become acquainted in London. Devin Drake, however, was not to be outdone. Exerting himself to charm the ladies, and

Brie in particular, he maintained a steady stream of light repartee to which even Lady Cordelia responded with a dry wit and calm good humor that was very greatly to her credit. Only James Pembroke maintained a quiet reserve, making no attempt to join in the conversation except to reply when spoken to.

Brie, sitting directly to his left, was moved to lean near at one point and inquire if he were not feeling quite the thing.

Startled, he glanced up at her through the thick lenses of his spectacles.

"I-I beg your pardon, milady?" he stammered, apparently jolted out of his thoughts. "I'm afraid I was woolgathering. What was it you said?"

"I said, sir, that you seem uncommonly quiet this evening. Is there anything amiss? Perhaps you are not feeling well."

"No. No, I'm fine, thank you." Seemingly nervously, he glanced around at the others at the table, and observing that their attention was all on Lady Cordelia, who was relating a humorous anecdote concerning a recent visit paid to Brighton by the prince regent, he appeared to relax ever so slightly. "I'm afraid I'm not very good at social gatherings, milady."

"Are you not? But I cannot see that this would fall in that category, sir. Those gathered here tonight are family, surely."

"Your family, ma'am, not mine," Pembroke shot back at her. Then immediately he seemed to recall himself. When he looked at her again, she could read nothing in the controlled mask of his face. "I beg your pardon, milady," he said stiffly. "You were only trying to be kind. But you see, I am the eldest of seven children. My father, who was a loyal officer in the King's Navy, was struck down off the coast of Spain. I was forced to seek employment to support the family he left behind. Something that you and the others at this table would scarcely understand."

"I see," murmured Brie, feeling the bitterness in the man. "How fortunate, then, that you should find yourself in the employ of my husband. He is, I believe, a fair man, and generous where it is warranted. Perhaps if you were to discuss with him the possibility of employment in a position elsewhere. One that offered greater opportunity for advancement? He is not, after all, without influence in London."

"No doubt you mean that to be kind," Pembroke cut in, his expression peculiarly hard, "and I thank you for your apparent concern. However, I am his lordship's private secretary, and I accepted long ago that that is all I can ever hope to be."

Turning back to his plate with a pointedness that was not lost on Brigida, he left her little choice but to drop the subject. Nor did she make any further attempts to engage him in conversation, but left him to enjoy his meal in silence.

When the sweetmeats and jellies had gone the rounds, Brie dutifully rose to signal it was time the ladies retired to the withdrawing room.

"I, for one, feel moved to protest," drawled the earl, much to everyone's surprise. "Rather than be deprived such scintillating company, I should prefer to forgo the lesser pleasures of brandy and cigars. Especially if we may prevail upon Lady Cordelia to play for us."

Devin, not to be outdone, was quick to rise to the occasion.

"Here, here," he seconded the motion.

Brie, meeting the earl's eyes across the length of the dinner table, felt herself momentarily covered with confusion.

"Perhaps, milord," she answered, quickly recovering herself, "you need be denied neither pleasure nor company. While I cannot presume to speak for Lady Cordelia, I myself have no objection to cigar smoke or brandy."

It transpired that Lady Cordelia had no objection either, and with the exception of Pembroke, who excused himself, claiming an early morning awaited him, the entire company removed to the music room.

Brigida, settling in a wing chair near the fireplace, was keenly aware when Malvern crossed with apparent deliberation to stand nearby, an elbow propped negligently on the mantelpiece. Indeed, it was only with the greatest effort that she was able to keep her mind off the slim, compelling figure, which she could see all too clearly out of the corner of her eye. Nor did it help her equilibrium to have Devin Drake sprawled on the divan, his back against the arm of the couch so that he was partially facing her. Steadily sipping at his brandy, he studied her clean-cut profile over the rim of his glass.

Lady Cordelia played with a real talent, producing one piece after another as the mood hit her, until at last a lively country tune prompted Devin to set his glass down. Unfolding himself from the couch, he crossed with cool deliberation to Brigida.

"Milady," he said, bowing with exaggerated gallantry. "I have been watching you, with the result that I am become convinced you entertain a wish to dance." A gleam of laughter sprang to his eyes at her incredulous look. "Your foot, ma'am, betrays you." His amusement broadened to a grin as Brigida, made thus aware that her toe was tapping to the music, hastily stilled the offending member. "Now then, may I not have the pleasure of this dance?"

Brie gazed askance at the devil in his eyes. He was a rogue, but he was a most engaging one when he chose to be. Laughing, she gave him her hand.

"Oh, very well, sir," she replied. "I suppose it would do no harm to humor you just this once."

She was breathless, and her cheeks glowed with pleasure when at length Devin escorted her back to her chair. She was not, however, to be given time to catch her breath. Devin, who had enjoyed his dance immensely, was not ready yet to relinquish his lovely partner. Retaining her hand in his, he glanced over his shoulder at Cordelia.

"Brava, dear lady." He applauded the musician. "That was marvelous. And now I think a waltz is in order. The evening, you must agree, would hardly be complete without it."

"Quite so," murmured a low, thrilling voice at Devin's shoulder. "Which is why I really think I must pull rank on you, Cousin."

Brie sensed Devin stiffen and felt her mouth go suddenly dry. Indeed, for the barest instant it seemed that Devin would take exception to his cousin's interference, but almost immediately he seemed to think better of it. Summoning a mocking smile, he bowed. "I relinquish the field, milord—under protest." Deliberately he looked at Brigida. "With your usual good luck, Cousin, you have netted a prize most men never dream of possessing. I wonder if you have the least notion how truly fortunate you are."

The earl's answering smile was edged with steel.

"Enough, I assure you," he said, "to make certain no harm should ever come to her." Coolly he turned his back on Devin, who was left no choice but to retreat. "And now, my dear Cordelia, if you would be so kind? I believe you were about to play a waltz."

Cordelia, who had been observing the exchange with something of apprehension, breathed an audible sigh of relief.

"Yes, so I was."

"Oh, but — but I couldn't possibly," Brie stammered. "I-I have never learned the waltz."

"Then, my love, it is perhaps time you did, is it not?" Smiling ironically, he held out his hand to her. "Come now, there is nothing to fear. I promise I shall not eat you."

A reluctant burble of laughter rose to her lips at that.

"Very well, milord. But do not say that I have not warned you."

Gamely, she placed her hand in his, determined to make the best of it. She was hardly prepared, however, to experience a sudden shock, like a lightning bolt, as her waist was encircled by a lean, masculine arm. Feeling the blood, hot in her cheeks, she waited for what would come next.

"No, no, my dear," admonished the earl. With his hand beneath her chin, he gently forced her head up. "Never look down at your feet. Your eyes are far too lovely to be denied your partner."

Brigida's breath caught in her throat as, half defiantly, she looked up and felt herself drawn into the unfathomable depths of his eyes. For a moment he held her, until at last, strangely, she felt the resistance melting from her. A faint smile touched his lips. "Yes," he murmured, "that is more like. You have only to trust me, *enfant*."

Never before had Brie experienced anything like this, her first waltz in the arms of the earl. Malvern, gifted with the natural suppleness and grace of the born athlete, swung her effortlessly through the dance steps. She felt melded to his strength, separate and yet one with him. It was a form of communication far more sublime than words, and when at length the music came to an end, she felt herself momentarily cut adrift from the rest of the world. Long after the final notes had died away, she still stood within the circle of his arm, her eyes riveted with a sort of wonder on his.

It was not until Cordelia gave a gentle cough that the moment was finally lost.

"It has been a most delightful evening," said that lady, getting up from the piano seat, "but I'm afraid I really must beg you all to excuse me. It has been a rather long day."

Brought back to reality, Brie blushed in confusion and dropped her eyes from Malvern's.

"But of course. I-I suppose it is getting rather late, she managed, torn between relief and disappointment that the evening had perforce to come to an end. "No doubt it is time I, too, retired."

She had reached her rooms and Fionna was helping her out of her green silk evening gown when she heard the low rumble of voices from the earl's adjoining suite. Only then did she realize with a start that she had forgotten Malcolm's visit and the purpose behind it. She had meant to arrange a meeting with Malvern before dinner with the intent of giving him the thing Malcolm had brought, and now it was too late. Oh, it was too bad of her. How *could* such a thing have slipped her mind! If only she dared take it to him now.

To her dismay she felt her pulse quicken at the notion. And why should she not? whispered a small, insidious voice. She was his wife, was she not? There could be little impropriety in the Countess of Malvern's seeking an audience with her husband, no matter what the time of night.

On sudden impulse, she dismissed Fionna when she had finished helping her mistress into a russet night dress and matching peignoir trimmed in swansdown. No sooner was she alone, however, than her nerve faltered.

It had all seemed so simple when she had first conceived the idea that afternoon after her encounter with Malvern in the west wing. But now she was not at all certain how he would take her meddling. He was so damnably proud. Very possibly he would resent her for it. And certainly he was more than apt to misconstrue her motives in choosing to summon him to her bedroom at such an hour and in such a costume. No, she told herself. It were better to wait for a more propitious time.

Vaguely dissatisfied with herself and finding that she was not in the least drowsy, she prowled fitfully about her room. At last it occurred to her that a book might help lull her to sleep. Changing her peignoir for a dressing gown designed more for warmth and practicality than for fashion, she took up a lighted candle and slipped into the hall. Moments later found her entering the earl's study.

The shadows cast by the flickering candlelight danced grotesquely about the room. Involuntarily, Brie shivered and considered lighting some of the lamps. Then disgusted with herself for feeling childishly frightened of the half dark, she resolutely discarded the notion. She would take only a moment or two to pick out a volume and then she would return to her bed.

Thinking to herself that it hardly mattered, after all, which book she took, she moved to the shelves behind the earl's desk and reached for a slender volume bound in leather. Upon discovering it was a collection of religious sermons, she grimaced wryly. Ah, well, the less stimulating, the better, she told herself and tucked the book under her arm.

The click of the door latch caught her unawares. With a gasp she whirled about, dousing the candle in her hurry. Plunged into darkness, she listened with a pounding heart as the door was shoved open. Prompted by an instinct she did not understand, she crouched down behind the desk just as the glow of a lantern filled the room. With bated breath she listened to footsteps cross the room, heard a creak of woodwork, and a soft susurrous of sound. Then the light flickered and was gone.

Hesitantly, Brie pulled herself up and groped her way to the fireplace, where the remnants of an earlier fire still smoldered. Trembling with excitement, she bent to light her candle among the glowing embers then made her way to the back of the study. Whoever it was had exited somewhere there. Yet on her earlier visit to the book room, she had seen no evidence of a door. Ergo, she reasoned, there must be a movable panel, beyond which, she doubted not, lay a secret stairway.

After several minutes of fruitless groping along the panel for some sign of a seam, she was about to give up in frustration. If there was a door there, it was deucedly well camouflaged.

"The devil!" she muttered, leaning her hand wearily against the embossed figure of a rose in one of the square panels. To her surprise, she felt it give way. The next instant a large section of paneling slid back to reveal a gaping hole, and, beyond, the winding steps of a spiral staircase.

Without pausing to weigh the possible risks, Brie lifted the candle high and stepped through.

Curious to see where the stairway emerged below, she decided to put the tower off for a later exploration. Besides, she little wished to encounter the mysterious prowler. Doubtless he had gone above to make more of his bothersome signals.

The stairs went only a short way before they emerged in a dungeon, whose original purpose had no doubt been for the storage of supplies in case of a siege. Some later earl had evidently transformed it into a wine cellar. The remnants of old wooden casks and a few bottles covered in dust were all that remained, suggesting that it had subsequently been abandoned, perhaps even forgotten. At the far end of the cell was a heavy wooden door left partially ajar. The secret tunnel, which Cordelia had said emerged beyond the outer wall, she thought, and started toward it.

Espying an oil lantern, hanging from a peg, she took it down and lit it with the stub of her candle. As the light flared, she caught sight of something else—a small casket of heavy wrought iron. Although it was undeniably old and battered and though it, like everything else, was covered in dust, she could not help but note that the cobwebs clinging to it had obviously been disturbed. As if someone had recently lifted the lid, she thought, her curiosity piqued. Setting the lamp down on the floor beside her, she opened the lid to find a purse, plump with coins, and a single scrap of paper bearing the cryptic message: "Tomorrow at midnight."

Frowning, she put everything back again and had reached for the lid when her blood ran cold at the distant rumble of voices beyond the half-open door. Good God, someone was coming! Her heart hammering beneath her breast, she closed the lid and, lighting her candle, doused the lantern. The next instant she had fled into the stairwell. Indeed, she did not pause until she had reached the study and sealed the secret panel.

It had been close. She had escaped being seen by only a bare second or two, but at least now she had enough to go to Malvern with what she knew. The smugglers were to meet tomorrow at midnight, and she would make sure there was a welcoming committee on hand to catch them in the act of whatever it was they were up to.

The clock on the mantel was striking the hour of two when she slipped into her room. Shoving the door to, she leaned her forehead against it, her eyes closed, as she sought to still the pounding of her heart. At last, drawing a deep breath, she straightened and turned.

A movement glimpsed out of the corner of her eye froze her into immobility. Breathlessly, she watched a slender figure unfold itself from one of the wing chairs.

"So, my love," came a soft, chilling voice. "You have decided to put in an appearance after all. I was beginning to think you intended to make a night of it."

Brie nearly sagged with relief.

"Malvern," she breathed. "You nearly frightened me out of half a year's growth."

"Indeed, madam? Then I beg your pardon. And now perhaps you would be good enough to explain just exactly why I should find you stealing to your bed in the dead of night."

Chapter Fifteen

Brie's eyes flashed with resentment. His was no request, but a demand, and one with the ring of accusation about it. What was more, he had obviously been waiting for her, and from the looks of the thin lips and hard bulge of the jaw, he was not in the best of moods. Indeed, a single glance at the grim cast of his countenance was enough to put her instantly on her guard.

"Well, my dear?" he prodded when it seemed no answer was to be forthcoming. "Surely I do not find you at a loss for words? It is, after all, a simple enough question. Where have you been for these past two hours?"

"Very well," she stated, feeling her way. "If you must know, I couldn't sleep." Deliberately she blew her candle out and set it down on the lowboy before turning around to face him once more. "It occurred to me that reading a book might help. So I went to the study to look for one."

The earl's smile was anything but encouraging.

"But naturally, and once there, you spent two hours browsing. How unfortunate that you found nothing to interest you in all that time."

"I-I beg your pardon?"

"The book, my love," he retorted in acerbic tones. "The one which was to lull you to sleep. It would appear you have returned empty-handed."

Brie blushed furiously, stung by his sarcasm. The book of sermons—she had forgotten all about it. She must have dropped it in all the excitement.

His lordship, contributing her heightened color to something entirely different, lifted a single arrogant eyebrow.

"Come now," he drawled coldly before she could find the words to tell him what had really happened, "I should have expected something more imaginative from you. If you are going to keep assignations, my dear, then you must learn to contrive your explanations beforehand. How unlike my cousin not to instruct you in that particular."

"Your cousin," Brie echoed incredulously. "But what has he to do with any of this?"

Malvern's laugh was singularly devoid of humor.

"Enough, Brigida," he said. "It is a trifle late to play the innocent."

At last the terrible significance of his words sank home. "Good God. You think that Devin and—and I . . ."

"I think there is little point in your denying it. It is, after all, what my cousin intended from the moment he saw you and realized I should never be content with a marriage of convenience. Dammit, Brigida. I found his note, entreating you to meet him. You were careless enough to drop it in your hurry to keep your assignation."

Contemptuously, Malvern flung the crumpled sheet of paper at her feet. Brie stared at it, stunned into speechlessness. Obviously Devin had slipped the note under her door while she was gone. Still, if Malvern could believe her so vile as to be capable of betraying him — good God, of betraying herself — then he would hardly accept her word she had never seen it before.

"You are quite right," she said at last in a voice that sounded hollow, even in her own ears. "There would seem little point in denying it. You appear to have all the evidence, do you not." Sickened, she started to turn away. "Now if you will excuse me. I find suddenly that I am really very tired."

His hand on her wrist yanked her back again.

"Oh, no, my love," he answered in icy tones. "I am not finished with you yet."

Shaking with anger and unbearable hurt, Brie felt something suddenly snap inside. Turning, she slapped him hard across the face.

With a terrible sinking feeling in the pit of her stomach, she beheld the marks of her fingers, red, against his skin, but she would not back down, could not stop herself had she wanted to.

"You — you are contemptible!" she cried, hardly knowing what she said, yet wanting to hurt him as much as he had hurt her. "It were better never to have been born than to have been forced into a marriage with a man I can only despise."

In awed fascination she watched the thin lips curl in a smile that seemed filled with bitter self-mockery.

"No doubt. And yet I think you will find I am the better bargain than the man you would choose as your lover."

"Perhaps," she flung furiously back at him. "But at least the choosing would be mine."

She almost quailed then before the terrible leap of his eyes. She had gone too far. She knew it with awful certainty, but it was too late. She could not snatch the words back now.

"If it is a lover you want," he uttered in a voice that sent chills down her spine, "then you will have one. But at least I shall have the satisfaction of knowing any heir you might bear me is mine."

Without warning, he let go of her wrist and, grasping her robe at the front, nearly ripped it from her. A flame leaped in his eyes at sight of her loveliness, revealingly clad in shimmering silk.

"Stop it!" White-faced and shaking, Brie backed before him. "I am not one of your lights of love to be treated so."

"No. You are my wife. A pity you apparently need reminding of that."

Brigida shuddered as she stared into pitiless black orbs. With a sense of helplessness, she watched him come toward her.

"D-don't do this," she whispered, forcing herself to meet his eyes. "I-I swear I shall never forgive you if you do this."

It was useless. He was calloused and hard, merciless in what he conceived as her betrayal. At the last her courage failed her, and she tried to pull away. Brutally he caught her.

A cry was torn from Brie's lips as he dragged her arm relentlessly behind her and pinned it in the small of her back. "I did try to warn you what Devin was," he uttered, his eyes flaying her with bitter condemnation. "But you, my little tart, had to find out the truth of it for yourself. And now you are about to pay the price of your education."

"Malvern, no," Brigida gasped. "It was not like that at all."

But already it was too late. Ruthlessly he forced his mouth down over hers.

A cry of rage sounded deep in her throat. She

struggled in his grasp. Not like this, she thought furiously. It must not happen like this. To her mounting horror she was helpless against the traitorous response of her body to his touch. A fire kindled in her depths and spread outward through her veins. Still, she fought, silently and with all the fierce passion of her soul, till at last her strength was spent and she sagged in his embrace.

She was half swooning when at last he released her. Bending low, he caught her beneath the knees and shoulders and swept her up in his arms.

For a moment he stared down into sea-green eyes, huge and unblinking in the pale oval of her face. Fleetingly something like bafflement flickered in his gaze. Then his face hardened. Cynically, he smiled.

"You belong to me, my deceitful little temptress," he murmured, his voice strangely husky. Deliberately he carried her to the bed and laid her on it. "It is time you were made to realize that."

Refusing to think, afraid to feel, she lay rigidly as he quickly disrobed. She was trembling when at last he came to her. In awed fascination she beheld his lean strength, the muscled hardness of his shoulders and chest, the raven mat of hair tapering to a V over the lean torso and firm, flat belly. He was beautiful. And yet there were scars, too, the mute record of a man who has flirted more than once with death and suffered horribly for it. She felt an irrational desire to smooth away the hurt, to minister to him till the lines of bitterness had been eased from his face.

Then he was beside her on the bed, and the nearness of his lean, strong body awakened a terrible ache within her breast. Dazed, she stared up into the steely glitter of his eyes and knew she was lost. She was his wife, and he would take her, but he would do so out of a false sense of injured pride. Never would she forgive him.

Then her thoughts scattered as he lowered his head to her.

He was merciless in his lovemaking, arousing her with the practiced ease of one who was no stranger to love. His kiss was cruel and demanding, his caress unrelenting. With his hand he stroked her, deliberately, sensuously, until she felt the resistance melting from her body. She shuddered, helpless against the flood of sensations sweeping over and through her. She writhed beneath him, wondering what was happening to her. His lips left hers to begin a feverish journey over her cheek, her eyes, her throat. Mindlessly she groaned and whispered his name. And when at last he pulled the gown up over her hips, she lifted herself to help him, glad to be free of the confining fabric, wanting to be near him. Irresistibly, as if possessed of a mind of their own, her arms stole up around his neck and clung there.

His mouth, molding itself to the pink thrust of her breast, awakened sigh upon sigh of pleasure. Compelled by a need she did not understand, she pressed urgently to him, felt the hard thrust of his manhood against her. His hand found the moist warmth between her legs, and a gasp burst from her lips. Never had she known anything like the molten fire that consumed her then. With a groan she arched against him, wanting him, loving him with an aching need she had never known she possessed. And at last he took her.

The sharp burst of pain as he thrust through the virginal membrane was as nothing compared to the fire that burned within her. She cried out as she felt him go suddenly still, a groan like a curse seemingly wrenched from his depths. In anguish she arched upward against him. "Brigida," he groaned, the muscles of his neck and shoulders standing out in ridges. Then he was moving, carrying her with him on a cresting wave of passion, striving toward some unknown release. And when at last it came, she cried out with the bittersweet agony of it. She shuddered as she felt his seed burst forth within her, felt shaken to the core as wave upon wave of pleasure rippled through her, until at last she collapsed, weak and trembling, beneath him.

"Brigida," he murmured huskily into the soft curve of her neck. "Brigida, love."

For a time he remained thus, his breath harsh in his throat, and when at length he raised himself up on one elbow to look at her, she could not bear to meet his gaze. He cursed at the sight of tears rolling unchecked down her cheeks.

"Dammit, Brigida," he uttered hoarsely. "I never meant to hurt you. Why, in God's name, did you lie to me?"

"I did not lie!" she choked, turning her head away from him. "Please. Just go away."

"The devil! I am not such a fool that I do not know when I have bedded a virgin. You were never with Devin tonight."

It was a statement, not a question, and at last she looked at him, her eyes bitterly accusing.

"I never said that I was."

Malvern's arm tightened with a convulsive leap of muscle. If she had meant to punish him for what he had done, she saw in the swift blaze of pained enlightenment that she had succeeded admirably. He pulled away, as if he could no longer bear the sight of her, and abruptly left the bed.

Feeling sick inside, she watched him dress. And when at last he stood, ready to leave her, she could not summon the words to call him back again. Pausing beside the bed, he did not look at her, but stared straight ahead, his profile seemingly carved from granite.

"I do not expect you to forgive me for having misjudged you," he said. "Nor do I excuse myself. But what came of it, I cannot regret." At last he turned unfathomable eyes on her. "Whatever else comes from this night, you belong to me, Brigida. And only me. Remember that. The next time you must come to me, my love, and there must be no secrets between us."

Without waiting for her to answer, he turned and strode quickly from the room.

Brie lay unmoving, unable to stop the tears streaming silently down her cheeks. There would never be a next time. It was over before ever it had begun, the love that might have been theirs, the happiness. The harm had been done. He had taken her, not out of love, but out of terrible anger and the need to punish. The knowledge was bitter gall to her.

Brie came sluggishly awake to the sound of birdsong and the sun streaming through her window. It must be close to midmorning, she realized, wondering that Fionna had not come to rouse her from her bed hours ago. Dully she thought of all the tasks awaiting her. The invitations to the ball had gone out, and there were still innumerable last-minute details to be completed, though in her present state, she could not bring her thoughts to bear on a single one of them. Instead, she lay abed, reluctant to face what lay before her—reluctant to face Malvern.

Good God, she did not know how she could bear even to look at him. She suffered a sharp pang at the thought that he would be distant and cold, a far cry from the charming nobleman who had waltzed with her only the evening before. Oh, why had he to spoil everything, just when she was beginning to think it was not such a bad thing to be the Countess of Malvern? Suddenly she groaned and, clutching the pillow to her breast, buried her face in it. The devil, she thought. Who was she trying to fool? Last night had changed nothing, except to grant her a glimpse of what life could be if only her love were returned! Long ago he had conquered her heart, and nothing he could do would ever change that.

And then it came to her that perhaps it was not too late to retrieve the happiness that might have been theirs. He had said that the next time she must come to him and that there must be no secrets between them. And, indeed, there must not be.

Tonight at midnight the smugglers were to meet in the cellar below, for what other meaning could the message have had? No doubt they were to make the final run, and this would be her last chance to discover the identity of the man she had overheard with Rory in the ballroom. Indeed, unless she managed somehow to catch him red-handed, she very much feared he would succeed not only in escaping unscathed, but in laying the blame on her brother, for she was no closer than before to knowing who he was. No matter how little she might like to admit it, this was one thing she could not carry off alone. She had to have help.

Oh, if only Collin had not been so foolish as to make himself scarce at the very time she needed him so desperately! And what if it had been Rory Gale's doing that he was gone off to the Lord only knew where? She trembled at the thought and knew that that was only one more reason why she could no longer keep what she knew to herself. Indeed, she must tell Malvern! She saw it all very clearly. No matter how distasteful in the wake of his own lack of faith, she knew she had no choice but to lay the whole before him and trust that this once he might be made to believe her.

Her mind made up, she flung out of bed and rang for her maid.

She was pacing impatiently when Fionna made her appearance.

"Be 'ee awake at last, mistress?" queried the maidservant, a knowing grin on her round face. "His lordship left orders belowstairs that 'ee wasn't to be disturbed."

"Did he," Brie murmured, assuming an indifference she was far from feeling. Good grief, no doubt the entire household was aware that the earl had bedded his bride during the night.

"Aye. Right before he rode out with Mr. Drake, he did," said Fionna. "Now what was 'ee wantin' me to lay out for 'ee, Miss Brie? 'Ee's yet to try the sprig muslin. Or the bronze shagreen."

But Brie was not listening.

"You say he rode out with—with Mr. Drake? When?"

"Just after he come down for breakfast, it were. Maybe an hour or so ago. Why, Miss Brie! What is it? 'Ee's white as a sheet."

Shaken, Brie turned away.

"I-It's nothing." For a moment she stood indecisively. Then suddenly she squared her shoulders. "Lay out my blue riding habit, Fionna. And hurry. I must go to Gullan Carn to see Grandfather."

Thirty minutes later, Brie, having hurriedly bathed and dressed, scribbled a note to Malvern and slipped it under his door. Then snatching up her riding crop, she hastened downstairs. She was on the point of congratulating herself on having achieved the entryway without encountering a soul when a low cough sounded significantly behind her.

"I beg your pardon, milady," intoned a voice, unmistakable for its nasal quality.

The devil, thought Brie. She might have known Griffith would be skulking somewhere about. The butler never missed anything that was going on in the house.

"Yes, Griffith?" she queried, hard put to hide her impatience. "Was there something you wanted?"

"No, milady, not exactly. It simply occurred to me to wonder when we might expect your return—in case his lordship should inquire," he was judicious to add.

The smug, square features of the butler were as carefully impassive as ever, and yet Brie had the distinct feeling that he was fishing for something.

"You may inform his lordship and anyone else who might inquire that I have gone to Gullan Carn. You may look for me in time for dinner. Now, was there anything else?"

"No, milady. I shall so inform the staff. No doubt the work on the ballroom will proceed apace. And, as I am sure you must already know, the men from the village arrived early this morning. Not having been informed to what purpose they were to be employed, I took the liberty of setting them to work pruning the hedges. I hope that meets with your approval."

Inwardly Brie groaned. Griffith knew very well that she had not realized the men had arrived. She had forgotten all about them, *and* the plans to strip the walls in the withdrawing room in preparation for new wall hangings. Well, it would just have to wait. She had more important matters to attend.

"Thank you, Griffith. I do most heartily approve." Moved by a sudden impulse, she placed her hand on the butler's sleeve. "I know we have not always seen eye to eye on things, but I have come to realize that I can rely on you to keep things running smoothly. For that I do thank you, Griffith."

Unexpectedly, she thought she detected a slight fissure in the man's stony façade. Indeed, for the barest instant she was almost certain she glimpsed a flicker of surprise in the normally expressionless eyes.

However, all he said in reply was, "Very good, milady," and, inclining his head, moved sedately past her in order to open the door for her.

In the norm, Brigida would have derived keen enjoyment from the ride across the down and through the deer park to Gullan Carn, but not today. In her morbid fancy, she visualized Malvern in some secluded place facing his cousin over drawn pistols. Indeed, she could think of no other reason why they should have left the castle together. Bitterly she cursed her stupid pride. If anything happened to either one of them, it would be her fault. Oh, *why* had she not made it plain to Malvern last night that she had not the least interest in Devin, nor ever could have? With all of her heart she wished she had told him about her excursion to the cellar.

Perhaps it was little wonder, then, that she should arrive at Gullan Carn in an overwrought state. Leaving her mount in the care of a stableboy, she went straight to the house where she was informed by Fionna's sister that the commodore was in his study.

"Gramfer," she exclaimed, bursting in on her grandsire without waiting to be announced. "Oh, Gramfer, I have been such a fool."

She stopped, her cheeks flaming, as she realized the commodore, seated behind his great oak desk, was not alone in the room. With a sudden sinking sensation in the pit of her stomach she beheld her brother, looking unnaturally pale and strained, and Rory Gale, sprawled carelessly in her grandfather's easy chair.

"Collin," she said. "So, you've come home at last. And where the devil have you been all this time?"

"Yes, Collin," said Rory, not bothering to get up, " 'fess up. It's damned inconsiderate of you to keep us in suspense."

The commodore, who appeared anything but gratified by this new intrusion, favored the squire's son with a fulminating eye.

"I'll thank 'ee to keep your nose out of what doesn't concern 'ee, Rory Gale," he growled. "This is betwixt me and me grandson. An' as for you, mistress. 'Ee'll keep a civil tongue in your head, or I'll know the reason why. And now that I've made meself clear, perhaps you, sir, would be kind enough to explain what in hellsfire 'ee's been up to."

Collin, thus finding himself once more the cynosure of all eyes, summoned a ghost of his old roguish grin.

"But of course, Grandfather. I never meant to keep 'ee in the dark. The truth of the matter is that I was kidnapped and have only just managed to escape."

"Kidnapped!" exclaimed the commodore in concert with Brie's "But why? Who could have done such a thing?" Indeed, it was some time before Collin could get a word in edgewise. It then transpired that on the night of Brie's wedding he had been taken unawares on his return from the inn at the Crossroads.

"I don't know who they were or why they nabbed me. There were two of them, one a giant of a man with the strength of a Goliath. And the other more my size. They wore masks and didn't say much, except to assure me that so long as I behaved myself, they'd do me no harm."

"Well, from the looks of 'ee, they kept their word," the commodore observed gruffly. " 'Ee doesn't appear much the worse for wear."

"Oh, you may be sure of it, Grandfather," replied Collin wryly. "Except for the fact that I was forced to spend the last se'ennight in a cellar, I was treated with all the courtesy commonly afforded a gentleman. The wine, I might add, was of excellent quality, as was the food. Nor were the furnishings anything to complain about. Had they provided me with a gaming companion, I might have been content to stay longer. As it was, I took the first opportunity that presented itself to knock my guard over the head and make my escape. That was this morning, following breakfast. You may imagine my surprise when I discovered I had been imprisoned in a deserted cottage less than a mile from Gullan Carn."

"And your captors?" demanded Brie, frowning. "Did you never see the faces of either of them?"

"I'm afraid I was in no mood to tarry when freedom lay before me. Not even to unmask the villain who had been careless enough to turn his back on me. I didn't stop running till I spotted Rory riding toward me on his way here."

"You were a sight for sore eyes, Collin lad," Rory admitted soulfully. "I'd begun to believe you'd fallen to a pressgang and were on your way to fight the French in a king's ship. You can have no idea how relieved I am to find you still on Cornish soil."

No, thought Brie, hardly able to conceal her disgust at Gale's duplicity, but *she* could hazard a pretty accurate guess. Without Collin, the blackguards would have been hard-pressed to come up with a scapegoat for their skulduggery.

"We must all be grateful that you are safely home," she said. "But the fact remains that we haven't the least notion why any of this has occurred. Until we do, we must assume they may try it again."

"Aye, the lass is right," rumbled the commodore, slamming the side of a fist down hard against the desktop. "The magistrate must be informed of these events at once. Until the matter is cleared up, lad, ee'll confine thyself to quarters."

"Oh, no, 'ee don't," protested Collin. "I've not escaped one prison only to be thrust into another, thank 'ee."

Brie groaned inwardly as the commodore's face took on a forbidding hue.

"Ee'll do as I say, boy," he thundered. "For your own protection, or I'll— I'll . . ."

"Thee'll do what, Grandfather?" Collin cut in, a firmness about his jaw that Brie had never seen there before. " 'Ee's wrong, sir. I'm not a boy anymore to be ordered around. I'm head of my father's house, and no one but me says what I will or will not do. Since I am presently of a mind to get blind, stinking drunk, I shall ask 'ee to excuse me." Stalking to the door, he paused and glanced over his shoulder at his friend, who had been observing the scene with a great deal of interest. "Well?" he demanded. "Be 'ee coming with me?"

Carelessly, Rory unfolded himself from the couch. "Wouldn't miss it, old boy," he said, and, bowing to the red-faced commodore and the countess, followed Collin out.

For a stunned moment, it seemed the commodore would go into an apoplectic fit. Then Brie, deeming it time to intervene, stepped toward him.

"He is right, Gramfer," she said quietly. "You can no longer order him about as if he were one of your sailors. Besides, he is not likely to be caught off guard again. And in a fight, you must know he is perfectly capable of taking care of himself. It was you, after all, who taught him."

"Aye, so I did," admitted the commodore grudgingly. "Little good though it may do him if he has not the sense enough to stay away from the gaming hells and taverns. A man in his cups is no match against the cunning of cutthroats and murderers."

"No, especially when they assume the guise of a friend."

"Eh? What's that?"

Brie, who had been merely thinking out loud, was quick to cover her lapse.

"Nothing, dearest Gramfer," she said, leaning down to give him a buss on the cheek. "And don't you worry about Collin. I'll go and talk to him."

She found him in his rooms, putting the finishing touches on a fresh neckcloth.

"Collin, thank heavens," she exclaimed, hastily closing the door behind her. "I was afraid you had gone off before I could talk to you. Are you alone? Where is Rory?"

"Gone downstairs to fetch a fresh decanter of brandy. But no matter. Brie, I warn 'ee, there's nothing 'ee can say that'll change me mind. I can bloody well take care of meself."

"Which is just what I told Gramfer. In any case, that's not why I'm here. I have discovered who is behind it—the smuggling, Duncan's murder, selling information to the French—everything. Or at least I shall have done after tonight—*if* you will agree to help me. Oh, Collin, I have made a terrible mull of everything. You must come back with me to Tal Carn and help me to set it all to rights again."

Collin, at hearing such an admission from his normally indomitable sister, was shaken to say the least.

"Brie, lass," he exclaimed, grasping her in alarm by the shoulders, "forgive me. I was only thinking of meself. Just tell me what I can do to help."

It all came out then, about the signal lights and her discovery in the castle dungeon, and about Malvern and Devin and her fear that even now one or both of them might lie dead or wounded—and finally about the men she had overheard talking in the ballroom.

"It was Rory," she said. "I recognized his voice right off, and then, later, I peeked over the banister and saw him. Collin, I heard him agree to help set you up to take the blame for everything."

Collin looked at her as if she had lost her mind. A hard bark of laughter seemed forced from him.

"Dammit, Brie," he choked, "this is nothing to joke about. Bloody hell, we've known Rory all of our lives."

"I know," murmured Brie, feeling miserable at having to be the one to break the news. "I wish it were all a jest, but believe me, it isn't."

She winced as he turned abruptly away.

"No, 'tis all a mistake. It couldn't have been Rory. Or, if it was, then 'ee heard it all wrong. Sure, he's done a little smuggling. Who hasn't? But it was a lark, that's all."

"Collin," Brie insisted, a hand reaching out to grasp him by the sleeve, "I saw him. I heard him agree to everything."

Angrily he shook her hand off.

"I don't care. D'you hear me? There has to be some other explanation."

In the tumult, neither of them heard the click of the latch or was aware that the door had swung open.

"I'm afraid not, old boy," murmured a new voice, from behind them. "But believe me, I am touched by your loyalty."

Startled, Brie and Collin turned as one to see Gale standing in the open doorway, a pocket gun trained on them with deadly intent.

"And now it seems I have no choice but to ask you to accompany me on a little ride."

Chapter Sixteen

No little time later, Brie found herself shoved in a corner amid empty crates and wooden barrels while she was forced to submit to being tied up like a prize package. She caught her lip between her teeth as the ropes bit painfully into her ankles.

"There," Gale grunted, coming to his feet to view his handiwork with obvious satisfaction, "that should hold you until we can decide how best to dispose of you. A pity you couldn't keep your nose out of things, Brigida. But then, you always were a meddling female."

Furiously, Collin strained against his bonds.

"*Dammit*, Rory! If 'ee dares to harm a hair on her head, I swear I'll kill 'ee with me own hands."

"I'm afraid you will never have the chance, old friend," Rory grinned callously. "Much as I regret it, you know too much to go on living. And, now, I am sorry I cannot stay to keep you company. No doubt you both have a deal to catch up on at any rate. In which case you must be heartily wishing me to perdition."

Laughing at his own feeble attempt at humor, Gale picked up the lantern and left them.

Brigida shivered as the darkness closed in around

them. Gale had not taken them to the cellar at Tâl Carn as she had half expected him to do. To her surprise, he had ordered them to turn on to the track that led to Men-aber and, once there, had forced Collin to row them to the trim vessel lying at anchor out in the bay. With the result that they now found themselves ignominiously trussed up hand and foot in the hold of the earl's private yacht. No doubt it was the one place to which he could be fairly certain no one would come to search for them.

" 'Tis all my fault we're in this mess," groaned Collin, leaning the back of his head against the bulkhead. "I should have listened to you. 'Ee tried to tell me what Rory is a long time ago. I guess I always really knew he was no good, but, God help me, Brie, I never thought he would do anything like this."

"No, of course you did not. How could you? Even now I can hardly believe it myself. The thing is, we cannot let ourselves give up hope. When I fail to make an appearance for dinner, they will know something is wrong. Malvern will come looking for us, and he'll find us, Collin. I know it."

"Aye, sure he will," agreed Collin, sensing the desperation behind her brave words. "He'll be here before we know it."

They found it increasingly more difficult to cling to what soon came to seem a vain hope, however, as the minutes stretched into hours and still help failed to arrive. The darkness and the discomfort of the ropes took their toll on their spirits as much as did the waiting in dread uncertainty. For a while, Brie felt as if she must go mad in the stifling confines of their prison, until, mercifully succumbing to weariness and the steady rocking of the ship, she fell at last into a fitful sleep.

It was not until much later that the yacht, pulling

against the anchor, awakened her. The tide, which had been well on its way out when they had first boarded, had turned, and with a slight shock, she realized it must be well after midnight. It was nearly over, the events going forth in the secret dungeon beneath Tal Carn, and soon Rory Gale and that other one, whoever he was, would be coming for them. No doubt they would make the end quick and painless. Somehow she felt nothing at the prospect, except a leaden weight about her heart that Malvern would never know the truth. He would never know that she had loved him.

The thought, rather than plunging her even deeper into despair, served instead to rouse her temper. Furiously, she began once more to tug at her ropes. Tears welled up in her eyes at the pain of her wrists, already raw and bleeding from trying to work the odious bonds loose, when suddenly Collin stiffened beside her.

"Listen, Brie. Do you hear it?"

Her heart pounding, she froze. At first she could hear nothing above the creak of timbers and the steady lap of the waves against the ship. Then, unmistakably, it carried to her—a hollow thud, as if something had bumped against the hull.

"A boat," she whispered. "Listen. There's someone coming aboard."

It was true. They could hear the sounds of voices issuing from the decks above, and at last the pound of hurried footsteps along the companionway. They were blinded by the shaft of lantern light leaping down at them as the hatch was flung open.

"Brigida!" called an anxious voice. "Brigida, answer me. Where are you?"

Brie's heart gave a wild leap.

"Malvern!" she gasped, nearly swooning with relief.

"We're over here. Please hurry."

He was already lowering the steep wooden stair, which was more of a ladder than anything else. An instant later he had reached her, and, ordering her to remain still, slashed the ropes with a sharp-bladed knife. Then at last she was in the blessed circle of his arms.

"Brigida," he uttered gruffly. "Thank God we found you in time."

"I-I had begun to be-believe you n-never would," she confessed, her teeth chattering from shock and the cold. "Indeed, I have n-never b-been so glad to see anyone in my whole life b-before."

"You can thank Pembroke there that we are here at all," commented a singularly grim voice at her back as someone thrust a coat around her shoulders. Only then did she become aware that the earl had not come alone. Devin had come with him, and James Pembroke, who was busy cutting her brother free. "He was the one who persuaded Gale to talk before he slipped his cable. A good thing, too, since Malvern and I had our hands full at the time."

"You—you mean Rory is dead?"

"Softly, *enfant*," said the earl, feeling her shudder against him. "It could not be avoided. When you did not return for dinner as you had said you would, Griffith became anxious. It was he who found your note and sent word to me. Which is why we were ready for them when the smugglers came ashore in the zawns below the perch. Gale tried to escape. I fear James had no choice but to shoot him."

"Just so," Devin muttered darkly. "And good riddance. He was ringleader of the smuggling gang who did for Duncan. He confessed everything to Pembroke before he died—how Duncan had stumbled on to them in the old passageway to Smugglers' Cave and figured out he was smuggling in more than French brandy. Gale had to kill him when he threatened to turn him in."

"Rory?" exclaimed Brie, looking from one to the other of the two men. "But that's impossible."

"I wish I could say you were right, my dear," Malvern said gravely. "I know you believed him your friend. But he did abduct the two of you, and there can be little doubt that he never meant to see you go free to turn him in to the authorities."

"And if that is not enough to convince you," Devin interjected, "then the fact that we caught him redhanded with a crop of smuggled goods and a French agent should."

Collin groaned.

"Rory, a traitor. Good God. What a blind fool I have been."

"But you don't understand," Brie insisted, turning the full force of her gaze upon Malvern. "I *know* Rory is not the man you are looking for. I lied to you about that day in the west wing. I was not frightened by a mouse. I overheard two men talking. Rory and somebody he called 'Bram.' I heard Rory say Bram had ordered Duncan's death. He is the one who was behind everything. Damion, you must believe me."

Malvern's grip on her arm tightened till she nearly cried out with the pain. Then she saw his face go suddenly granite hard, like a door closing, shutting her out.

"Oh, but I do believe you," he said in a voice, all the more chilling for its steely softness. Deliberately he put her from him and turned to face Devin and Pembroke, his hand drawing a pistol forth from the waistband of his breeches. "Indeed, it all makes perfect sense. I think, Cousin, it would be best if you stepped to one side."

As in a dream, Brie saw Devin's face go white with sudden terrible certainty.

"Easy, Damion," he answered, "don't do anything hasty." Never taking his eyes off the earl, he started to do as he had been ordered.

"Hold it!" Pembroke's shout froze Devin in his tracks.

In the sudden ensuing silence, Malvern raised his arm with chilling deliberation and thumbed back the hammer.

"Give it up," he said, the gun trained and ready. "It's over, James. Your father paid the price for his mistakes. Don't make it any worse than it already is. Enough men have died because of what happened off Cadiz."

In stunned bewilderment, Brie realized the gun was pointed not at Devin, but at Pembroke. Cadiz, she thought, and James. In a flash it came to her that 'Bram' must be short for Bramwell, the name she had heard Malvern curse in his sleep. It had been Bramwell who refused to engage the enemy, and James Pembroke must be his son.

"I wondered when you would finally get around to figuring it out," sneered Pembroke, his eyes on the earl coldly calculating his chances. "Clever of you to have your own brother-in-law kidnapped. With his disappearance, I was forced to look elsewhere for a scapegoat. I was certain when you left this morning with Drake that I had succeeded in making you think he was the one. Just out of curiosity, what made you change your mind?"

No fool, Malvern was keenly aware that Pembroke was only talking to buy time. Cornered and dangerous, he would not give up without a fight, and yet there were still questions that needed answers. His own sealed orders had been to the point. The man he was to find and apprehend was a spy for the French, and the admiralty wanted him taken alive.

"The note you slipped under my wife's door," drawled the earl, playing along. "There happens to be a tavern keeper who is willing to swear my cousin arrived at the Crossroads Inn shortly after midnight. Nor did he leave until an hour or two before dawn. Obviously, he could not have written it. It was apparent someone wanted me to believe that Devin had planned everything—including Duncan's untimely demise—to obtain the title for himself. I almost fell for it, too, in spite of the fact that I was certain he stood not a chance against me in a duel."

Pembroke's laugh sounded harsh in the quiet.

"How careless of me to underestimate your cursed sense of honor. But then, how many men would have done as you did? I'd have killed the man I suspected of dishonoring my wife, without asking a lot of bloody questions. But what would you." He shrugged. "You have yet to tell me how you knew I lied about Gale."

Malvern could see him gauging the distance to the hatchway. He meant to make a break for it, and Devin was still in the line of fire, leaving only Pembroke's head as a target. Steeling himself for the right moment, Malvern smiled.

"Trying to pin it on Gale was even more clever still. The morning I was to go to Plymouth, Hartwell and I spotted him entering the underground passage. It was not unreasonable to suppose he might have done the same last night in order to leave the note incriminating my wife and my cousin. You might have pulled it off, were it not for the fact that Brigida overheard you and Gale talking that same morning in the west wing. When she told me he called you 'Bram,' I knew it had to be you. Pembroke is your mother's name, is it not?" Malvern smiled coldly at the flicker of surprise in the other man's face. "Oh, yes. I knew. You see, it was no accident that Duncan took you on at Malvern. He did so at my request — because your father was once my friend. I've known from the beginning who you were. And now it is over. Finished. There is no place left for you to run."

Pembroke appeared suddenly to leap before them.

"You're wrong. It'll never be over, Captain bloody Demon Drake. Not till one or both of us are dead."

What came next happened with bewildering swiftness.

Brie screamed as Pembroke flung himself hard against Drake and sent him stumbling into Malvern. Without waiting to see more, he bolted for the hatchway. There was a deafening explosion as Malvern's gun went off. In horror, Brie saw Pembroke pitch forward on the wooden stair, then, catching himself, drag himself to his feet. In awed fascination she watched him press his hand to his midriff just under the ribs, saw it come away, wet with blood. Then he looked at the earl, his face distorted with bitter hatred terrible to behold.

"You have done for me just as you did for my father. You and the bloody King's Navy."

"No," said Malvern, with a certain pitying sadness. "Not I. Or the navy. Phillip Bramwell brought disgrace down upon himself — when he refused to engage the enemy."

"It's a lie! All lies! You stripped him of everything — his ship, his name, his honor. And then, when there was nothing left, he killed himself. I swore I'd make you and your precious admiralty pay for what you did. I shall see you in hell, Demon Drake!"

Too late they saw the gun, saw him raise it with

deadly intent and bring it to bear on the earl. A scream rose to Brie's throat, even as she heard Devin's shout.

"Pembroke, *no!* Don't be a bloody fool!"

From out of nowhere came a silvery flash, followed by the sickening thud of metal striking flesh. Pembroke jerked, flung up his arms, and in slow motion hurtled forward as the gun went off, sending the bullet crashing harmlessly into the decks above. Brie gagged and turned away, sickened, as he landed, facedown at the bottom of the stair, and in his back, imbedded to the hilt, the knife that had killed him.

In the stunned silence that followed, Hartwell's homely face appeared, peering down at them through the open hatchway.

"That were a close 'un, Cap'n," he said, "an' that's no lie. I expect he won't be botherin' you nor anyone else from now on."

Wearily, Malvern glanced up at his former coxswain, his smile feeling tight against his teeth.

"Again, Hartwell?" he murmured. "Still protecting my back? I had thought those days were behind us. Obviously I was wrong."

"Aye, sir." Hartwell grinned widely. "I expect I'd not be comfortable any other place. And now if you and your lady are ready, sir?"

Malvern nodded, his gaze going to his wife, standing white-faced and trembling in her brother's arms.

"Yes, let us go home. There is nothing more for us here tonight."

At last, as if freed of a paralyzing hand, Brie tore herself away from Collin.

"Damion!" she choked, flinging herself against his chest. "Oh, God, he meant to kill you."

She felt his muscles tense with surprise. Then, with a hesitancy that hurt and bewildered her somehow, his arms closed around her.

"Would it have mattered so much to you if he had?" he queried with an odd sort of weariness. "After last night, I should have thought you might gladly wish me to the devil."

Brie swallowed, unable to still the trembling in her limbs. How close she had come to losing him! And yet she could not mistake the coolness in his embrace, like a barrier he had deliberately erected between them. With what bitter anguish did it come to her then that indeed he *was* lost to her. Now that it was over and Duncan's murderers lay dead, he had no more use for her. Already he must be regretting the impulse that had led him to take her as his wife. Feeling her heart frozen within her, she pulled away.

"And so I might, milord," she answered stiffly. "And still I could not wish you dead. Never that." She felt weary and more than a little sickened, and she was finding it difficult to order her thoughts. Indeed, she suddenly wanted nothing more than simply to be away from there. At last lifting her head, she looked at him. "You saved my life, and my brother's. For that I must naturally be grateful and—and . . . relieved . . . that you were not made to pay the price of it with your own."

At the end, she felt herself sway and caught herself, a hand going distractedly to her forehead.

Malvern's curse sounded harshly, then his arm was about her shoulders, steadying her.

"No." As if stung, she tried to push him away. "I am all right—truly."

"Don't be a fool," he growled and, holding her, half carried her to the wooden stairs. She felt strong hands grasp her from above and lift her, and as from a distance, heard Hartwell's voice, comforting somehow.

"I've got her, sir. Don't you worry none."

She remembered little after that of the short ride in the pitching boat or of the arm that cradled her against a hard chest the rest of the way home on horseback. Vaguely she recalled Griffith, opening the door for them, and noting that his stony expression had curiously given way to what appeared very like concern. Then she was carried upstairs and laid with an odd sort of tenderness on her bed. Only then, as Lady Cordelia ushered the earl firmly from the room, did she realize it was he who had borne her there.

For once Fionna appeared to have lost her tongue as she set grimly about the task of disrobing her mistress and getting her ready for bed. Save for a sharp exclamation at the sight of Brie's torn wrists, she said hardly a word. When at last her wounds had been treated and bandaged and she had been safely settled beneath the bedcovers, Brie sighed and embraced the beckoning darkness.

"Tomorrow," she muttered, unaware, as sleep closed in on her, of Lady Cordelia bending over her. "Go tomorrow. Home, to Gullan Carn."

She did not see Lady Cordelia's troubled frown or know when she left her to cross purposefully to the door connecting the chamber to Malvern's.

It was late afternoon when Brie finally awakened, time enough to reach Gullan Carn before nightfall had she wanted to, and yet somehow she could not rouse herself to pack the few things she could truly call her own. When at last she could not force herself to lie abed any longer, she rose and dressed without ringing for Fionna, only to stand uncertainly in the center of the room when she had finished.

What was she to do now? she wondered, wandering at last to the window to gaze out over the bay toward Gullan Carn. Somehow the prospect of nurturing her growing flock of sheep had lost its former allure. Indeed, everything that had once been dear and familiar about her old life now seemed reduced to little more than fond memories. With a shock she realized just how far she had grown away from them.

Once, she had believed she could wish for nothing more than a stiff wind at her back and her hand upon the helm—the freedom to go her own way without answering to anyone, least of all to a man. How empty it all seemed now, the dreams of a child. How could she go back to what she had been, now that she knew what it was to love? And yet how much less could she stay here, where that love could never be returned!

With a groan, she sank down on the window seat. Good God, she had lost herself. She did not know who or what she was anymore.

The low rap at the door caught her unawares. Startled, she lifted her head.

"Yes? Who is it?" she called and hastily brushed a hand over her eyes to clear the mist away.

The door to the sitting room swung open and Collin, looking little the worse for wear after their recent ordeal, stuck his head in.

"Hello, so 'ee's awake. 'Ee slept so long, we were all a mite worried. Mind if I come in?"

Her smile a trifle off center, she shook her head.

"No, of course not. Though I fear I am not very good company. Here." She patted the window seat beside her. "Come and sit down. Tell me what has been going on while I have been a slugabed."

She felt his eyes on her, sharp with concern, but for the life of her she could not keep the dullness from her voice. Then he was beside her, the same old Collin, and yet different somehow, older it seemed.

" 'Ee'd be surprised. It has been sort of quiet. In fact, 'ee'd hardly know anything untoward had ever happened. I expect that's due in large part to this Griffith of yours. A queer duck, he is. He has practically stood guard outside your door to make certain nothing or no one disturbed 'ee. I was forced to sneak by him just to get in here to see how 'ee was doing."

"Funny how things turn out," Brie murmured. "I actually suspected for a time that he might be the man I overheard talking to Rory. Not only did it seem odd that he should have left London for the wilds of Cornwall, but Duncan was killed shortly after his arrival. I could not help but be suspicious of him, though it all seems rather absurd now. Especially in light of the fact that for all practical purposes he saved our lives."

"But didn't 'ee know? Your Mr. Griffith was accused of aiding in the robbery of his former employer's home. Duncan made no secret about it He used to laugh about it when he was in his cups. No doubt 'tis why the poor man has such a sourpuss about him."

Brie started in surprise. Indeed, a great deal about Griffith began to make sense. "But he was tried and found innocent, surely?" she exclaimed. "Else, why is he not in prison?"

"There wasn't evidence enough to send him to Newgate, only to dismiss him without a reference. Which, when 'ee thinks on it, amounts nearly to the same thing. And though, in the end, the brigands were caught and confessed that Griffith was guiltless, his reputation in London was ruined. He had no choice but to accept what employment he could. I don't know what 'ee did, lass, to win him over, but he would seem to have developed a doglike devotion for 'ee."

Brie smiled a trifle whimsically.

"It was quite simple, really," she said, remembering her last encounter with Griffith. "I placed my trust in him."

"Aye," mumbled Collin, "and no doubt 'twas better placed there than in me."

Having exhausted the subject of Griffith, an uncomfortable silence fell over them then. At last Collin shifted his weight and coughed to clear his throat.

"Dammit, Brie," he blurted, "there's so much I'd like to say. I just can't seem to find the words."

"I know," she answered quickly, putting her hand over his. "You don't need to say anything. It's all over now, thank God, and it's time we—you take hold of your life. Do you not think you have kept a certain young lady waiting long enough?"

To her surprise a ruddy tinge invaded his cheeks.

"As a matter of fact, that was one of the things I wanted to talk about. I popped the question—when I was at Hessenford for the house party—and Elsbeth has accepted."

"Oh, Collin, but that is wonderful news. Indeed, I could not be happier for you both. It is what I have hoped for you. A home and—and children for whom I may play the role of aunt."

His glance narrowed sharply on her face.

"Aye, well, that's all very fine," he said. "But I expect 'ee'll have children of your own before very long."

Brie stilled, then, glancing hastily away, withdrew her hand from his.

"No, I-I am afraid that is something which can never be. I am going home—to Gullan Carn." She could feel his eyes on her in startled concern. Laughing shakily, she got up and moved away. "If, of course, you and Elsbeth will have me."

"Of course we would have 'ee," he retorted impatiently, "but, why, Brie? And don't tell me it's because thee's no fondness for his lordship. 'Tis plain as the nose on your face that 'ee's eating your heart out. 'Ee love him, now, admit it."

Brie felt her heart wrung in two at her brother's unexpected sympathy.

"Yes, I love him," she cried, her brittle composure broken at last. "More than you can ever know. But it changes nothing. I-I cannot stay here. Oh, don't you understand? He cares . . . nothing for me. It is my fault. I-I drove him away."

Haltingly, it all came out then, how he had believed her capable of betraying him and how her pride had kept her from forcing him to hear the truth. In her anguish, she magnified what she conceived as her own ignominy, her guilt, in failing to avert what had happened in the wake of his anger.

"I-I told him I should never forgive him," she ended, her eyes tormented with the memory. "And it is I who am to blame."

"But that's nonsense, Brie." Taking her in his arms, Collin laid her head against his shoulder. "Don't y'see? 'Tis a man of rare honor that 'ee's taken as thy husband. 'Tis himself he can't forgive. Go to him, Brie. Tell him what 'ee's told me. Tell him, lass, that your heart's breaking in two for love of him."

Brie, her throat constricted with emotion, wordlessly shook her head.

"Ah, well," sighed her brother, "at least promise to think about it before 'ee does something to regret all the rest of your days." Patting her on the back, he stood up and after a moment's hesitation, finally left her to herself.

She was to have no time for her less than rewarding thoughts, however. Hardly had Collin shut the door behind him than Lady Cordelia put in an appearance.

"Brigida. Child," she exclaimed, taken aback at the sight of the girl's wan aspect. But almost immediately she caught herself. A look of resolve in the fine eyes, she crossed to Brigida and took both her hands in hers. "You poor dear. You have had a very bad time of it, I know. But it is over now, and you must pull yourself together."

Brie suffered a frisson of warning at something she sensed in the other woman.

"Something is wrong. What? Please, you must tell me. 'Tis Malvern, isn't it? Something has happened to him."

"Softly, child. It was not my intention to alarm you. Only, a naval officer has arrived with orders for Damion."

"Orders?" echoed Brie, giving her a blank look. "But I don't understand. I-I was led to believe he was through with—with all of that."

"I know. That is what all of us thought. Indeed, from what Damion has told me, he believed himself that it would never again be given to him to command a king's ship. But he never resigned his commission. He was under orders to return home. To discover the truth of rumors that had reached the admiralty, rumors to the effect that information was being passed on to the enemy out of Cornwall. I am afraid that he not only is still very much an officer in the navy, but that the admiralty has seen fit to make him a commodore. He is to leave immediately for Plymouth to assume command of a squadron of ships. Unless *you* can persuade him to do otherwise."

"I?" Brie queried, feeling her heart withering inside

her. "What could I possibly do?"

"Go to him. Tell him you want him to stay. He loves you, Brigida. You must know that. Whatever else has happened between you, that at least has not changed."

"No, you don't understand." Unable to bear the pity in the other woman's eyes, she turned away. "It is not like that all. He married me out of an absurd sense of duty—because of the marriage contract drawn up between our fathers. And—and even if he could l-love me, it would change nothing. Can you not see I could not ask him to make such a sacrifice? It is everything he has been hoping for—a command and a ship to take him back into the thick of things."

Behind her, Lady Cordelia threw up her hands in exasperation.

"No, my dear, I do not see," she answered. "It is not as if he has not given enough for king and country, for he has. And if he is so enamored of leaving you for his precious navy, then perhaps you can explain why he spends his time brooding in his study over a decanter of brandy. At least you might have the courage to face him and discover for yourself what his true feelings are. Do you not owe him that much at least?"

When Brigida showed no signs of answering, Cordelia sighed and crossed with a heavy heart to the door. There she paused, compelled to make one last try.

"Life is too short, too precious, to waste, my dear," she said quietly. "If you love him, Brigida, you must fight for him—for your happiness and his."

Then without waiting for an answer, she turned and left, shutting the door softly behind her.

For a long time, Brie stood where she was, Lady Cordelia's final words seeming endlessly to mock her.

And yet how could she go to him, when he cared nothing for her, when, indeed, he must be filled with impatience to be away from here, away from her? It was his life, the sea, and if she had had the power, she yet would not have had the right to deny him the very thing that made him what he was.

In an agony of indecision, she flung herself across the bed. Upon which, she suddenly found herself staring at a bundle set on the lowboy near the bedside.

All at once she straightened, remembering Malvern as he had been that day in the west wing, the black eyes boring holes through her—remembering his bitterness as it came to him that she must be ashamed to be seen in his company. From somewhere she had found the courage to speak her heart then and with a brazenness she had not known she possessed had proven him wrong. What she had done once, she could do again. This one last time she would indeed go to him and banish forever the last of the secrets that lay between them. If nothing else, it would be her farewell gift to him.

Her mind made up at last, Brie went about laying her plans.

Chapter Seventeen

The sea was awash with the silvery light of a full moon when Brie stole from the castle on to the parapet. Gazing out over the cliffs, she saw with a vague feeling of surprise that the beach swarmed with dancing flames—the torches of the villagers combing the rocks for shellfish. It was the springtide harvest, she realized with a slow pang in the region of her heart, and a full two fortnights since she had made her way to the grottoes and stumbled on to the smugglers sunken cache of goods. Faith, it seemed more like a lifetime.

Shivering a little in the chill breeze, she hugged her coat more firmly about her and listened to the music wafting to her from the ballroom.

The ball was a *success fou,* she realized with a small, somewhat wistful, smile. It seemed as if nearly half the county were present to see for themselves the Earl of Malvern and his new countess. Proud that the hero of countless tales of daring should have chosen one of their own for his wife, they had treated her both with warmth and kindness. Indeed, a chorus of murmured approval had gone up when the nobleman had appeared with his lady on his arm. And how handsome he had looked in white breeches and the blue dress coat bearing the single white stripe of a commodore in the King's Navy!

For a long moment Brie stood perfectly still, remembering their single waltz together, the one that had signaled the opening of the ball. In her cream-colored ball gown of shimmering satin, the Drake diamonds about her slim throat and dangling from her ears, she had felt like a fairy princess. And for the length of the dance she had even been able to pretend that like a fairy tale, hers, too, might have a happy ending. But then the music had died away, leaving her gazing up into black, unreadable eyes, and the moment had been irretrievably lost. Malvern, brushing his lips to the backs of her knuckles, had left her to disappear in the crowd.

It had been all she could do after that to conceal the ache in her heart behind a façade of gaiety and laughter, until at last she had found the opportunity to slip away to her room to change. It must be near midnight, she thought as she waited in the shadows, her senses attuned to the sights and sounds around her.

Nevertheless, she was taken unawares by the sudden appearance of a lone figure striding past her toward the battlements. Her breath hard in her throat, she watched him come to a halt and stand staring out over the parapet—a lonely sentinel, his cloak, billowing around him.

She breathed a long sigh of relief. The Demon of Malvern had come at last to his perch overlooking the sea!

He had not seen her, crouched in the shadows, she realized, feeling her heart pounding madly beneath her breast. It was not too late. She could still slip away if she wanted to. And, indeed, she thought, observing the forbidding cast of that lean profile, she was almost tempted to do that very thing.

How stern he looked, and yet how compelling! The raven hair, ruffled in the wind, in sharp contrast to the pallid brow, he presented the aspect of a man lost in brooding thought. What was he thinking about? she wondered. About the squadron, waiting for him at Plymouth—the ships and the men who would look to him to lead them?

Unwittingly, she suffered a sharp stab of jealousy at the thought. If only it were she he were thinking of!

She must have made some sound, for suddenly he turned, his glance seeming to pierce the shadows.

"Who's there?" he called, his voice lashing out at her through the silence. Gathering her courage around her like a cloak, Brie swallowed and stepped boldly into the moonlight.

"I might be the ghost of Inness Glen," she said, thinking of that first fateful meeting in the depths of Smugglers' Cave. "Or some other spirit come to pay his respects."

She saw him go instantly still. Then a tremor appeared to shake the lithe frame, and in spite of herself she experienced a bittersweet sense of her own power to awaken painful memories.

His eyes were like black coals in the pale mask of his face as he swept her breeches-clad form a piercing glance.

"But thee's not," he answered on cue. Almost her courage failed her.

"Can 'ee be so certain, gov'nor?" she made herself go on. "Behold the pallid complexion and reflect: Is it in truth a creature of flesh and blood who stands before 'ee or rather the poor remnants of a lad 'ee once knew?"

He smiled mirthlessly, his face hard-cast in the

moonlight.

"I should judge both and neither to be closer to the truth. But no matter. More to the point is the purpose behind this visit."

Brie shrugged, though, inside, she felt herself taut with uncertainty.

"To lay to rest the ghost of Brian Murdoch," she answered simply.

For the space of a heartbeat, he looked at her with eyes that seemed to see right through her.

"Then so be it," he said as though pronouncing judgment on her or himself.

In a single swift stride he had reached her and without warning, yanked the wig from her head.

"Did you think to bam the likes of me, my girl," he growled, crushing her ruthlessly to his breast, "with naught but a wig and the garb of a street urchin? I am not such a blind fool, I assure you."

Stifling a gasp, Brie stared up into the lean, handsome countenance.

"You knew," she breathed accusingly. "All the time you knew I was Brian Murdoch."

With his eyes he devoured her.

"And how not? Your grandfather, after all, had been kind enough to send me a likeness of my promised bride. One look into those glorious, flashing eyes, and I knew 'twas no lad come to beard the Demon in his lair."

He grinned, reading in her face the dawning realization of the enormity of his deception.

"How dared you play such a despicable trick on me?" she furiously demanded. "All—all the talk about the pact we had made. You *swore* to play it straight with me. You—you gave me your word!"

A devilish gleam ignited in the depths of his spellbinding orbs.

283

"And so I did, my love. No tricks, on my word of honor, for just as long as Brian Murdoch should choose to deal in plain pounds with me. How unfortunate that *he* should have been a deception from the very beginning. By the very nature of our contract, I had no choice but to be as devious as he. You cannot deny that I, at least, kept my part of the bargain."

Brie stared at him, momentarily speechless with the knowledge that indeed she could not deny it. Then, with realization came a terrible, rending hurt. How dared he use her so! lanced through her brain. He was loathsome and vile. Furiously she shoved against his chest and, catching him off guard, wrenched herself free of his grasp.

"Oh! And to think I have been dying of love for you," she choked, trembling in humiliation and rage, "tormented with the thought that I dared not tell you the truth lest it convict my brother of crimes you knew very well he had never committed. How you must have enjoyed casting me as the fool in your little farce. And how much greater shall be your enjoyment upon learning to what lengths I was willing to go to win a measure of your regard. I came here tonight, milord, to humble myself before you. To—to confess the truth and beg your forgiveness. And—and finally, to give you this."

Producing the bundle from beneath her coat, she fairly flung it at him.

"It is for your lamed hand, milord," she stated bitterly. "In the way of a going-away present. A brace to help stretch the muscles and sinews and, in so doing, straighten the fingers."

For what seemed an eternity, but which in reality could not have been more than a few seconds, Malvern stared at the cleverly wrought contraption. It was made up of a wooden splint and leather straps to hold it in place about the forearm. In addition, there was a stout leather glove to the fingers of which were attached coil springs of the sort used in harnesses. These, in turn, were made to fasten to the top of the splint in such a manner as to straighten the fingers and yet still allow the wearer a certain amount of flexibility.

"Malcolm designed it for you at my request," she added gruffly, when it seemed that no comment was to be forthcoming. "Naive fool that I was, I thought to give you something in return for having been forced to wed where you had no wish to have done. In my childish fancy, I even imagined it might in some way soften your heart toward me. And, *now,* as far as I am concerned, you can go join your precious squadron off Plymouth. Indeed, for all I care you can go to the devil!"

The back of her hand to her mouth, she spun on her heel and broke for the castle.

"Brie! Wait!"

Something in his voice froze her in her tracks. Nor did she move as she felt Malvern come up behind her.

"Brie," he murmured huskily. "My poor sweet love, I never meant to hurt you. Can you truly think I should have played such a game merely to render you foolish in my eyes?"

"I-I think you are despicable and mean," she retorted, unable to stop herself. "I think you meant to use me from the very first. And when my brother was foolish enough to remove the pretense of Brian Murdoch from your manipulations, you had no choice but to marry me." Suddenly she stiffened as the implications of what he had done struck her fully. "Good God," she gasped, wheeling to impale him with accusing eyes. "You raised your sword against him, knowing he had not murdered anyone! You — you might have killed him, and for what? Merely to further your precious scheme? To what lengths were you willing to go, milord, to have your way with me?"

In awed fascination she beheld the leap of anger in his face. Then bending near her, he pierced her with his gaze.

"To any lengths, short of murder, I assure you," he answered in a steely voice. "Your brother was never in any danger of dying at my hand. I guessed the minute I saw him who he was."

"Then why—?"

"Because I judged it time somebody taught him a lesson, for your sake if nothing else. I have seen others like him go to the devil for lack of a steadying influence. Next time he thinks to throw his lot in with desperate men, he will have the scar I gave him to remind him where it might lead."

Brie stared at him doubtfully, afraid to believe. Afraid to grasp to her the slender thread of hope he seemed to hold out to her, lest in the end it prove illusory.

"And if I am fool enough to accept that as the truth," she said grudgingly, "it still does not explain why you should have used it as you did. You forced me to wed you. Why? What did you possibly think to gain by it?"

"A wife," he answered, his thin-lipped smile sardonic. "Surely that at least requires no explanation. Dammit, Brie! Why do you think I should have done it?"

"Why indeed?" she echoed, feeling an odd sort of giddiness as she sensed her wall of defenses on the point of being tumbled down.

Her breath caught as he took a step toward her.

"Because, my impossible green-eyed beauty," he growled. "I fell in love with you almost from the first moment I saw you. Even in that ridiculous garb, you bewitched me with your sweet fire and innocence, your generosity—your damned irrepressible courage. I thought never to find a woman such as you, one who, rather than being frightened or repulsed at the sight of my disfigurements, should dismiss them as though they were matters of little consequence. I wanted you, Brigida, more than I have ever wanted anything before. And, yes, I should have gone to any lengths to have you, even go so far as to trick you into marrying me."

He had been moving steadily toward her as he talked, forcing her to retreat, until with a start she felt the castle wall at her back. A grim look of triumph flashed in his eyes, and then he grabbed her and yanked her to his chest.

Hungrily he bent his head to hers and kissed her lingeringly, passionately—with all the pent-up fury of his love.

When at last he released her no little time later, Brie clung to him, feeling shaken and weak and yet suffused with a glorious feeling of happiness. Her eyes huge and dusky, she let her head loll back against his shoulder to find him watching her, a question in his gaze.

"Brigida—love," he groaned, touching her face with fingers that trembled slightly. "I have been driven mad with the fear that you could not forgive me for taking you the way I did." A wry smile twisted at his lips. "Pembroke did his best to convince me Devin was courting you secretly. And, like a fool, I believed him."

Brie silenced him with her fingers pressed lightly to his lips.

"Hush," she murmured. "It does not matter anymore. I love you, and that is all that is important."

"No, it is not all!" he said roughly, a fierce light of pain in the look he bent upon her. "Brigida, my own sweet love. If only I had known before what miracle of happiness awaited me here in your arms. I should have quit that other life long ago, and nothing should have called me away. Now it is too late."

"No, my darling." Smiling at him through her tears, she gazed at him with her whole heart in her eyes. "It is never too late. This war cannot last forever. I shall be here for you always — waiting, watching for the ships to return. And you must promise you will always come back to me. Promise me, Damion. Swear it. It shall be the final pact between us."

Her courage almost failed her then as, crushing her once more in his embrace, he pledged his word always to return. For in truth, she did not know how she could bear to surrender him to that most importunate of mistresses — the sea, which long ago had claimed him as her own. And yet she must! she bitterly told herself, for was she not a Cornish woman, born and bred? And was not that the lot of her kind — to be ever the safe harbor, the "someone" her man could always come back to?

But no, she thought rebelliously, that was wrong. *She* must be more than that. She would be his equal, sending him forth because she herself could not go, and in her heart, she would be with him. Always it would be so, for, indeed, she had made a pact with the devil. Heart and soul, she belonged to the despicable Demon of Malvern!